**monsoon**books

# MATARAM

Tony Reid is better k~~...~~, author of ten historical works ~~...~~ e much-read and translated *Sou~~...~~erce*. He has taught Southeast Asian history at universities in the US (Yale, UCLA, Hawaii) and Australia (ANU), as well as in Malaysia, Indonesia and Singapore. He now lives in Canberra, Australia. *Mataram* is his first work of fiction.

### Praise for *Mataram*

'Romance, intrigue, warfare, adventure – *Mataram* has all the ingredients necessary to bring seventeenth-century Java to life. A young Englishman and his Javanese translator struggle to find cultural acceptance during a time of far-reaching religious and political change. Written by an eminent historian, *Mataram* will be welcomed by all those who see historical fiction as a means of illuminating the past.' – Barbara Watson Andaya, University of Hawai'i, an authority on gender relations in Southeast Asia

# MATARAM

## A NOVEL OF LOVE, FAITH
## AND POWER IN EARLY JAVA

TONY REID

**monsoon**books

First published in 2018
by Monsoon Books Ltd
www.monsoonbooks.co.uk

No.1 Duke of Windsor Suite, Burrough Court,
Burrough on the Hill, Leicestershire LE14 2QS, UK

This updated second edition published in 2019.

ISBN (paperback): 9781912049127
ISBN (ebook): 9781912049134

Cover design by Cover Kitchen.
Cover painting courtesy of KITLV, Leiden. 'The Tiger Fight or Rampok
Party on Java' by J.S.G. Gramberg in 'The Indian Archipelago: scenes
from nature and folk life in the Dutch East Indies'.

A Cataloguing-in-Publication data record is available from the British
Library.

Printed and bound in Great Britain by Clays Ltd, Elcograf S.p.A.
21 20 19          2 3

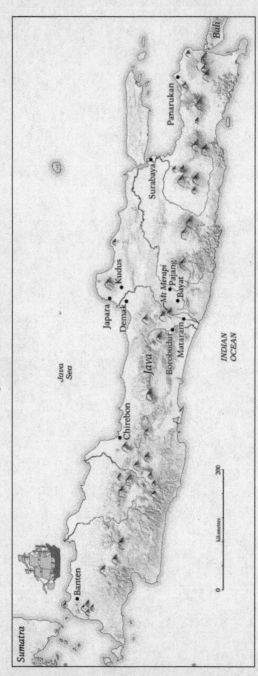

JAVA CIRCA 1610

Sumatra

Java Sea

Banten

Chirebon

Japara
Demak
Kudus

Surabaya

Bali

Panarukan

Java

Borobudur
Mataram

Mt Merapi
Pajang
Bayat

INDIAN
OCEAN

0        200
kilometers

# Banten ("Bantam")

He smelt it first. Sweet, heavy; carrying a hint of the promised spices amidst simple putrefaction. Bantam struck Thomas Hodges as he staggered up on deck, weak from the scurvy and foul food. After the heat, squalor and mounting despair of the voyage, the busy harbour overwhelmed his senses. Here at last was the reason for their suffering – the jewel of Java, where pepper was to be had for four Spanish reals a hundredweight, so they said. A good cargo could make his fortune, and give the crew the hope they needed to get the cursed ship home again without a mutiny. Bantam was his one chance to make a decent life for himself; to make his bitter wife and her whining family show him some respect.

Now he saw huts here and there among the trees on shore, and everywhere there were boats. Most were the little fishing canoes he had already seen on the Sumatran coast, with their single sails and an outrigger on one side. They had none of the bulk of an English fishing boat. It was amazing how quickly they sped over the water, but you wouldn't want to face a North Sea squall in one of those. Then there were bigger vessels that seemed to be carrying cargo, something like the size of a Thames riverboat. One large sail was slung in front of the mast, with a big oar at the stern for a rudder. There were hundreds of these coming and going, but not many ships that came close to the *Red Dragon* or even the *Susan* in size. Only the Dutch men-of-war he could now see anchored in the roads, and half a dozen large ships of Asian type – *junks*, they called them.

'See that three-master,' said a voice beside him, 'that's Chinese, you can tell by the folding sail, like a fan.' It was Jason, one of the Cornish deckhands who had survived the *Red Dragon's* first voyage to Bantam. He pointed to a large ship at anchor near the shore, surrounded by small lighters. 'God knows how those Chinamen find their way here in those clumsy hulks, but we're lucky they do. If you want to fill your belly, rot your gut with their firewater, find a whore, or get your boots fixed, first find your Chinaman.'

Talking of Chinamen, Uncte himself was now on deck, and looked excitedly at the Chinese ship. He had lived in Bantam half his life, before being taken to England by Henry Middleton in the second English voyage. 'China *junk*,' he shouted to Hodges. 'China *kampong* backside. My house!' He pointed eagerly to a jumble of roofs on the west side of what appeared to be the walled centre, near where the junk was anchored.

Though the sailors made fun of his comical English, Hodges had found Uncte indispensable. He appeared to know everything about Bantam, which he called Banten, even if he couldn't express it clearly. He corrected the Malay phrases Hodges was trying to learn from Jason and the other Cornishman, who seemed to have learned their few words in the Bantam whorehouses.

Jason said Malay was all you needed, but Uncte knew Chinese and Javanese as well and kept confusing Hodges with too many words.

'Why are the Chinese not inside the city?' Hodges asked him now.

'Banten no like pigs, China like.'

Most of the town could now be seen, with a jagged wall along the seafront. 'So that's Bantam,' mused Hodges. 'Doesn't look as if it could stand a siege by good English musketeers for more than a day or two.' One building projected far above it, with what appeared to be a series of thatched roofs, one on top of the other. 'Is that the king's palace?' he asked Uncte, 'The one that looks like three hats piled up on a single head?'

'No palace. They call *masjid*, like church. Mussulmen pray.' He mimed bowing down.

'Look lively, now,' shouted a voice behind, and all the fit men busied themselves stowing the last sails. The anchor was rattling down, and the *Red Dragon* came to rest a healthy distance from the city and the larger ships. The guns were readied and the fittest men positioned with muskets on the poop. You never knew where danger might lurk in a strange port. It was reassuring to see that the biggest ships were Dutch, not Portuguese, but even so you could take nothing for granted.

Their presence had been noticed. There was scurrying among the small fishing boats nearest to them and on the Dutch ships. The first to arrive were a pair of the fast sailing boats with outriggers, with only two men aboard each. They fairly flew across the water. As they approached the *Dragon* they lowered their sails and paddled closer. One of the men stood in the prow holding some large fruit aloft. Two of the crew held them in the sights of their muskets, but the bosun beckoned them on. He called on Jason to ask their business. Hodges was pleased to recognise two words Jason and Uncte had already taught him – '*Mau apa?* Want what?'

They shouted something back and waved their fruits in the air. It was obvious enough they wanted to sell the fruit.

'See what you can get for two crowns,' offered the bosun. This proved too much for Jason, and Uncte intervened with a stream of Malay evidently explaining the English and their money. He had more trouble explaining the boatmen's answer in English, and it was Hodges who summed it up. 'They know nothing of crowns; they want Spanish reals.'

'The devil take them,' muttered the bosun, 'as he'll take those Spanish coxcombs. Very well then, two reals.'

After more shouting it was agreed they could have the whole contents of the two boats. The Bantammers started clambering up the ropes like cats, a huge pile of fruit on their backs. The bosun stopped them dead with a roar. 'Not with those cursed choppers. Get those heathen things out of here.' In truth the knives they wore at their belts were fearsome things, like butchers' cleavers but twice as long. After more shouting these were left in the boats, the men came aboard, and the crew started grabbing and testing the strange fruit.

Next to arrive was a skiff under a Dutch ensign, carrying a smartly dressed pair of officers, a barrel of water, some vegetables and a squealing pig trussed in the stern beneath the feet of two oarsmen. These were hoisted aboard as the fruit sellers fled in apparent horror.

'Welcome,' proclaimed the elder officer stiffly as he stood in the boat below. 'You will need fresh food if you've come from the Cape. Keep that pig away from the Bantammers if you value your lives; but cook it well and you'll find nothing sweeter. May we come aboard?'

The master, Pickering, invited them up and sat them in the shade of the poop. Since the Dutch were speaking Portuguese, Hodges was permitted to join them. His seniors had to admit he spoke the language better than any of them except the Commander himself.

Thank god he had escaped the village as a lad and talked his way onto a ship in the wine trade between Portsmouth and Porto. Three more years he had spent the whole of the wine-buying season there. It turned out he had an ear for language that made him useful to the English wine-merchants. That same talent had brought him to the attention of William Keeling, newly appointed General of the third East India Company fleet, who was looking for a promising young master's mate. A linguist himself, Keeling knew Portuguese was the only Christian tongue spoken in the East, and without it there was no talking to the natives. 'I can get plenty of men who can crew a ship or cut a throat,' he had said, 'but men who know how to survive among a strange people are hard to find. Keep your eyes open on shipboard, and learn as much Malay as you can from those deckhands.'

Now Pickering apologised to the Dutch. Commander Keeling could not leave his bed, he said, and the chief merchant was not much better. It had been a miserable passage since the Cape, between hostile Muslim ports and the fickle winds. They were becalmed for a month with the men growing sicker every day and five already dead. He thanked the Hollanders for the water and provisions, desperately needed. 'Is it safe to go ashore? Are there medicines here for men near death? How can we get more provisions? What news of our Englishmen? Are the Portuguese papists in town?'

'One thing at a time,' laughed the older Dutchman, who had introduced himself as an *onderkoopman* - would that be a junior merchant? 'Your Englishman is well enough, and probably on his way to greet you. But don't believe all his stories. As for the Portuguese, we have dealt with them. There were two ships here when our fleet arrived. They tried to put up a fight but we gave them no chance. We took a pretty cargo of Chinese silks and porcelain before burning the ships. The Portuguese will be no trouble as long as we are in port. There are a few in the town, but they are not so pompous since we sank their ships. Of course, they tell the Javanese all sorts of ridiculous stories about us – that we have no king and no god but money. But our guns speak louder than their prating.

'The Javanese found soon enough what nonsense the Portuguese have been feeding them all these years. Would you believe they claimed that the kings of Spain and Portugal ruled the whole world between them, so there was no point fighting them? When they saw the papist galleons burning in the roads the Javanese could hardly believe their eyes, and when we made the Portuguese women follow us in chains through the city, along with the others we didn't put to the sword, they began to give us a little respect.

'As for the city, you should have no trouble moving about, once these men of yours can walk. Wait until you're fit enough to put on a spectacle, or they'll think you beggars. It's all show here. Those who don't have slaves to follow them about will pay all they have to hire some, especially when they go to the court. Your man Scott has been telling the Javanese some pretty tales about the English, so you had better not disappoint them.'

He was interrupted by a faint cheer from the men on the watch, as they hailed the approach of a small native boat flying a tattered English ensign.

'That will be Scott, sure enough,' said the Dutchman. 'We will take our leave – he wouldn't want us to spoil his stories. But remember we're not as bad as he will tell you. He's had a rough time, and the grog has begun to turn his head, poor fellow. He thinks everybody is trying to kill him.

'He can't do much to help you with water and supplies. Don't worry. We'll have our men fetch a couple of extra barrels for you from the stream we found in the hills. Anchor your ship next to ours in the morning, and we'll see you back on your feet.'

Hodges rushed to the gunwale to get a look at Scott. He was the one who had been left virtually alone in Bantam when Middleton's ships moved on. He had evidently survived, but at what cost? Scott sat in a Bantam outrigger canoe, and without the ensign Hodges would have taken him for a bedraggled Javanese. A half-naked savage behind him held a tattered umbrella over his head. He sat stiffly in the small vessel, only his eyes flashing, with an occasional gruff command to the Javanese boatman.

Once aboard, his composure suddenly broke. He fell on his knees and sobbed: 'At last, thank god! At last!' He threw himself upon Pickering, crying that he thought they would never come.

Once he had calmed down and joined the officers for a glass of wine, the stories came pouring out about the place he called in the native way 'Banten' – usually with an expletive. Fire seemed to be the stuff of most of them, since the houses at Banten, he said, were all made of thatch and straw, and the favourite sport of knaves was to set them alight to make their thieving easier.

'Fire, *fogo*, *api*,' he said, 'Learn that word in every language, so you hear it even in your sleep. You must have cloth to trade with these villains, but protecting it from fire and thievery is the very devil.'

Scott's house was in the Chinese quarter of town, since the Banten people distrusted all foreigners and placed them outside the wall of the citadel. He spoke as though every Chinese and Javanese in the town took his turn to try to burn the English out, or get at what little silver and cloth they kept there.

Scott would have gone on all night with stories of the villainy he had lived though in the city. Hodges began to hope the Dutch were right that the grog had got to him, for if his stories were even half true it would be a fool who would try to live here. When Pickering told him he was planning to move the ship's mooring in the morning to be near the Dutch, Scott let out a string of curses. 'Better be near the devil!' he shouted. 'Be on your guard every minute, especially when they talk all friendly. It's us English they want to destroy. The damned Portuguese is only a clapped-out braggart whose guns don't shoot straight. They know it is only we who can rob them of the prize out here. Watch every move.'

While Scott was spinning his stories, a galley had pulled up with some smartly dressed Bantammers aboard. Their leader was barefoot like the rest but was the only one with a tunic. He spoke enough Portuguese to convey his message. He announced his name at length but Hodges caught only Ali. A lively woman came with him, wearing what looked like a loose Portuguese *camisa* above her sarong. She was able to clarify Ali's remarks when needed in much better Portuguese, and even saluted Scott with what seemed to be English - 'Hello, ol' fren'. He admitted he had known her 'too well' in his first year here.

Ali made known he was sent by the *Shahbandar*, the ruler of the port. He asked plenty of questions about the English, whom he called *Inggeris*. He knew that the Portuguese and Dutch hated each other. Which side were the Inggeris on?

In response to Pickering's questions, Ali made clear that there would be no buying pepper or anything else without what he called the *chop* of the Shahbandar, which seemed to involve some kind of seal from the king. One of the English must negotiate with this great official and seek his favour. After that, they might seek a base in the city and hope to meet the king himself. He was only a boy, but still honoured as a god even if others made the decisions. Admission to his palace would be the sign that the great ones had accepted the English.

The woman had seen that Hodges understood her Portuguese better than Pickering did, and she took him aside. She explained the importance of dressing well and having the right gifts for the Shahbandar – impressive, but not as impressive as those to be given to the king or there would be even more trouble. The Dutch had done well with clocks, she said, and if the English wanted to impress they should bring something at least as new and intriguing. When he asked how she learned her few words of English, she just grinned and glanced at Scott.

Scott himself was allowed only a few minutes at the Commander's bedside, but that was enough to convince Keeling that this wreck of a man was a menace to his plan for smooth relations with the Bantam court. He was looking for somebody who could make a fresh start. Hodges saw it at once: this was his big chance. It was obvious that Pickering and the other officers had no taste for being the first to step among the cutthroats, even if they resented Hodges as an inexperienced intruder dropped onto the ship by Keeling.

He would take the risk – if only he were chosen. What had he left to lose anyway? Life with Margaret had become wretched since their boy had died. She seemed to blame him for the accident, rather than face the guilt of her own carelessness. He might die, yes; but if he succeeded and somehow got back to England, he would be a great man with a fortune. Life would be worth living.

He whispered to the woman. She in turn said something in Javanese to Ali, who looked Hodges up and down before nodding. Ali quietly spoke to Pickering, 'If you send someone with decent Portuguese, like this red-beard here, things will go better.'

Pickering scowled, but disappeared for a few words with the Commander. When he returned he barked, 'Smarten up, Hodges. Grab your kit and go ashore with these fellows, NOW. Come back as soon as you're sure it's safe for us to follow. The sooner we get off this stinking boat the better.'

Hodges did not hesitate. 'What about the gifts? I'll get nowhere without them.'

Pickering allowed one telescope for the *Shahbandar*, some of the English broadcloth they had hoped would be acceptable in the market; and just enough English and Spanish silver to buy essential food for the ship. 'Find out what others are paying for pepper, but say nothing about our price.'

So there it was. Glory and riches or death and dishonour. His moment had come.

# Shahbandar

A cock crowed, as if in the Hampshire village of his childhood; the one oddly familiar thing in an absurdly alien land where no one spoke his tongue. He stretched on the unaccustomed mat and knew this was not that village, nor his cold marital bed in Portsmouth. Bantam, yes, Bantam – or was it Banten? Ashore at last and with some decent food in his belly, even if mostly rice. What a day. It had landed him alone among a barbarous people. He felt for the silver and gifts Pickering had entrusted him with. He must defend them with his life until he could use them to get access to the pepper.

So here he was, with no friends in a dangerous land. Hodges felt for the sword beside him, and the dagger in his belt – the only true friends in a crisis. This was Ali's own compound, where the Bantam official had showed him a hut to doss down in and a hole in the ground to do his business. He had had no choice but to trust his own wits in this place where he had no friends, rather than relying on the wretched Scott or the perfidious Dutch. Ali had made Hodges take off his shoes before entering the hut and wash his stinking feet with a great jar of water standing nearby.

The Portuguese-speaking woman who had come to the *Dragon* with Scott had told him bluntly, 'You *feringgi* from Europe, you stink to us, especially when just off a ship. Here we wash, *mandi*, and you had better do the same if you want us to think you better than an animal.'

Hodges didn't like the idea of taking off his clothes and parting company with his sword. What a chance to cut his throat and steal his precious things! But having sweated in the stifling heat for months on shipboard, the touch of cool water sounded good before he again donned the doublet and hose that would make him hot again. He put on his sword and crept out to check out the compound.

There was plenty of life stirring, with people moving about dressed only with a cloth around their waist – was that the *sarong* he'd heard about? They looked calm and cool. There was a sound of splashing on one side of the compound nearest a small creek, close to the hole in the ground Ali had shown him. A man came out from behind one partition, all wet, including the cloth around his hips. So the sarong was the key to the mandi?

Hodges was assailed by some giggling children, laughing and shouting at him. He could only catch 'feringgi', but there must have been much ruder things said. One gestured a long nose, and another tried to pull the hairs of his arm and his beard. It was true they had flattish noses; yet judging by the way they held them while gesturing rudely at him, they smelled something about him that he couldn't.

He tried his new word: 'Mandi?' One girl gestured to where the man had emerged. She then darted to the next corner of the compound with similar partitions and came out with a woman still drying her long black hair. She seemed oblivious to her nakedness above the sarong until she saw the foreigner. Hodges looked away in alarmed embarrassment -- it was years since he had seen a female breast, even Margaret's. When he looked back the sarong was pulled up over her breasts and under the armpits, though still revealing enough of her smooth brown arms and shoulders to gladden Hodges' eyes. He tried a cautious smile and a Portuguese *bom dia* and got a smile back, though with teeth darkly discoloured. A flow of words came out, and when he looked blank she repeated just one – *makan*, with gestures of putting food delicately in her mouth. Hodges nodded eagerly, remembering how welcome a solid meal had been the previous night.

Back in his hut Hodges noticed a cloth neatly folded by the mat where he had slept; a sarong, perhaps. He decided to trust himself to the dagger, tucking it into the sarong he wrapped awkwardly around his lower body. Not willing to show his embarrassingly white and hairy upper body as the Javanese had, he put his jacket over the bare skin, clutched the bundle of presents and set off for his mandi. When he returned, a meal had been laid out in the hut – rice, as before, on a banana-leaf, with some eggs, a violently spicy sauce he had to push aside, and warm water. It was welcome to his belly, even though obliged to sit on the floor and make do with his dagger and hands for want of a spoon. He felt ready for whatever Bantam could throw at him.

It arrived soon enough when a young man came and told him in gestures to get ready. He led Hodges to the larger house at the back of the compound, where Ali greeted him cheerfully on the veranda. 'Ah, thank God you have learned how to mandi. I had warned my wife we might have to wash the place after you brought all the smells of that stinking ship ashore. The children had a good laugh at you trying to keep that sarong on you, but you'll learn soon enough.' He unfolded and refolded his own sarong with a few deft gestures, leaving it miraculously in place.

'Now. Are you ready to meet the *Shahbandar*?' He led Hodges out, clutching his bundle of presents. A couple of Ali's men followed. They were naked above their sarongs, and barefoot, but well-armed like Ali himself with the ornamented dagger they called *kris*. Ali led the way slowly along dirt paths to a broader road, past little stalls selling foodstuffs and changing money. There were as many women as men out on the streets and selling their wares. Eventually they passed through an ornamented gateway with some fiercer-looking guards who acknowledged Ali. They were then in a quieter, grander walled space which Ali called a *kraton*, where all the great men of Bantam lived.

The Shahbandar's compound was a big one with many wooden buildings, the grandest of which were elevated a little off the ground on wooden stilts. Ali headed for the largest of these, which he indicated was called the *pendopo,* the audience hall of the Shahbandar. Many men were waiting there, and even Hodges' unpractised eye could see how varied they were in dress, hairstyle and hue. Ali indicated that Hodges should join them while he went further in to talk with the Shahbandar's men. The arrival of an unfamiliar Englishman caused a stir, and several addressed him in languages he could make nothing of. One addressed him in tolerable Portuguese, introduced himself as Ah Pong, and was eager to establish the identity of this newcomer.

'I myself am from the great empire the Portuguese and Malays called "China". In fact there are many languages and peoples in the vast land ruled by the Ming. Nobody there has heard this word "China".

'Banten,' like Ali he used the local pronunciation, 'is full of all the world's people. There are hundreds of us "China" here, but that one over there,' he indicated one dressed like himself in a gown-like garment with long hair tied up in a knot, 'I speak to if I must in Malay, since he is from Canton where their language is like birds twittering. There are many too from what people here call "above the winds" – *di-atas angin*. Here,' pointing to a tall, fair man in a turban, 'is one from Gujarat, and there,' a darker man in sarong and tunic, 'from Kling. They bring the Indian cloth that people here will exchange their goods for. Did you bring some on your ships?'

'We have cloth from England,' said Hodges. 'The finest woollen cloth in the world.'

'Like your jacket? It looks grand, but people here will find it too hot. If you have silver they will sell you their pepper and spices soon enough.'

'At what price?' Hodges now eagerly plied him with questions about the market, and how to get hold of a shipload of cheap pepper.

'Everything will depend on the Shahbandar here,' was all Ah Pong would tell him. 'But you need to go to the market with somebody to guide you. When you have finished with the great man, I can take you there and show you the way.'

Ali returned and motioned to Hodges to follow him inside. 'But leave your shoes here,' he warned sharply, pointing to a row of strangely diverse footwear on the step. Hodges hesitated, but saw that nobody inside the pendopo wore shoes. These barefoot barbarians have their own ways, he reasoned, and he was in no position to argue.

The Shahbandar had been sitting on the floor but rose to greet Hodges and pointed to two chairs. 'I understand you feringgi have got so used to chairs that you have lost the art of sitting properly. So I bought some chairs from the Chinese for you.'

'Thank you,' said Hodges. 'You are most kind.' Gently he unrolled the telescope from its cloth, showed how it extended, and offered it to the Shahbandar. 'This is fine English craftsmanship, and very helpful at sea in spotting friend or foe.'

The Shahbandar put it to his eye, played with it, and gave it to a servant squatting nearby with a flow of Javanese instructions. 'Thank you. I am glad to see that the English make useful things. So tell me: you speak Portuguese but dress more like a Dutchman. What are you Inggeris? Do you have a king like the Portuguese, or do the merchants rule as with the Hollanders?'

'We have a good king, James, and before that a queen. Like the Dutch we fought against the Spanish king who tried to rule the whole world and force us to accept his religious tyranny. We believe Portugal should be our friend, but since their queen married the King of Spain they had to pretend to hate us as the Spanish do. The Dutch are more like us, and value their freedom. But Holland is a small country of traders and fishermen at the mouth of great rivers. There the merchants may be able to govern themselves, but not in a great kingdom like England.'

'Why do you feringgi hate each other so much, even when far from your home and your king? You all say you want to trade in peace, but you have little peace with each other.'

'We English will have peace with all who leave us in peace.

We live on an island, like you in Java, and believe we can be free of the wars and tyrannies of bigger lands. But Spain has attacked us, and we must defend ourselves.'

'So why have you come to Java,' the Shahbandar asked, 'and how can I help you?'

'We need pepper at a fair price, and other spices your land produces. Ours is a cold land suitable for sheep and their fine wool, but we cannot grow your pepper and cloves. And we would like a chance to sell our woollen cloth here, in exchange for your products.'

'I have seen some of what you call *wol*,' the Shahbandar responded. 'The Dutch gave me a coat of it, but it was hot and scratchy.' He mimed the itchy feeling. 'Have you nothing else to offer? You have fine ships and guns – they will be more popular here. I liked Dutch pistols better than their woollen coats.'

'I am sure we will find English products that are good for your market,' replied Hodges, trying to sound more confident than he was. 'But first we need your permission to buy pepper in the market.'

'You are free to visit the market for the supplies you need, *senhor*. But if you wish to fill your ships with our pepper, you will need the sultan's approval, or at least that of the old Protector who governs in his name. You must seek an appointment with one of them, and make sure you please them. I may warn you that they have grown tired of both the unruly Portuguese, who have attacked too many peaceful Muslim ships but have at least learned our ways, and the arrogant Dutch who honour no king. Perhaps you can convince him that the English would be more faithful friends for our sultan.'

'And how may I do that? Men say that you have the key to his door. Can you arrange for me or my commander to see him?'

'That may take time,' replied the Shahbandar ominously. 'Of course I will report to him that you are here and wish to see him, but he has his own ideas and I cannot answer for them.'

Hodges could see that his time was up, and another supplicant was being prepared for his turn. He made his attempts at polite thanks, and crept out. He had failed.

# Ah Pong

Feeling defeated, Hodges was glad to find Ah Pong still outside, conversing in what seemed to be Malay, but with very different sounds coming out of the mouths of the motley group of traders around him. He broke away to agree to take Hodges to the market the next day. 'Bring some Spanish dollars if you want to get supplies,' he warned. 'And practise your Malay if you hope for a decent price. You want *murah,* cheap, not *mahal*, expensive – got it?'

They were at the market early the next day, with a crew from the ship to transport supplies. Hodges could hardly have missed it even on his own, since the whole town seemed headed that way, some with huge bundles of fruit or coconuts, bags of mysterious herbs, knives or cloths. They started in the fruit area, where they were at once assailed by noisy women. *'Belanda? – Kom Koop'* one shouted. 'No Dutch, English,' he replied in English, not wanting to be taken for either Dutch or Portuguese.

Ah Pong said something in Malay that set them all cackling, and soon something like 'Inggeris' was going around the market. Hodges' eye was caught by the prettiest of the women selling little oranges. He decided to try his Malay: *'Berapa -* how much?' Her grin in reply was enthusiastic but disappointing, as he saw the row of blackened teeth. But despite his stumbling language he was able to put together a few barrow loads of fruit and vegetables at prices that seemed cheap. Ah Pong helped him out in translating for the biggest deals, and explaining the unfamiliar items. He felt sure the captain would like the large fleshy fruit called mango, and threw in a few others just for curiosity – the hairy red *rambutan* and the purplish *mangosteen*. There was more giggling when a cheeky young fruit-seller compared his hairy arms to the rambutan. Only later, after a few drinks, did Ah Pong tell Hodges what had been proposed about other aspects of his anatomy that set the women cackling and hooting again.

A couple of attractive young women seemed not to be selling anything except the betelnut they chewed all the time, but they were particularly attentive to Hodges and his men. They questioned the strangers in a mix of Malay, Portuguese and Dutch that they could make little sense of. The most persistent question seemed to be one to which he did not know the answer – 'How long are you staying in Banten?'

The Englishmen were happy enough to try to communicate with these beauties with their long black hair and warm brown skin. Simmons, an older Norfolk man who had been the quickest to find women in other ports, was getting very friendly with one of these, to the cackling appreciation of the fruit-sellers.

Hodges looked to Ah Pong for help to understand what was being said and whether this was going to lead to trouble. 'Are these whores? They look much like the other market women. Do they have protectors or pimps?'

'If your men need women for one night there are those here who keep slaves for that, and make good money from the Dutch and some Chinese. But the Banten people don't think well of that business, and won't let their own women engage in it. These girls are local Javanese or Malays, and they are looking for a trader-husband for at least a few months. This is not like China, where women are married for life. Here, there are many who boast how many husbands they have had – I know of one who had a dozen before she was thirty. It's handy for the Chinese traders, here for the trading season. My Javanese wife knows the market far better than me, and stays and trades for me while I go back to Amoy.'

'And do you have a wife there too?'

'Of course – who else would look after my old parents? She's a good woman, and the mother of my children. I am always pleased to see her when I get home – especially for her noodle soup. But these Javanese women know how to pleasure a man – so much more passionate than our China women. It's always good to come back.'

'And do these Javanese women take another husband while you are gone?'

'No, or if they do there is trouble when the Chinese comes back. If we tell them to expect us next season, and provide the goods to live on meanwhile, they will be faithful. If the man dies at sea, or doesn't come back with the fleet next year, then the wives are free to marry another if they choose, keeping the house and goods of the first. How is it in the land of the Inggeris?'

Hodges thought of the dockside at Portsmouth, and the women who came to greet an incoming ship – not as respectable-looking as these women talking to Simmons. 'There are some good-hearted whores, I'm sure, who would like well enough to stick with one man for a year or more. But the seamen in England are not traders, they have little money and no home except the ship. They may long for a wife but they must make do with a whore when they can afford one for a few hours. In England a marriage is forever; there's no ending it.'

'As in China,' sighed Ah Pong. 'The system here is better, especially for us who have to stay for a few months to wait for the winds to take us home.'

'Our men must be back on the ship tonight; they have little money and no trade goods. They may be gone in a few days. They will be easier to manage if they can do some quick drinking and whoring in safety. Can that be arranged here in the market?'

'Not with these women, if you value your life. My friend Kwee might be able to fix something for them. Tell them to come to the furniture market over there in the afternoon and ask for Kwee.'

Hodges spoke sternly to Simmons and the others. Ah Pong said something to the women that made them slip quietly away.

'Where do they sell the pepper?' asked Hodges. 'I need to tell my master what he's likely to get for his silver.'

'Over here you'll find some pepper and spice stalls, in what we call the free market. You could buy a measure of pepper there to show him. But that is just for local needs. The big sellers are all aristocrats – *orangkaya* – or relatives of the king. They can't sell without seeing your chop from the Shahbandar. Still, let's have a look.'

Sure enough, the women in the spice market would sell no more than the amount that one segment of bamboo would hold. Their prices were cheap enough to make a miraculous profit in Europe, but the woman who sold a portion to Hodges warned him darkly that the Shahbandar's men kept a close eye on her. She and her friends dared sell no more to the English, no matter what the price.

The English moved on to the animal section of the market, where Hodges hoped to find a fat heifer he could send to the desperate crew. There were many black squat buffalo there they called *kerbau*, but they looked like tough eating compared with the Devon cattle of home. Ah Pong pointed to a darker slim man with long hair he called a Kling, tending a couple of white cattle with a hump behind their shoulders. 'Unless you're ready to cook the buffalo meat all day, one of those will suit you better. Don't look too interested or you will pay a bucket of reals.'

The Kling indeed drove a hard bargain, in his mix of Malay and Portuguese. 'Dutch buy everything,' he said. 'You no like, Dutch pay more.' Only when Hodges walked off to show more interest in the buffaloes did he get a price that seemed fair. His men eventually walked away with a large cow, the first beef they would be tasting since they left England.

This done, the men thought they had earned a good drink. 'You'll not get one here,' Ah Pong advised. 'Some of the preachy Muslims gave a beating to the Javanese toddy-seller who used to be over by the fruit-sellers, and nobody dared stop them. He's more careful now to sell only from his house.'

'With so many sailors in town, there must be an ale-house somewhere.'

'I don't know about your ale, but we Chinese know how to drink. The preachers don't bother with us since we don't pretend to be Muslim like the Javanese. You'll find plenty of arak houses in the Chinese quarter, and they're happy to empty the pockets of the Dutch and Portuguese. Your Scott is there most nights, drunk out of his mind. Get your purchases onto the ship and meet me at dusk at the main gate of the Chinese camp over in that corner of the city.' He waved towards the southwest. 'Just ask for *kampong China*. I'll show you the arak house where most of the Dutch go. Your men might find Kwee there too if the liquor makes them think of women. He makes sure to visit the arak houses where the feringgi are drinking when their ships are in port.'

Simmons and the men cheered up at this news, and set about hauling supplies towards the waiting longboat. They returned before dusk with more of the crew.

'Ready for some action, I see. But remember,' Hodges warned, 'you're in a town with no friends and little law. Watch your money, and above all don't start a fight.'

He taught them the basics of bargaining in Malay as they strode through the town, but only a few were listening. It was all he could do to pull some of them away from the women selling fruit at a corner near the city wall.

'You'll be safer in the Chinese camp,' he said with more hope than conviction. 'I'm told they are less quick to put a dagger in your ribs, and readier to settle things with money.'

When they reached the gate in the western wall that led to the Chinese camp, Hodges saw with relief that Ah Pong was there. But from their hats and swords, the men he was chatting with were clearly Portuguese. 'Papist pigs,' Simmons muttered. One of the Portuguese understood the tone if not the English, and spat out, '*bandidos heréticas!*'

Ah Pong reacted quickly to the threatening tone. He took one of the Portuguese by the hand and introduced him to Hodges, whom he called 'Senhor Hod' – he seemed to have decided this was all the locals could get their tongues around. 'This is Senhor de Castro, who has lived here long enough to know the Java ways. He knows the Banteners are tolerant enough of the feringgi. In many ways they like you better than us Chinese, since you part more easily with your money. But they don't have any time for the way you fight all the time among yourselves, even when you are guests in a peaceful port like Banten. So as long as there are Banteners about,' he nodded in the direction of a couple of Javanese with their krisses tucked neatly into their sarongs, and wearing little else, 'you had better behave.'

'*Encantado, senhor,*' said de Castro, pleased to see that Hodges spoke Portuguese. 'I hear that you English have a king again, who is not so hostile to the true faith as that Elizabeth. What are your plans here? Will you play the mad Dutch game of trying to control all the spices, or do you plot your own course?'

'England is a free country under the noble King James, as it was before with our gracious queen. You will find us as ready as ever to defend our freedom, whether against the arrogance of the pope, the tyranny of Spain or the greed of the Dutch. And what of Portugal? Do you allow the King of Castile to trample on your liberties, or do you too plot your own course?'

De Castro snarled at this, but their exchange was disrupted by the rowdy English sailors.

'Enough of this papist lingo! Shall we cut their throats now, or will you show us where to drink?'

Hodges told his men tersely that there was to be no fighting ashore in Banten. 'Save your bravado for when we need it and have a chance of winning: at sea. Let's find the ale-house.'

Ah Pong excused himself from de Castro, and hustled the English out of the gate and into the palisaded Chinese camp – a different world. By contrast with the spaciousness within the walls, here all was clamour and congestion. The lanes were narrower, with no trees, and no chickens running about. The houses for the first time resembled those of a proper town, solid brick, with shops below and dwellings above.

'Where are the women?" asked Simmons. 'Are you sure this is the right place? I liked the look of those dusky lasses at the market better.'

Sure enough this looked like a man's town, with Chinese men selling everything one might need – furniture here, pots there, tools and knives across the road, various cloths further down the street. The only women they could see were inside the houses, or helping one of the Chinese men with his wares. Several of the sailors began bargaining for the clever wooden toys, colourful China bowls and small knives set out for sale.

'Later,' bellowed Simmons. 'Let's find the grog first, and you can come back and spend your money here if you prefer trinkets to trollops.'

Ah Pong took the English past numerous stalls selling food and what appeared to be liquor, and dived into a small lane where they heard the familiar sound of rowdy sailors. The arak house was distinguished only by some Chinese lanterns outside its narrow doorway, but inside was a kind of hall with tables and benches, lit by torches and leading onto an open area stretching down to a creek, where some revellers were relieving themselves. A Chinese man came over and greeted Ah Pong, who now spoke in a strange language about the new customers he had brought. Switching to Portuguese, he introduced Hodges.

'This is Hong, owner of this arak house. Hong, you should meet Tuan Hod, who speaks Portuguese and is trying to learn Malay. His men need to learn how to drink in Banten.'

Hong quickly escorted the men to an empty table, and looked puzzled as they began to shout for wine, brandy and grog.

'I will order one glass of your arak for all the men,' confided Hodges to Ah Pong, 'if you get me the correct price before these fellows are too drunk to care.' Some exchanges followed with Hong, a small sum was handed over and a jug of liquor appeared with a dozen small bowls to drink from.

The English began cautiously, but gulped it down eagerly once they felt its warmth in their bellies. When Hong returned with a second jug, Hodges asked him what it was. 'Do you bring it from China?'

Hong needed the help of Ah Pong to explain that it was all made locally, except the most precious Chinese *baijiu* kept for his rich Chinese customers. It seemed to be made from the juice of a palm like a coconut, but with a smaller nut they called *lontar*.

In simple Malay Hong said, 'Lontar juice is *tuak*, sweet. Heat *tuak* with fire, make arak.'

'Ah, like turning wine into brandy – "burnt wine". Is this Javanese or Chinese?'

'Tuak is Javanese, but Chinese know how to make fiery strong. The word arak not Chinese. Maybe them.'

He pointed to a group of the darker Indians they called Kling. Ah Pong recognised one with a European-looking face but well-dressed with a Muslim gown. He introduced him to Hodges in Portuguese as Murad, from Gujarat. 'This arak is almost good enough to be Chinese, but the word arak doesn't come from China. Is it yours?'

'The Arabs invented everything worth having unless it came from India,' said Murad, 'not you Chinese. Of course arak is from Arabic, just like alcohol. First it meant just sweat, like what your English friend is doing. Then they figured out that if you can make the wine sweat by boiling it, the sweat is stronger, like the kick of a camel.'

'So how come your Prophet condemned it?'

'Just because the Arabs were the first to invent these pleasures, our Prophet was the first to see its dangers. When you Chinese and feringgi have all seen reason and accepted Islam, no doubt the world will be a better place of peace and harmony, without alcohol. Meanwhile, you infidels have your uses. You can buy me another drink.'

Ah Pong guffawed, but Hodges was distracted by the uproar from the English corner. They seemed to have got into a contest with some Dutch sailors in downing the arak and were now shouting for Kwee and women. A long-haired Chinese had emerged to try to talk to them, but was making no headway amidst a Babel of languages. Simmons had him by the shirt and was looking menacing.

Hodges dragged Ah Pong over to mediate. 'What's the fuss, lads?'

'Does this fellow have the women or not? He makes no sense.'

Hodges pulled Simmons away and asked Ah Pong to explain what the deal was. Kwee's voluble Chinese was translated into Portuguese for Hodges, and then into English for the crew. 'He has a couple of women available this evening, but they can't cope with all these men. At most two for each girl, if the money is right and your men behave themselves. The others can come back another night and he might try to get more.'

The men erupted into pandemonium. Some feared to trust themselves to the sinister-looking Kwee, but there were a half-dozen who were starting to fight for the first experiment. Hodges asked Ah Pong to plead a little harder to keep the peace by accommodating them.

Another flood of Chinese followed, with Ah Pong looking increasingly sceptical. Eventually he turned to Hodges. 'Some of these southern barbarians have strange customs. Kwee says he has one or two other women, the pick of the Bugis slaves, but they are particular about who they accept. They seem to regard only men with something extra in their manhood as able to get them interested. I've heard of such things, but told him I doubt you English have anything to offer in that line. He said the addition could be arranged for a price.'

'*Filho da puta!* I can't tell these men there's something wrong with their pricks. What does he mean, exactly?'

More Chinese. Kwee gestured to Hodges to follow him across to another table where some locals were speaking in Malay.

Kwee and Ah Pong joined in, and soon had them chortling and slapping each other. Eventually one of the men produced his penis for inspection. Hodges saw small round lumps under the skin. When the man shook it they made a tinkling sound. Even without understanding the words, it was obvious he was proud of his exhibit and the conquests he had made with it.

Sensing an opportunity, Kwee offered, 'Depending what quality you want, some balls of bone can be inserted for one real, or of silver for five. Very nice.'

Simmons had joined the crowd of spectators and roared, 'No wench is going to mess with my prick. This is black heathenry!'

When the sailors had finished their incredulous merriment about this episode, urging each other to go first, their ardour for women seemed diminished. Only three eventually went off with Kwee, the others preferring to let them try the local wares and report back.

Hodges warned them to be back on the ship by midnight, and left them to it.

# Bintara and Sri

Hodges returned several times to the Chinese camp. It was not only the easiest way to purchase the small comforts of life, its arak houses were the places to learn how this town worked: what ships were in port, what pepper and spice was expected, and who was paying what price. Malay was the best way to start every conversation, if only with the ubiquitous *dari mana,* where from? He was always surprised at the answer. There were so many places he had never heard of – Masulipatnam, Tennasserim, Pegu, Johor, Patani, Cambodia, Palembang, Acheh, Banjarmasin, Banda. Then there were the Chinese ports that all sounded the same.

The English seamen were also eager to return, and had their share of the fights that broke out around the drinking houses. One evening Ah Pong grabbed Hodges urgently as he was trying to understand what a Kling trader was telling him about the cloth trade.

'You must come at once, Tuan Hod, if you want to save your men. You must tell them *never* to provoke the Javanese.'

Hodges recognised some of the troublemakers among the crew, evidently allowed on shore for the first time. They looked both drunk and confused, but ready to take on a group of Javanese men with their krisses drawn. Some local women were screaming at them, but they continued tipsily cursing everybody as if oblivious to the looming disaster.

'Stand back!' Hodges shouted. 'Just keep quiet if you value

your lives.' Turning to the best dressed of the Javanese, he summoned all the polite Malay words he knew, larded with more exaggeratedly apologetic Portuguese. 'I am sorry if these Inggeris have given offence. They have just arrived below the winds and know nothing of customs and language. If they have offended I will make sure not happen again. We wish to learn your way and trade peaceful here.'

Various languages erupted from both women and men, shouting at each other and at Hodges. It seemed clear enough that the sailors had laid hands on some of the women, who had come to buy at the nearby furniture shop. The English were saying the women were ready for play, but the women looked far from happy and their men ferocious.

'These women may look frisky enough, but they are out of bounds. If you want to play at hot cockles I will show where you can pay for it. Any man who gets in a fight over women will be in irons for a week,' Hodges bluffed, without much hope that Pickering would back him up.

'I apologise for their misbehaviour,' he continued, now speaking gravely in his pidgin Malay. 'I punish these men hard. We English want be friends Banten people. This not happen again.'

He drove the men off in the direction of Hong's arak house, acting as fiercely with them as he dared. As he cursed them loudly and cuffed the ear of one of the drunkest he whispered, 'Ask for Kwee if you want a woman without trouble.'

As the hubbub subsided, Hodges thought he heard a gentle, 'Obrigado senhor.' He turned back to find a lovely young Javanese woman being pushed forward by an older one, who evidently had much more to say than the young beauty herself. After another volley of Javanese from the older woman, the young one said in polite Portuguese, mocking his pidgin Malay, 'My mother wants to thank you for keeping these sailors in order, and to ask if our family can help you in your business here. Perhaps her husband, my father, can help you to "learn our way and trade peaceful here".'

Hodges eagerly agreed to visit at the first opportunity. He was running out of time to secure that chop from the palace, and every chance must be taken. He was in any case mesmerised by the exquisite young woman with her strangely elegant Portuguese. How could the rough male cacophony of this trader's town have given rise to such an enchanting apparition?

The way to Bintara's compound led through a maze of paths, the larger ones muddied by the passage of cattle and horses. Ah Pong had given him the general direction, envying his good fortune in finding an opening to one of Banten's most respected *orangkaya*, as they called the leading merchants. Hodges had to ask the way half a dozen times of the betel-stained old women selling fruit or pots at the junctions of these paths. He was learning to respond to their ribaldry in kind, as they made fun of his faltering Malay and pointed to his long nose, beard and hat. '*Lain kali,*' another time, seemed the safest response to all their invitations to buy, to dally, or whatever other indecent suggestions they were making through their cackles.

Finally he reached a raised gateway in a brick wall that stood out from the surrounding congestion. A man wearing a European jacket over his sarong stiffened as he saw the foreigner, grabbed his spear and disengaged himself from the group around a Chinese food-seller outside the gate. When Hodges explained his business with Bintara in a few rehearsed Malay phrases, the guard shouted something through the gate. A head soon appeared, then another, and soon a small crowd of men and children were gathered at the gate, pointing to his apparel and ginger beard as if he were from another world. And so he was, he reminded himself. He struggled to think what the villagers in Hampshire might have made of one of these swarthy fellows with sarong and kris appearing at their door. The children would think him a monster, no doubt, just as some of these frightened-looking children appeared to regard him, peeking around the legs of the braver boys.

The crowd of children scattered as an older man appeared at the gate and said, 'Please come in, sir,' in passable Portuguese. He ushered Hodges up the few steps to the open ceremonial gate, and into a compound as ordered as the space outside was messy. In the centre was a raised platform with a high roof, open on three sides. It was the structure Hodges knew they called a pendopo, like that of the Shahbandar. Two men there were playing softly on an arrangement of gongs.

On two sides of the compound were neat rows of the fragile houses on stilts he had seen everywhere. On a third was the only solid brick building, which must be what they called a *gudang*, or warehouse, where Bintara kept his trade goods. In a corner was a small open building, elevated a few feet off the ground and distinguished by its three-tier roof – a miniature version of the great mosque of the Sultan. To this the old man, who had introduced himself as Karim, motioned as he led Hodges to the pendopo. 'The Bintara is saying his evening prayer – it is *maghrib*.' He nodded towards the west where the sun had just set. 'Please sit down.'

With a sinking feeling Hodges saw that, as in the Sultan's palace, there was nowhere to sit – only some mats on the polished floor of the pendopo, to one of which Karim was gesturing. Remembering the agony of his legs after sitting on the floor there, he opted to remain standing. This forced Karim to do the same.

'He is a follower of Muhammad then, your master?'

'Of course, we are all Muslims here – people who submit to God. But we do not all pray as Bintara does. He likes to say that he has to make up for his Chinese ancestors, who ate pork and who knows what else.'

'Chinese? I thought he was a Javanese aristocrat, and close friend of the Protector.'

'He is, he is,' Karim insisted. 'Many people here have strange ancestors – that is not to be held against them. I myself had one Indian grandfather and the other Japanese, but I believe I am a good Javanese. Of course our mothers are all islanders – Javanese, Malay, Bugis – and that's what counts, isn't it? Bintara's father was a great Chinese merchant called Chong Poh, but when he settled here he became a Muslim, married a beautiful Javanese lady and became a Javanese. Bintara himself does not speak that barbarous language at all, except when he has to swear at the coolies on the wharf. Please do not suggest he is anything but Javanese, or he will not be pleased.'

He whispered these last words, as the tall figure of Bintara made its way from the little mosque to the pendopo where they sat. '*Senhor Inggeris*,' he called a Portuguese welcome as Hodges mounted the stairs. '*Boa-vinda casa Bintara*.'

Hodges thought he could do almost as well in Malay as Bintara's pidgin Portuguese, and muttered a few words of greeting. This produced a flood of Malay to which Hodges could only look expectantly at Karim. 'He says you are most welcome to his house, and he is delighted that you have begun to learn our languages. He hopes you will in time come to appreciate our customs also, and see the wisdom of the religion of Muhammad. He has heard that the English are good people, neither grasping like the Dutch nor swaggering like the Portuguese.'

'Please tell him I am grateful for his kind words, but that I believe the English are good people because they are true to their own religion, that of Jesus.' Bintara frowned when this was translated to him, so Hodges hurried on to more promising subjects.

'I too have heard much praise of Bintara's fair dealing with all. I have come far in the hope of trading our goods fairly with yours. But there seem to be some in Banten who have no wish to see fair trade. I believe that Bintara can help me, so that I do not have to tell my king that Banten is a port unfit for civilised traders.'

Karim delivered a lengthy speech to render this, and when he had finished Bintara smiled, began to settle himself cross-legged on a mat, and gestured to Hodges to do likewise. Hodges was about to continue, but was stopped short by the low but firm words of Karim.

'I gave you a chance, by embroidering your kind words about Bintara. If I translated your other remarks you would be thrown out for insolence. You feringgi will get nowhere unless you learn patience in doing business. For us, trading is part of the art of civilised living. If Tuan Hod wants Bintara's favour, he will sit down, talk about agreeable matters that interest Bintara, and wait until he is ready to learn what you want. Then he will decide whether he wishes to help you.'

Hodges struggled to restrain his desire to walk straight out. Much as he detested the thought of another senseless torturing of his legs, he had no other options he could think of. Karim talked like one who knew. Hodges lowered himself very carefully to the floor, and did his best to imitate the graceful posture of the Javanese.

Bintara had said something quiet but firm in what Hodges was sure was Javanese, for it had none of the sounds he recognised. A servant crept soundlessly to the back of the pendopo and disappeared behind a curtain. Hodges pondered how to cope with the etiquette quickly enough to get to the point before his legs betrayed him. He forgot the discomfort, however, the moment the young woman who had spoken to him outside the Chinese camp appeared.

She approached in a soundless, half-crouching glide, accompanied by an even younger girl carrying a bronze tray. Both quietly knelt behind Bintara, heads respectfully lowered. Now he had a chance to admire the mysterious beauty, exquisitely finely featured with straight black hair down to her waist. A sarong of expensive Indian cloth covered her lower body completely, but only a loose scarf graced her light brown shoulders and arms, allowing him to marvel at their liquid movement. The younger girl may have been a servant, from the humble pose she adopted and the local cloth she wore.

As Hodges was admiring this vision, Bintara was returning to his pidgin Portuguese. 'Since we are amigos, we chew *pinang* together. The Portuguese call it betel. I show you how.'

The betel idea did not appeal. Hodges had tried it in the market and found it bitter, and that red juice was a messy business. Any thought of demurring was forgotten, however, as he was transfixed by the delicate movements of the young woman. She flowed forward somehow in a crouch, took a betel leaf from her assistant and proceeded to fill it with lime and the betel nut. With deft movements she folded the little package together and offered it to Bintara in a graceful dance of homage. As he began slowly to chew it he visibly relaxed, closing his eyes for a moment and smiling. 'Now, Tuan Inggeris, you must learn how we surround business with pleasure in Java.'

The same delicate performance was performed for Hodges, the girl managing this without ever raising her eyes to him. Tentatively he took a small bite, and winced with the bitterness of it. With much urging from the Javanese he managed to get it all in his mouth, and found it tolerable if he chewed little but kept it in the side of his mouth. It was not easy, however, to manage this while answering the questions with which the Bintara began to ply him. How many ships did England have? How many did the Dutch? How were the cannons on shipboard made, and where did the best ones come from?

To his dismay, the girl had withdrawn as these questions began. She soon glided back, however, and whispered something in Bintara's ear. He nodded, and she moved to the curtains as Hodges struggled to regain his focus on what Bintara was saying. Now an older woman appeared – was she the more voluble one from their previous encounter? He'd had eyes at the time only for the daughter. But yes, this must be she, for she walked confidently forward to take up a position almost beside Bintara. The girl sat coyly at the older woman's elbow, almost out of Hodge's sight.

'This is my wife, Tuan Inggeris, and my daughter Sri,' said Bintara expansively. 'It seems you have met them already. They ask me too many questions about the strange foreigners who come, and I cannot answer them all. So, if you are willing, I shall let them speak for themselves.'

'I am delighted,' said Hodges. 'In my country, the fine people dine together in their great houses, the men beside the women. It makes men's tongues looser when they have to charm the ladies. And does *Senhora* also speak Portuguese?'

He could see that both women were listening as if they understood, but at this the older woman grinned: '*Pouco*, Tuan,' she giggled, making a sign of how little with her fingers. She went on in Malay: 'My daughter is clever, and she has friends among the children of the Portuguese with our local women. She will explain for me what strange things you tell.'

Bintara pressed forward again. 'My daughter is indeed a headstrong child, and gives me no peace with her questions. She has a better head on her shoulders for language and for figures than her brother, though, so I let her help me with my affairs. She was asking me why you English and Dutch come so far only to buy pepper and spices. Are you so desperate for these things in your country? Perhaps you can explain.'

'Our country is cold, and different plants grow there than here. Few of them are as spicy as yours. Pepper, cloves, nutmeg, ginger, cinnamon cannot grow in our fields, often covered with frozen water called snow. The Portuguese brought these spices from your country to sell us, but they charged high prices and supported our enemies. The Dutch should be our allies, but they charge even higher prices and try to control the whole supply. So we have come to deal fairly with you who grow these spices. But it seems we need a chop from the Shahbandar, and he says only the Sultan or the Protector can approve that. Every day the Dutch buy more of the pepper in the market, and I fear there may be nothing left for us.'

'And what does your cold country produce that you can bring in exchange?'

'We have the finest wool in the world from which we make clothes.' Seeing their puzzled looks Hodges explained that a sheep was something like a goat, but that its hair was softer and more abundant. Seeing this was failing to impress his audience, he tried another tack.

'We are a clever people, and make things, as the Chinese do. Much more than the Dutch and Portuguese.' He pulled out an eyeglass and presented it to Bintara. 'This makes things bigger, so that even ageing eyes can see small writing. There are many such inventions in Europe that we can bring here. The German towns make the best of these glasses and clocks, but they have no big ships as we do. We can bring you all the best inventions of Europe, even weapons, without bullying as the Portuguese and Dutch try to do.'

Bintara looked unconvinced. 'Yes, this glass is wonderful, thank you. I will use it to read the Quran. But I think you do not have enough of such gadgets to pay for all our pepper. The Dutch had the same ideas when they first arrived. They tried to sell this *wol*, and gave clever things as presents. But now they have realised that we people below the winds love the Indian cloth. See how beautiful it is.' He pointed to his own checked sarong, and the highly coloured designs with horses and elephants worn by his women. 'My wife and daughter want to bankrupt me by outdoing their friends with more beautiful patterns. But fortunately they have little taste for your *wol* or your gadgets.'

Sri whispered this exchange to her mother, who directed a torrent of Javanese protest at her husband. She then tried to ask Hodges something in her mixture of languages, but he only caught enough to realise he was on delicate territory, so paused in uncertainty. This finally provoked Sri to address him directly in her beautiful Portuguese, with the same gently mocking manner she had used outside the Chinese camp.

'My mother, Raden Ayu, wants to know about your English women. We have seen Portuguese women, both the mixed ones and a few who are fairer and come from Portugal. Some of them are pretty, she says, although their hair is not good. But the Dutch and you English come here with only men. Why is that? She believes you also must have had mothers and therefore wives. Are your women kept closeted in the house, as with the Arabs? Do they wear hats, shoes and too many clothes, like you men?'

Hodges rummaged again in his bag, and looked through some cheap engravings he had picked up in London for such a moment. Finding one of Mary Queen of Scots, he passed it over for the ladies' examination, with apologies for its torn and grubby look.

'This is a picture of the mother of our present king, known as a beauty in her day, with many admirers. Our ladies wear no hats. Don't ask me why. Perhaps they count their hair their glory and like to braid and display it. Do you find the queen pretty?'

'Mm – what a strange costume, more like the gods we see in theatre than a real person. It must be hard to move. Do all your women have such narrow waists? And why is her hair all curly like that? Is it a disease?'

'It is true they wear more clothing than you here, and great ladies like this queen spend much time and money dressing with stays and ruffs, making their waists small and their hips wide, as you see. Even that famous red hair of the queen turned out to be false when they cut her head off, and the wig came off in the executioner's hand.'

'Cut her head off! Even queens are not safe in your country! It must be a scary place for ordinary women.'

As Sri explained this exchange with her mother, Hodges bit his lip and wondered how to put things right. 'No, no. We take great care of our women. It is true that both kings and queens were caught up in the fight between the false religion of the Spanish and Portuguese with their tyrannical pope, and our freedom to follow the truth we find in Jesus. But now we are at peace, and the country is united.'

'We too have some religious problems, when the Muslims say only their religion is true and fight with those who practise the old beliefs of our country. Too many people were killed, but nobody thought of cutting the heads off women over these matters, let alone queens!'

Bintara was clearly not pleased with this direction. 'Enough of this nonsense, daughter! Whatever they do in England, we live in peace here, even these quarrelsome feringgi. You have pestered our guest enough. He came to ask our help to trade peacefully, and we should give him some advice.

'Tuan Hod,' he turned to Hodges, 'if the Shahbandar is not giving you what you want, you must find some way to the palace. As you know, our king is a young boy, and carefully guided by the Protector and the others around him. As it happens, our queen, the boy's mother, is one of the most influential. Women here have much to say, and their heads are in no danger. If she receives you and likes your story, you will have no trouble with the Shahbandar.'

'But how could I approach her?'

'Well, you could ask my wife,' he nodded to Ayu. 'She goes often to the palace to join the queen in what they call *tapak*. It is an old Javanese practice that should have disappeared now that we know the truths of our Prophet Muhammad. I try to forbid it, but my wife is stubborn, and the queen more so.'

A sharp exchange of Javanese followed between Bintara and his wife, with Sri interposing what sounded like sweet reasonableness to Hodges. Eventually it was Sri who conveyed the conclusion to him. 'My mother knows the queen well, and much admires her wisdom and generosity. She will speak to her about your problem. Since the queen is also very interested in the new knowledge brought by many visitors to our land, she may be curious about these Inggeris. If she agrees, my mother will send Karim to bring you to the palace on Thursday afternoon, when she usually receives visitors.'

'And how will I speak to her?'

'The queen has her favourite translators, since she is curious about foreign ways. She sometimes asks me to the palace to help, and sometimes others. She will decide. You should bring some gift that will interest her in your new knowledge or your arts. Better not mention the queen who lost her head,' she smiled coyly.

Hodges made his exit as gracefully and gratefully as he could, given that his legs barely functioned after sitting on them for two hours. For the first time since he set foot in this extraordinary, frustrating place, there was music in his heart.

# The Palace

Hodges fought hard with Pickering over a suitable present. Only by appealing to the General, promising that this was the key, the only sure way to gain access to the pepper market, did he win the right to present the only elegant clock left on the ship. Pickering was not pleased. 'That's it, Hodges. If you waste this treasure, it's back on shipboard for you. There are better ways to get what we need.'

He tried desperately to focus on the right approach and the right Malay words to convince the queen and the court she inhabited. Instead his mind turned constantly to the black-haired, barefoot beauty who had so delicately folded the betel leaf. Was it the thirst for a woman's touch that so distracted him? He thought he had long ago tamed that beast amid the rigours of shipboard life. Once, it had sufficed to call to mind the image of Margaret in their first weeks together, when the softness of her flesh had been a source of endless wonder. That image had long gone. All that her name evoked now was the memory of her bitter tears and reproaches. She had wallowed in the grief that followed the damned fire that had killed their son, until she convinced herself it had been his fault rather than her own. She had made their house a place of misery where laughter was forbidden.

It was this mysterious Sri who now slid constantly into his mind. How could she be so demure and deferential with her father, yet so lively and curious in conversation? That voice gently mocked his clumsiness and ignorance. By some magic she had made her barbarous, cursed, hot land seem warm and welcoming, and his own dear England cruel and peculiar. As he planned his words to the queen, it was only her response he anticipated. It was her, not the queen, his rehearsed explanations were designed to impress. But what if she was not there? He must be prepared for that, even if the thought now cast a chill on him.

Karim came as promised. Hodges, dressed in his English finest, followed him through the streets, clutching the clock wrapped in a fine Indian cloth. Ah Pong had pointed out that the wrapping was part of the gift brought by foreign traders. The Gujarati cloths indeed made the English fabrics look drab, and he had spent his last reals buying one to wrap the clock.

Karim explained they were not going to the great front gate foreign envoys were allowed to use, but to a side door giving access to a middle section between the northern side of the sultan and his courtiers, and the southern, or women's section of the palace. 'No men are permitted there,' Karim explained, 'except the young sultan and some *sida-sida*.'

'What are they?'

Karim answered with cutting gestures at the level of his genitals.

'You have *capado*, eunuchs, like the Turks?'

'Indeed, it is a new idea the foreign Muslims have brought; some of the sida-sida were gifts from Arab and Turkish shipowners.'

Karim spoke to a couple of guards in respectful Javanese, indicating Hodges with a downward-pointing thumb. He had seen Sri and her mother do this, apparently in polite deference.

One guard hurried off, and returned with a plump older man dressed in a beautiful sarong.

'You wish to see Sri Ratu,' he addressed Hodges in Malay. 'Come with me, but leave your shoes here, and your sword with Endang there.' He pointed thumb-wise to one of the guards. 'It will be returned when you leave. Do you have other weapons?'

Hodges was ushered through several gateways with steps up one side and down the other, until the sound of female laughter welcomed him to a courtyard in which a group of women sat on a raised platform. They surrounded an older woman seated cross-legged on a slightly higher level. The eunuch (if such he was) indicated that Hodges should stand silently until called. He tried to look respectfully downward, while involuntarily searching for Sri. She was not there!

Gradually the group on the floor began rising to a crouching position and backing outwards, bidding their respectful farewells. When only two younger women remained at her side, the queen gestured for Hodges to come forward.

He had rehearsed his opening lines in Malay: 'I bring greetings, Kanjeng Ratu, from the King and Queen of England. They have heard of the glory of Banten and wish to befriend its rulers and trade with its people.'

'Ah, you speak some of our language, however badly,' she laughed. 'No doubt you will learn more. Come closer and sit there so I can see you.'

Hodges carefully placed the clock as close to the lady as he dared, before settling his reluctant legs in the place she indicated.

'This is the unworthy gift we have brought from across the vast oceans.'

One of the attendants picked it up and placed it before the queen, who kept up a rapid commentary in Javanese as it was unwrapped and opened, to her apparent puzzlement. Hodges had wound it up and tested it, and to his relief its delicate spring mechanism was intact. It was still ticking, but when the attendants turned it upside down in their curiosity to see what made the noise, it stopped. Most interesting to the queen were the gold figures on top of it, representing the sun and the moon. Eventually the queen turned back to Hodges in Malay. 'Is it alive or dead, this clever box? What is the message it brings from England?'

He struggled to explain with his few Malay words, many gestures and some Portuguese what a clock was, how it measured time and why it had stopped making a noise. '*Boleh cakap Portugis?*' she asked, and when he nodded enthusiastically that he indeed spoke Portuguese, she whispered to an attendant.

Soundlessly and mysteriously, Sri appeared at her side and exchanged a few pleasantries with the queen without appearing to notice Hodges. Finally she turned to him with head lowered and said, 'The queen thanks you for this strange box with its pretty illustrations and figures. She would like you to explain what the pictures show, what noise it made and why it stopped.'

With obvious relief, Hodges poured out what a 'clock' was. He used the English word to appear to claim it, and got around the word Nuremberg clearly visible on the face by implying this was an English town full of clever craftsmen. He explained the agricultural scene on its cover, imagined Greek nymphs amidst

English farmland, and how important it was to measure the hours of the day.

'Wait, wait, impatient Englishman,' Sri gently mocked him. 'I will try to explain to her what you say a "clock" is, and the decorations.'

After much back and forth with the queen, she turned back to Hodges. 'The queen likes the pictures of English life, and the strange creatures you have there. But why did it make a ticking noise and then stop, and what are the numbers on its face? Is it some kind of tool for prophesying good times and bad?'

Hodges seized with too much enthusiasm his chance to impress the girl. He explained how the sun defined the day, the moon the month, and how the clock measured the hours of the day precisely. Its energy to do this was provided by a spring, which he must now reset. Sri's smile grew ever more long-suffering, but this time it was the queen who interrupted to demand a simple explanation. Hodges had too obviously forgotten it was she to whom he was speaking. Javanese exchanges followed, briefer and more spirited than Hodges' explanation.

Finally Sri turned to him again: 'The queen respectfully points out that the farmers watch the rains and the sun to know when to plant; the astrologers watch the movement of the stars to know the favourable dates and to mark the passage of times; the Muslims know when to pray by the movement of the sun and the moon. What more can this machine do?'

Hodges hesitated, his confidence vanishing. 'In England the sun rises at very different times in summer and winter, but we may still wish to dine, or meet with others, at the same time.'

This was clearly unconvincing. He tried again, pleading to Sri: 'We live in a time of many discoveries. Measuring things is important to know our world. How long does it take a star or moon to move across the heavens? How long for a man to run around the walls of Banten and return? How long to boil away a pot of water? Is it the same in a hot country, Banten, as a cold one, England? Just as we have discovered new countries that open our eyes to new things, we can discover more things about our natural world. For our ship to find its way to Banten, we must be exact in measuring the route by the stars. If we are to understand our amazing world, we must learn to measure things precisely, including time.'

Sri's eyes widened as he grew more passionate on this, his favourite subject. Her translation now appeared to hit the mark. The reply that came back gave him hope.

'The queen is glad to see your zeal for knowing new things. She agrees that this is a time for new knowledge; we must be open to learning something from every source, even from a faraway, cold island. We have learned the world is round like a ball, and that England can be on the other side of it without falling off. Her parents did not know such things, but she hopes her children will understand even more.'

Sri now had trouble keeping up with the queen's flow of questions. 'Tell us about your king, and the queen you had before him. Can women rule equally with men in England? And your religion? The Portuguese say that the holiest authority of the Christians is in Roma, but the Arabs say the Turks have conquered the old empire *Rum* and it is now a great Muslim empire. Where is the centre of your English religion?'

Hodges now appreciated limiting himself to one thought at a time, allowing Sri to translate while he pondered the next. Much depended on hitting the right note.

'The old empire of Rome broke into two, and Constantinople ruled the eastern part. The great city the Turks conquered was Constantinople, and that is now their capital. The rest of the old Roman Empire remained Christian.'

The queen queried Sri several times about this, going back and forth about the words *Rum*, *Rumi* and *Roma*. Finally she seemed satisfied, and he continued.

'The Christians in Rome tried to make a new kind of religious empire. Their bishop called himself pope and tried to rule all the Christians. The popes became corrupt and pretended that if people gave them money they could buy their way to heaven. We English are Christians, and believe that Jesus showed the way to God. Good people in the cities learned to read the holy book of Jesus, the Bible, for themselves. They saw that the pope had distorted his teaching. He was a fraud, and Jesus never meant to have a tyrant ruling his church. Many good people, especially in Holland and England and Germany, showed a better way to honour Jesus and worship God as free men. But the kings of Spain and Portugal cruelly destroyed this belief and killed its upholders. Only the King of England was strong enough to resist, and protect the reformers.'

'Was this Jesus a god? How many gods are there? The Muslims say that you Christians are no better than the old believers here who acknowledge many gods, and that the truth is that only one god made the whole world, us brown people as well as you pale ones.'

'We too believe that! There is only one god who made everything. Perhaps he is the same as who the Muslims call Allah. Jesus was part of god, the part that showed us how to live as men. The learned men say that god has three personalities, like a father, a son, Jesus, and a spirit. But he is one.'

'Your learned men sound confused. And so all your gods – father, son and spirit – are men? We Javanese know that cannot be right. If god has more than one personality, they must be male and female. Could Jesus have a father but not a mother? The Muslims and the Christians make the same mistake. They think that god is all male and has no need of women, so they feel free to fight and kill like men instead of to nurture and protect like women. I hope you learn at least, from your time in Java, that all creatures are either male or female, and only the unity of both can be god.'

Taken aback, Hodges looked from one woman to another and decided on a different tack. 'I was told that Banten was all Muslim. But does Your Majesty favour a different religion of the Javanese?'

'Difference is only on the surface, is it not? I am a Muslim, and I am a Javanese. You Christians and Muslims have taught us one thing; that this new world is all one, so it probably had one creator whom we should all worship. But since you fight so much among yourselves about it, we know none of you have the whole truth.

'We Javanese are not so eager to spread our ideas to others. We even talk to you Christians in Portuguese and to the Muslims in Malay, because our language and ideas seem difficult for others to understand. But we know that truth does not lie in division, or in any book in only one language, since this god made us so various in our languages and ideas. We must all work to find the truth that is within us. That cannot be expressed in Malay or Arabic or Portuguese. '

'But in Javanese?'

'Perhaps not even,' the queen conceded after a pause.

Hodges was not sure he understood the lady, but since her thoughts were delivered so sweetly and confidently by Sri, he did not want to disagree. Instead he mumbled his gratitude for her guidance, and his hope to learn more about Java.

'Now tell us more about your English country. If you reject this Rome and its pope, who decides how you worship? Do you have priests like the Portuguese, who claim to work miracles and to control the path to god? Or are you more like the Dutch, who seem to have no priest and no king, and to side with the Muslims against the Portuguese?'

Relieved to be on safer ground, Hodges took up the challenge. 'It is true that the Dutch have no king. When they fought against the Spanish and the pope, it was the merchants of Amsterdam who led the fight and took charge of the country. So although they have many Christian reformers, the religion that holds them together is only the pursuit of money. In England we have a king, who governs a church to which all must belong. We have priests and bishops, but they only preside over spiritual matters and do not attempt to become little tyrants like the Portuguese priests. We believe we have the best of both freedom and order. And so we have the freedom to trade with your kingdom. I hope Your

Majesty will help me in this matter.'

'Yes, yes. We have had problems with the unruly foreigners who want to fight in our port – Portuguese against Muslims, Dutch against Portuguese. But you English have only one ship, and I believe you pose no threat to our country. If you continue to trade peacefully, to respect our customs and the freedom of trade for all here, then you may buy your pepper. The more buyers the better for us, and the easier to resist the greedy demands of the Dutch. The king will issue your chop tomorrow.'

Hodges repeated his words of gratitude, and promised the English would be found honourable and peaceful if not attacked. As he prepared to untangle his aching legs and make a decorous exit, the queen stopped him with a stern command: '*Tunggu*, Tuan Hod – wait.' Sri then translated what followed.

'You say you wish to learn more of Java. Before you leave the palace, you should experience something of our beliefs. Perhaps you will understand then that we are Muslims, but also something deeper and truer. There is a ceremony taking place this evening which you should attend, and watch and listen carefully.'

'The queen,' Sri added, with lowered head, 'has commanded me to accompany you and explain as best I can what is taking place. I must obey, as must you.'

There could be no argument. As the eunuch reappeared and led them through more courtyards, he tried to question Sri about the queen, her beliefs, and what lay in store. She only answered softly, '*Paciência; paciência*,' and when he persisted: 'Our wise queen thinks you are too restless, and you need to learn how to become quiet, quiet on your inside.'

# Possession

Sri and Hodges came to another raised platform where a performance was taking place amidst much merriment. Two misshapen figures with masks were clowning about, hitting one another and exchanging comments in what appeared to be different languages. One saw Hodges as he was trying to sit unobtrusively on his protesting legs. He mimicked the ungainly foreigner, and focussed attention on him with an exaggerated welcome dotted with quasi-Portuguese words. Hodges sensed that Sri discreetly shared the mirth of the small crowd. Once attention shifted back to their slapstick routine, he asked her what had been said.

'The clown, we call him Petruk, welcomed Senhor Big-nose to join the performance. He thought you must be related since he too has an awkward body and a large nose.' Suppressed giggles followed before she could get out the rest. 'He thought you may be an envoy from the land of the monkeys, and feel more at home swinging from trees, since you do not appear to have the habit of sitting in our way.'

Her sweetness disarmed all protest. They turned back to the antics of the clowns. 'Is this a comedy, only to amuse, or is it part of what the queen intends me to learn?'

'The clowns amuse, yes, but they are not only clowns. They are the spirit of Java; they have magic powers like seeing into men's hearts. The king over there,' pointing delicately with her thumb to a motionless figure, 'will soon speak his words of wisdom, but those words are hard to understand. The clowns will do his will, even if they appear to misunderstand and joke about it. Like us, they can understand only enough to do right and avoid evil.'

Sure enough, the king began to speak as the clowns sat before him. Sri strained to catch his low, steady voice and difficult words. The antics of the children in the audience, who lost interest as soon as he started speaking, made it even harder.

At last she turned to him. 'This is Arjuna, who is very wise but speaks with difficult old words, hard for us to understand. I think he is questioning whether it is necessary to fight one of his relatives who has fallen under the spell of an evil monster. He must consider duty, honour, the love for his relative, the terrible cost of war, and the danger of evil in the form of the monster. In the end we know there will have to be fighting. That is the most exciting part, when he shows his skill with puppets and everybody wakes up. Although I don't fully understand Arjuna's wisdom, I suppose the queen wants you to hear the kind of values he represents, and how to maintain balance and harmony in the kingdom, and in men's inner being.'

'If you don't understand it, who does? In my country we have had enough of so-called expert priests using difficult language to hide their ignorance. So is that all the queen wanted me to hear?'

Sri questioned an older woman in the audience before replying. 'This is part of it, and perhaps we have seen enough for her purpose. This performance has been arranged as part of a process of healing, or restoring harmony to the spirit of the daughter of one of the courtiers in the palace. That will happen in another place later – I will show you.

'But first you must eat, not only because you are hungry, but because you must share in this ceremony. Eating together is part of the healing, showing that nobody is alone and the community has forgiven and put right whatever is out of order. This *wayang* – theatre – is also part of the healing, and explains the deeper meaning of things for those who will listen. But,' she smiled softly, 'most of us know that we will never understand. It is enough to learn how we must behave in order to maintain balance in ourselves and with others.'

They came to a larger pavilion where many men were again seated on the floor in a large circle, each with a banana leaf which they were using to eat from a series of small bowls of fish and garnishes. Large baskets of rice were brought around by two women on their knees to add to what was on the leaves.

'Here you must join the men and use your words of Malay. They will speak slowly and politely, so you need not fear being made fun of. Later they will find out all about you from their women, who will question and make fun of me mercilessly. I will tell them some of the truth – enough to make them laugh but still to understand that you are human too. Do what the other men do, use only your right hand for eating, and try not to make too much mess. Later they will bring some water for you to wash your hand.'

Hodges did as he was told as two older men made room for him and welcomed him to the feast. He tried several positions for his aching legs, but still found himself too far from the banana leaf to eat. One old man, who announced himself as Ketut, showed him how it was done. '*Begini Tuan* – like this,' as he deftly rolled some rice into a neat little ball, dipped it in garnish and popped it into his mouth. Sure enough, the other men politely pretended not to notice his disastrous attempts to transfer the rice from leaf to mouth. But from the adjoining kitchen area, where the women were both preparing the meal and eating it, there were guffaws aplenty. Sri had disappeared into a huddle of women where the cackling was loudest. Giving up on the rice, Hodges spied some chicken legs being brought around. He helped himself to two. This he could handle with one hand, and never mind the eruption of laughter from the women's section.

Hodges' Malay could by now cope with Ketut's inevitable question, 'Dari mana – where from?' but not so well with the answer. 'Not Hollander, not Portuguese – Inggeris,' he repeated. 'Far away ... many months ... cold ... good people.' He tried all the words he knew. In despair, he turned the question back to Ketut, and was relieved this took the pressure off for long enough for him to devour some chicken.

'From Bali,' was the answer, and when Hodges looked suitably puzzled, a stream of Malay followed with many accompanying gestures. Bali, it seemed, was an island, and very beautiful. But it had a great fire mountain, gunung api, that exploded; many died, rice crops destroyed, nothing to eat; joined a ship to trade; came to Banten.

A great drumming began from a nearby courtyard. 'What's that?' he asked Ketut, but understood nothing of the reply.

'Come, see.'

Hodges need not have worried he would lose Sri; he was obviously the centre of attention for the women. As Ketut led him towards the noise, she again appeared at his side, accompanied by some young women who could not contain their curiosity.

'Where are we going?'

'You will see. Please watch what happens with an open mind. My father has closed his mind to the Javanese rituals because the foreign Muslims say they are from the devil. My mother, like the queen, knows that they are a window to the deeper world, where there is evil but also good. I love both my father and my mother, but on this they will never agree. My father would be angry if he knew I came here, and if you talk to him about it, you must not say that I did.'

They entered a courtyard crowded with people, some of whom were dancing in a cleared space in the middle. A Javanese orchestra of drums and gongs was playing at the side, but faster and more rhythmically than those elsewhere in the palace. A fire had been burning in the middle of the cleared space, but was now largely embers and smoke, which some of the dancers appeared to inhale.

Gradually Hodges discerned a pattern in the seeming chaos. There were well-dressed young girls dancing slowly with studied concentration, older men dancing demonically, some with strange masks. Was this the *amok* he had heard about, when normally restrained and polite Javanese became suddenly crazy and violent, heedless of pain to themselves or death to others? Fearful devilry!

One unkempt old woman danced in a different way, appearing heavy and clumsy. One by one the young girls jerked suddenly upright and the rhythm of their movements grew faster. Two of them were picked up by male dancers and placed precariously on their shoulders. There they continued to dance ever more energetically as the tempo increased, somehow keeping their balance with eyes closed. The male dancers now walked through the glowing embers, oblivious to the heat. The crowd seemed absorbed, but tittered when one man got tired of carrying his girl, made some jocular remark and transferred her to a younger man.

'What are they doing? Is this some sacred thing, or just an entertainment?'

'It is very serious, though we call it play. The girls are sacred. They are now not themselves, but like gods or spirits. It is hard to explain, but we can all feel their presence. Can you?'

Hodges felt only confusion and alarm at what might happen next. But now attention shifted to the older female dancer, who also jerked suddenly upright. She danced towards the embers, seized a handful in her naked hands and rubbed them together, seemingly in a trance where she felt nothing.

'She is a *balian*, a person able to become a vehicle for the spirits of those who have already died. The woman here told me that she will try to contact a high-born lady who died, leaving her married daughter not just upset but disturbed, crazy. Her Muslim husband would not let her perform the old rituals where sacrifices must be made to ensure that the soul is at peace. Her husband and his Muslim friends think she is possessed by the devil, but their prayers did not help. Then she began dreaming about her mother being unhappy. So her sister was allowed to organise the ceremony to talk to her, although the husband refused any part of it.'

After some violent movements and reckless handling of the

hot embers, the priestess became suddenly still and grave. She spoke slowly, seated now on the floor in the Javanese manner. Hodges noticed for the first time a well-dressed younger woman who approached her, took the balian's hand and pressed it to her forehead repeatedly, muttering tearfully as she did so. After uttering something in a reassuring tone the priestess suddenly sat up and surveyed the crowd. She announced something loudly, looked straight at Hodges and beckoned to him imperiously.

He turned in alarm to Sri for an explanation. This was getting out of control.

'She thinks there is a stranger here who does not understand our ways. She must speak with you first, before she can talk more to her daughter. She commands you to come forward. Please do as she asks, or there could be serious trouble. I will come behind you and explain what she wants.'

Terrified, Hodges looked for an escape but saw none. The courtyard was packed with people blocking the exits, and all were now looking at him. Sri pushed him gently forward and he reluctantly moved to stand before the priestess. She directed some solemn words to him, which appeared to end with a question.

Sri whispered urgently. 'She needs to know why you are here and whether your motives are good. Please say something in any language, maybe English so it sounds strange, and I will tell her what she needs to hear, that you have come from far to learn the wisdom of the Javanese. '

Panicking, Hodges eventually managed to mumble something about his long voyage and many troubles.

'Enough,' Sri hissed. She bowed low and spoke to the medium

in a register he had not heard, low and slow. This appeared to satisfy the balian, but she was not finished. Looking intently at Hodges, she spoke again at length, and appeared to end with a question. This time Sri answered for him, to the evident satisfaction of all.

'It's alright. She accepts you. Please step back and let her attend to her daughter.'

'What did she say?' Hodges whispered when they were safely back in the crowd, 'and what did *you* pretend I said?'

'Later,' was all he could get from Sri. She was intent on listening to the priestess, who was now addressing the tearful young woman, sometimes questioning her, but mostly speaking reassuringly in a low voice. As the woman at her feet continued sobbing, she spoke some sharp instruction to her and then suddenly collapsed. Her 'daughter' rose and rushed about the small circle, before being restrained by some of the older guests. She quietened and was still.

Hodges' hair was standing on end as this last drama was enacted. It was a kind of popish devilry, he thought, and yet was clearly deemed a success by the young woman and the crowd, who now began talking excitedly. Sri seemed more remote and inaccessible as she was drawn into the drama, while he wanted only to escape.

'That's enough. Let's get out of here.' he spoke roughly, in a voice that surprised him.

'Yes, it is done, she is well.' Her calm only added to his disquiet. He tried to push his way to safety, but quickly realised he had little chance of finding his shoes and his sword without

Sri. Brusquely he turned back to her: 'So, was it god's work or the devil's?'

'There are Muslims who ask that question, as if there were two, but only two, forces in the universe. Wiser ones know that god is not god unless he is the whole of our world.' Struggling for words, she made an expansive gesture. 'The world is full of the many spirits of living and dead people. Some people, like that balian, are wise and strong enough to move among them and help them to get closer to ...' She struggled for the Portuguese words again.

'To what? To god or the devil?' Hodges demanded.

'To god, of course, but everyone has a different idea of what god is. I am not sure I would like your god if he is as restless, aggressive and male as you say, always fighting this devil as if fighting was the way to understanding.'

She paused, now looking at him with a mixture of concern and alarm. 'Perhaps it is hard for you feringgi men to be still – I don't know if your women are different. That balian spent all last night and this morning being still, meditating – *tapak*. Only that enabled her to empty herself and grow closer to what she probably calls *sunya* – something like emptiness. Muslims say their *ikhlas* is the same thing but better. Perhaps you would call it god. Only then could she be useful to other spirits who have something to say to us ... even to you.'

'What did she say to me, damn it?' Her calmness only inflamed his fury.

'It was the young woman's dead mother who spoke to you, and seemed to know something about you. She knew that you were troubled about your family. She asked you not to worry about your dead son. He was at peace, and blamed no one for his death – neither you nor your wife. Although your ways are not ours, she understood you gave him a ritual that was good for him.'

'God's blood!' A cold sweat overcame Hodges as the blood drained from him.

Since he was evidently struck dumb, Sri continued. 'It was the same with the mother of the young woman. She told her daughter that it did not matter whether she was Muslim with her husband or followed the old way of Java like her mother. What mattered was that she continued to honour her parents after they died, as she had in life, and to be sincere in seeking union with god through whatever path. If her husband forbade the old rituals, she could achieve the same peace, safety, *sunya*, through his Muslim ones. Her husband was a good man, and she should be a good wife to him.'

Hodges hardly heard these strange words; he was back in England wondering whether his son was in the bosom of Abraham, as the preacher had said, or with the angels. Might he somehow still communicate? How could the cursed priest-woman know about poor, doomed Timothy? He had shared his private misery with nobody, not even on the *Dragon*.

Sri pointed him towards the entrance where he had come in. When she ducked away to report to the queen, he was still too shattered to protest. Only once outside, with the reassurance of shoes and sword and a familiar bustle of people, did he wonder if he would see her again. There were so many questions. Despite his denial of her devilry, that damned witch had opened the wound in his heart about Timothy. He must have an explanation. How could beguiling, level-headed Sri be mixed up in this nonsense?

Although there was much to do for the ship now that he had the *chop*, he instead lingered in a small market near the palace entrance. He needed answers. Would she come out by the same gate? He allowed one of the women food-sellers to engage him in conversation, and even accepted her offer of fried rice he didn't need.

Finally a small group of women emerged and hurried past the little food stall. He called out to Sri in Portuguese, 'Wait, I need to ask you about that performance. Who was that woman – some kind of sorcerer?'

Sri tried to pay no attention, but as he persisted she stopped and spoke coldly in Malay: '*Permainan sudah habis. Pulang rumah.*' She seemed to be telling him it was over, and he should go home; but why so cold, and in a language he barely understood?

As she turned back to her companions, shouting erupted from a group of angry young men. They seemed to be directing abuse at Hodges, but still more at Sri. He could catch nothing but the tone of contempt and the word *Portugis*. When he grabbed his sword and looked menacing they backed off from him, but there was no stopping their lunging at Sri. She shouted back at them and pointed to the palace, but one of them grabbed her and tried to pull her away from the others, while two other lads drew their kris and menaced the other women.

Hodges leapt into the fray and found himself facing the two kris-wielders, while the other screaming women came to Sri's rescue and pulled off her assailant. Hodges forgot all the good advice against fighting onshore and went for the attackers in fury. Only when one was badly wounded in his kris arm did the two men flee, and Hodges realised his arm was also bleeding. Worse, there was no sign of the women. He presumed they had scurried to safety, but without even a word of thanks.

He was walking grimly back to his house when he remembered the talkative woman with the fried rice. His job was to leave a good impression of the reliability of the English, but he had not paid her. He turned back. She was still there, and when she saw his money welcomed him with motherly attention to his wound. 'Muslims,' she said with a shrug, pointing towards a mosque he had not noticed just outside the palace wall. Brushing aside his protestations, she had in no time washed his wound, wrapped it in some leaves and tied it around with a bandage of cloth. She pronounced it good, *baik*.

Now she was trying to convey something else, which she said several times in a low voice until finally he caught some of the words. 'Pretty lady say ... you come ... Bintara house ... *kliwon*.'

He could not understand that last word, but she counted on her fingers – one, two three, four. Could it mean he should call in four days? Anyway, worth a try, he reasoned, since he should thank Bintara for his help. There was confusion in his head, and throbbing in his wounded arm, which would take some explaining to Pickering. Yet there was a spring in his step as he found his way back to his hut.

# Enchanted

The next days were busy. Hodges had acquired the royal chop, and even an agreement that his general could meet the young boy king and present his gifts. There was much to explain to the ship's merchants about the pepper they had come so far to seek, but also cloves from the eastern islands that he had learned could be had from some of the Malay traders.

Yet amidst this activity he needed to find Ah Pong, to try make sense of the extraordinary events in the palace. Most urgently, what was this kliwon when he should meet Sri?

Ah Pong explained that it was the last day of the old Javanese week of five days – *lege, pahing, pon, wage, kliwo*n. Nobody had told Hodges about this confusing calendrical phenomenon before. To cater for the numerous foreigners, Banten had officially adopted the seven-day week of the Christians, Muslims and even Chinese. It had been hard enough for Hodges to learn the Malay names of the familiar week, and to get his head around the way the 28-day Muslim months kept changing their relationship to Christian ones. Now he had to cope with a cycle of five days. It apparently still governed the thinking of Javanese, and the way markets moved around from village to village and back again in five days. His mother in her Hampshire village would have liked this; he remembered her complaints about stale food as she waited for Thursday market day.

'How can anybody deal with all these systems?' he demanded

of Ah Pong. 'There must be some authority who could impose a sensible method.'

'Who? Java has many kings, many religions, and many foreigners. We Chinese have our own system of months and years, and nobody can tell us to abandon it. The Muslims are the same. But auspicious days are very important to the Javanese, and they seem to keep at least both Javanese and Muslim in their heads.'

Sure enough, when Hodges tested this with the woman in Ali's compound who supplied his meals, she told him today was *selasa pahing*, citing both the Tuesday of the seven-day week and the second day of the Javanese. In three days it would be *jumat kliwon*, a powerful combination of the Muslim Friday and Javanese day for meditation. It was the day Sri had assigned for their meeting, and he hoped it would be auspicious also for him.

He shared with his friend some of his confusion about the strange religious ideas the queen and Sri had introduced to him. Ah Pong was unsurprised by the spirit possession, thinking it was the foreign Christians and Muslims who were strange in their reluctance to accept such things. But there was nevertheless a dangerous conflict between the old Javanese ways and the new Muslim ones. The queen was a powerful protector of the many who clung to the old ways even when calling themselves Muslims to satisfy the state. The foreign Muslims feared her, and put their faith in the boy king to shake off her influence and fully embrace the religion of Muhammad like his dead father. Even families were divided, and Bintara's was no exception. 'Be careful,' Ah Pong cautioned with a glance at his bandaged arm. 'We Chinese try to stay out of their conflicts, and agree with both sides.'

The conflict was palpable enough in Sri's household, and Hodges found himself divided. His head supported the men of the household against the hocus-pocus he had been through in the palace; but his heart was with the women. As he sought an appropriate thank you gift for Bintara's help in getting the chop, he worried most about Sri's reaction. He looked through the engravings brought out to impress the Asians, but decided the graphic depictions of human anatomy, or Foxe's martyrs, would only confirm Sri's idea of quarrelsome Europeans. The 'overdressed queens' had not been a great success.

There were some musical instruments which would surely be new to them – their music was all gongs with different pitches; agreeable enough, but monotonous to his ears. He had seen the interest the Javanese showed in the poor instruments the Portuguese had introduced. The English instruments were surely more impressive, especially the violin that the purser sometimes played after a fashion. But Hodges knew it was beyond him to make an agreeable sound with that, or to teach anyone to play it, even had he somehow persuaded the purser to part with it. He opted instead for a finely polished recorder. His mother had taught him to play some tunes as a child, and even to read the music sheets with new tunes from Italy. Having persuaded Pickering that this was essential to the success of their pepper trading, he took the recorder and some sheets to practise in his hut until it began to sound like music.

When the visiting hour, the late afternoon of kliwon finally came, he was surprised to find little activity at the Bintara's house. Abdullah was there again, and explained that his master would soon need to go out but could perhaps find time to see him briefly.

Had Hodges misunderstood Sri's instructions? The great man duly appeared, and graciously heard Hodges' practised Malay words of gratitude. He appeared only polite on unwrapping the recorder. 'Is it your English *seruling*?'

Hodges assumed he was referring to the bamboo pipe he had seen played in the market, but insisted it gave a finer and more varied sound. As he demonstrated the Italian tune he had rehearsed, Bintara's wife appeared and showed more interest in the performance. But Bintara was clearly in a hurry. He stood and gestured for Hodges to depart.

'Unfortunately, I must leave you for some religious duties. I am glad your mission has been a success, and trust that you will pay fair prices and keep the peace here in Banten. We look forward to seeing your English ships in future years.'

'*Tunggu,* Tuan Hodges, wait,' Ayu interrupted, and directed some Javanese to her husband. He hesitated and then conceded.

'My wife is interested in the paper you read when you play those notes, and wishes you to explain what that is for. I will leave you with her and Abdullah, and bid my farewell.'

No sooner had he departed than Sri glided into the reception hall and sat beside her mother. She explained her mother's interest as if she had been listening all along.

'We have heard that the Portuguese have a way to write music on paper the way one might write a story in words. It seems that you also have this system. Can you explain how it works?'

Relieved at this change of mood, Hodges delighted in explaining the five lines and the notes that danced along them.

When he tried to explain the octave, mysterious to the women, he had to shift from his unsuccessful demonstration of the higher pitch of the recorder to using his voice. As he demonstrated the seven notes of the octave and how it started again, Sri laughed.

'I understand. It is like *slendro*, but you feringgi make it different. We also know how the cycle repeats at a higher register. But it takes only five notes to get there.' She demonstrated with her voice, sweet and true, but strange to his ear. 'God gave us five fingers, to show the harmony of his creation. Why do you make it more complicated?'

After more giggles and discussion with her mother, she spoke more quietly. 'My mother says that the written notes are an interesting idea, but not necessary. Our musicians can easily remember their tunes; more easily than the words of the poets, in fact. Are yours less skilled that they need this paper?'

'I am less skilled, indeed, and needed to read this paper to learn the tune. True musicians can remember very much, and play for hours without reading. This writing is a new thing also in Europe, but a wonderful part of the new knowledge of our age. In Venice, in Italy, there are clever people who create new tunes and new ways of combining tunes, and write music for high voices and low voices to sing together, or high and low recorders to sing in harmony. Even though we are far away in England, their music can be written down and brought by traders, so that we too can learn new tunes. Soon our English musicians will be better than theirs, and they will be able to read our music.'

'My mother, and also my father when I explain it to him, will be grateful for this music-writing. They will ask our musicians if they can do the same thing.'

After checking that Abdullah was well out of earshot, Sri continued. 'Now I must thank you for endangering yourself on my behalf outside the palace, and explain why I was rude to you. The mosque is close to the exit of the palace, and many hot-headed young men gather there, Javanese as well as foreigners. They sometimes fight with the Portuguese, who are as bad as they are. They do not like to hear the Portuguese language, and hate to see a local woman like me speaking it to the feringgi as if I were on their side.

'My father is much wiser, and knows that we must learn from all foreigners. He likes to quote the Prophet's saying, "seek knowledge even unto China". But he tries to be a good Muslim, and frequents the same mosque as these young men. My brother Khalid has had a good Muslim education, and cares even less than his father for the old Javanese ways. He is at the mosque now for his religious class, where they may be talking about the incident with a feringgi who spoke Portuguese. I hope nobody knew I was Bintara's daughter; please do not tell anybody about it. He also worries about getting me safely married to a good Muslim. This is not easy.'

She broke off to explain to her mother, who then unleashed a torrent of angry-sounding Javanese. Finally Sri turned back to Hodges.

'My mother and father do not agree in this matter of my future husband. Of course my mother, Raden Ayu, is Muslim too, and appreciates the changes Islam has brought. But she fears to lose her daughter if a Muslim husband is as strict as some are about keeping women in the house. She feels she has already lost Khalid. And the man my father favours for my husband is one of Khalid's older friends, one of the devout, strict kind of Muslims with an Arab father.' She puckered her pretty lips at this.

'And you?'

'As long as my parents disagree I do not have to make a choice. And I am certainly not easy to please.' She smiled mischievously at him. 'But now you must go, so I do not have to explain to my father what we were talking about.'

He wanted to stay, to pry further beneath the tantalising surface of this beguiling young woman. How could he see her again? But she called Abdullah, who unceremoniously led him back to his shoes and the gateway of the compound.

# Accused

Hodges could not get this woman out of his mind. His heart racing, he was not ready to return to his hut. He paced the city, drawn towards the thought of a stiff drink in the Chinese camp. Trying a new alley that seemed to lead in the right direction, he found himself in an unfamiliar quarter. The smells were different, with something like incense carried in the air. The familiar rhythm of the *gamelan* gongs was interrupted by staccato drumming. It was coming from inside another walled compound with an ornamented brick gateway like a little split mountain, doorless but with four steps on either side.

Curious, he went up and down the stairs into an incense-filled courtyard, where a motley group of people were engaged in different activities. Some were prostrate before statues, others were chatting and drinking. There were many Javanese, but also what looked to be Chinese, some Indians and a few Portuguese. In the centre of the courtyard, women were making offerings to a statue of an elephant-headed god, before which a drummer was performing. But there were other statues also getting more or less attention. One being garlanded by two women was strangely familiar. Surely it was a papist Madonna, carved in wood and partly painted? Hodges peered closer: yes, she definitely held a rosary with a cross in her hand.

Near the entrance were some women selling garlands of flowers and candles. He asked one, '*Apa ini*, what is this – Islam?'

The woman emphatically shook her head. 'Old religion. Muslim not like.'

She offered Hodges a garland and began the usual bargaining. 'Make your wish. Can get.'

On impulse he took the garland, paid the woman and placed it at the foot of the Madonna. For the first time in months he quietly prayed, he knew not why, that Sri would not marry her strict Muslim.

One of the Portuguese greeted him when he was finished. 'Welcome, stranger. I am Gomez. Are you also Portuguese and Catholic?'

Hodges recoiled: 'Certainly not. I am English, and will have none of a pope who wants to enslave us.'

Gomez gestured to the Madonna with a raising of the eyebrows.

'She is still the mother of Our Lord. I was surprised to see her in this place, which looks far from Christian.'

'We Christians have no church or priest here in Banten, but we come to this place where the old-style Javanese can retain their worship. They are tolerant enough to honour all that is holy, and especially seem to like the Madonna. What's more, they protect us against the Muslims, and we them.'

As Hodges began to protest at this confusion of ideas, a clamour outside the gate interrupted them. A group of young men were shouting angrily in Malay, of which he could only catch the words *allah* and *kafir*. One had begun to attack the demonic-looking figures ornamenting the gateway with an axe. Muttering 'Here they come again,' Gomez pulled his sword and rushed out to defend the gate.

Others joined him, including a number of Javanese with their krisses. They seized the attacker and grabbed his axe. His Muslim friends came to his aid, many in white garments and headbands. The whole lane outside the gateway was filled with struggling bodies, some duelling with their krisses.

A long-haired older Javanese emerged from the compound and stood at the top of the stairs, before dancing down them in a kind of trance like the spirit-possessed men Hodges had witnessed in the palace. He chanted slowly in a strange language as he wielded his kris in slow, ritualistic movements. Now he became a prime target of the Muslims, though somehow managing to parry the first kris-thrusts as if he believed himself invulnerable.

One tall, turbaned attacker rushed at him with a long blade, shouting 'Allahu Akbar'. The old Javanese barely interrupted his chanting as he collapsed in a pool of blood. This enraged the other defenders so much that they lost all control in the fight.

Hodges stood aside, horrified at the savagery of both sides. He was spurred to action only by hearing the strong, unmistakable voice of Bintara above the melee. Though the words were unclear, there could be no doubt that he was seeking to restrain the Muslim hotheads. 'Don't stain our holy faith with blood,' seemed to be his message, but it was nearly drowned out by the shouting. Hodges sprang to the defence of Sri's father, as he seemed in danger of attack from both the warring sides.

He shouted in Portuguese at Gomez, who appeared to have assumed the leadership of the defenders. 'This man is good, our protector. We will all lose if this continues. Call your men off.'

Hodges backed up his words with his sword, forgetting the ache in his arm. He pushed Gomez's group back, trying to frighten rather than draw blood with his sword. Bintara was less successful in restraining his fellow Muslims with hands and words, and soon the two of them were swallowed in the chaos.

The fighting stopped suddenly as the word *jawara* was shouted through the melee. A group of men dressed in black were shoving people aside and thumping with bamboo sticks any who resisted. As the fighters fell back, Hodges saw to his horror that Bintara was among the crumpled, motionless bodies. He rushed to his aid but was roughly pushed aside by one of the black-shirted men.

The man who bent over the fallen Bintara was Khalid. He embraced his father, and mournfully pronounced his death: *"Mati."* Accusingly he gazed around, looking darkly at Hodges. But it was Gomez, standing bloodied but defiant, on whom he fixed, shouting and pointing. Three of the jawara seized the Portuguese roughly, disarmed him and marched him off.

'*Lari, Tuan!* Run for it,' muttered the woman who had sold Hodges the flowers. 'The jawara show no mercy, and care little for truth.'

Hodges had to tell Khalid what had happened, to make sure that Sri also knew he had done his best to protect her father. But there was no chance of getting past the menacing jawara, even if he had the Malay words to express his grief. He sheathed his sword and backed away from the jawara into the curious crowd of onlookers.

If he rushed to Bintara's house now he might be able to explain to Sri and her mother what had happened, and how he had tried to stop it. Terrible as it would be to bring such dreadful news, it would be worse if Khalid got there first. He would think the worst of all the feringgi.

He had been wounded also, but hardly noticed it in his despair at how everything had turned to ashes. Meeting Bintara and his amazing daughter had transformed his life, reconciled him to Java, and even made him a hero for his countrymen on the ship. How could it all have gone so tragically wrong so quickly? Logically, he should escape to the safety of the ship before the jawara or the Muslim zealots blamed something on him. But then he would never see Sri again, and she would believe him a heartless enemy. It was unthinkable!

He stumbled back as fast as he could in the direction he thought he had come from. He must explain to Sri how her father had died a hero, and how they had struggled together for peace and reason against savagery.

But in his despair he became lost in the narrow alleys. He stumbled about, reversing direction many times before calming down enough to ask directions from one of the fruit-sellers. By the time he approached the familiar area of Bintara's compound he could hear that he was too late. There was wailing from a procession carrying Bintara's body towards the compound. As they approached its gateway he saw with anguish Sri rushing out, seeing her father's lifeless body and flinging herself upon it.

He hung back in the shadows wondering how he could possibly speak to her now. The procession moved inside, with Sri holding her father's head and sobbing. She had some angry exchanges with Khalid, punctuated by her cries. Hodges waited some time after all had moved inside before moving cautiously to the gateway. He could see that the body had been placed on the little pendopo, and was now being attended by a tearful Raden Ayu and numerous other women, while Khalid was giving instructions to servants.

Where was Sri?

# Hate-Love

This was his chance. If only he could talk to Sri alone, surely she would understand. But where? Behind that curtain was a forbidden area, where only his imagination had previously been allowed to enter. This time he cared nothing for propriety. He must see her, comfort her, explain to her, or die in the attempt.

It would be impossible to cross the courtyard and pass that curtain without being noticed. There must be a back entrance to the domestic quarters, however; he had seen in other compounds serving women coming and going to market.

He circled around the compound and found that there was a small door. Thank god it was not locked, and there was little sound of activity within. He removed his shoes and sidled inside as quietly as he knew how. He caught a faint moan from one room, then a deep breath, a sob. Quickly he entered, needing to console her broken heart, whatever the risks of being where he should not.

Sri lay face down on a mat, her back heaving with stifled sobs. The room was dark and lined with cloth, so it was a moment before he saw that she was holding something. As he began to speak, she sprang up and flung it at him; it was the broken half of the recorder he had given Bintara.

'Traitor!' she cried. 'Murderer. Infidel. Slave of Satan. You have killed him!'

She stood there trembling with rage, her eyes narrowed with

hate, her long hair for once unkempt. A loose garment fastened with two brooches covered her heaving breasts but her sarong, as always, was elegantly fastened around that tiny waist.

'No.' Hodges tried to be calm. 'No, Sri, your father and I tried together to keep the peace, but the fanatics wanted blood. He died a hero.'

The words sounded limp in his mouth, but before he could explain more she was at him. She sprang like a crazed cat, hissing and hitting his face, his chest. He staggered back and tried to dodge the blows, but winced in pain as she tugged a handful of his hair.

'Steady, Sri, this will not help your father.' Clasping her thrashing arms, he wrenched his hair free and tried to pin her arms to her sides to oblige her to listen to his explanation. But she seemed possessed, oblivious to the calming words he tried to find. Grief he understood, but this wild rage made no sense. It came from some crazed Javanese darkness that terrified him. Would this mad woman never listen to reason?

He could barely hold her arms but not her legs, and dared not hold her any closer against him. Already the pain of her blows was submerged in a quite different sensation stirring his body with its closeness to hers. She kicked, stamped and kneed him till he could hold her no more. With the sound of ripping cloth she was free, glaring at him and then at the torn garment. As she stepped back to spring at him again, a single effortless movement slipped the garment over her head and flung it in a corner.

He gasped as the round breasts bounced free, a little paler than the rest of that smooth oak-dark skin. Their invitation to him seemed quite contrary to the murderous look in her eyes. Instinctively he lowered his gaze from the astonishing sight, and was caught completely off balance by her lightning charge. This time her head rammed his stomach, bowling him over and leaving him gasping in pain. Now she was on top of him, stamping on his arms, then dropping to her knees to better pummel his chest, scratch his face and knee him in the stomach. '*Kafir*, infidel, barbarian ...' The hate-filled words kept coming, but while they had first been spat at him, they now seem to have sunk to somewhere deep within her, issuing as a kind of moaning mantra to accompany her blows.

Her nails tore at him, turning the ache of his wounds from the fight into agonizing jabs of pain. His angry reaction was instinctive, snapping him out of his stunned incomprehension. Now he didn't care if he hurt the demented Javanese – nothing else would work. He grabbed the flailing arms fiercely and made her yelp with pain as he pinned her to him.

'Control yourself, you mad beast!' he cried in involuntary English, before he realised the words were addressed as much to himself as to her; for he was rapidly losing the self-control that was his greatest pride. There was no escaping her extraordinary body. It was against him, her face in his shoulder, her long black hair all over his face, her miraculous round breasts swelling against his chest, rising and falling with each breath. His arms were across her bare brown back, while further south his loins had begun their own response to the warm, wriggling body on top of them. This time as she threshed her legs to knee him again he held her tighter, telling himself he had to keep her quiet long enough to finish his explanation.

But before he could speak her teeth were in his shoulder, biting as if to sever a tendon. He grabbed her hair and pulled her head back, but this had an even more startling effect. He could look straight into her eyes, now filled with puzzled tears rather than hatred. Below them the full lips were trembling, and as he held her head back her breasts stood out taut and full, the dark brown nipples erect against the pale firm flesh around them. Perhaps he should die now, after seeing such wonders.

With a great effort of will he held her very tight, and hoarsely tried to explain how he had tried desperately to defend her father and stop the fight. She grew still and tearful, reminding him of the balian who could switch so quickly from Javanese calm to demonic possession and back again. Now it was he who had to fight to control the beast within. Falteringly, he explained how the terrible fight had broken out, how her father had bravely tried to stop it, and how Hodges himself had risked all to try to help him. He not did not dare to look into her eyes or move the arms that held her amazing body in their grip.

'Khalid did not really see what happened. He just wanted to believe it was all the fault of the feringgi. Is it true that you were the one trying to save my father?'

'It is true, Sri. Your father was at his noblest, insisting that conflicts be solved peacefully. I always admired him, but at that moment he was magnificent and I had to join him in trying to stop the foolishness. But this only enraged some of the Muslims, and I'm afraid the other side were just as crazy. Khalid only came later, and it must have been hard for him to understand the chaos.'

'You are a good man and a brave man. I knew that, and so what Khalid said broke my heart. I'm sorry I hated you and hurt you. It was foolish. Now I will be a good woman and tend your wounds. But it is not safe here until I explain somehow why I cannot be at my father's side for a moment.'

She slipped quickly away from him, retrieved her upper garment, and deftly transformed back into the elegantly reserved Javanese woman he knew. Having directed him to hide in a partitioned area at the side of the room, she seized a tub of water and took it out to where Bintara's body was being mourned.

Hodges scarcely had time to recover himself before she was back. He was so paralysed by confusion that he let her tend to his wounds with bathing, poultices and herbs. He should be fleeing back to the safety of the *Red Dragon*, his usefulness as a mediator here at an end. But he had no desire to move anywhere away from Sri and her gentle ministrations.

As his body responded again to her touch, he ventured to share some of his confusion.

'I can understand that you hated me for what happened to your father, since you would not listen to my explanation. What I cannot understand is, if you hated me, why you took off your breast-cloth.'

'You would have torn it. When I was a girl we never wore an upper *baju*, only a sarong. Even when we started to get breasts and covered them outside, we would always take the jacket off when we had a fight or a rough game. It tears too easily.'

'In my country nobody would take off their clothes like that unless they were crazy, or a whore, or perhaps mad with love.'

He made this last up, because he didn't like the first two options. In reality, Hodges had great difficulty imagining the ladies of Hampshire ever tearing their clothes off.

'Yours is a cold country. You have to have a reason to take your clothes off. Ours is a hot one where you have to have a reason not to.'

'Isn't it enough reason that a man would go wild with lust if he saw your beauty?'

'You did not go wild. You just stood there.'

'My body may have. My mind was on fire. I could not understand why you would want to make me want you so much while you were trying to kill me.'

Sri wrinkled her brow as she applied a leaf to his arm. 'My grandmother followed all the old Javanese ways, and often left her breasts bare. She said she did the same when she was young and beautiful. I believe where Islam has not yet gained the upper hand they still go to the market with no *baju*. I don't think the men go wild with lust. But you Christians are perhaps like the strict Muslims. You cover your women with clothes and lock them inside, and then have all kinds of silly thoughts about them.' At this point, she stretched behind him to wash a welt she had scratched on his back, making sure as she did that her breasts brushed against his face. 'There's nothing so special about them, is there?' she asked coyly.

Hodges could barely control himself. 'You know perfectly well that you drive me wild. I cannot believe there is a man in the universe who would be unmoved by your perfection.'

She rubbed his back thoughtfully and smiled. 'Of course, if I had really wanted to kill you I would have done it, with a knife. So perhaps what upset me was the thought that I should be hating you when somewhere within I still wanted you to like me. It felt very good when you held me tight, protecting instead of fighting me. I do not want you to go away, Thomas, at this terrible time.'

It was the first time she, or anyone in Banten, had used his personal name.

# A Plan

'What are we to do?'

Sri was thinking fast now, taking in the harsh realities of her position.

'You must go quickly, you should not be here. Khalid would kill you if he found you now. I must explain first to him and my mother that you were wounded trying to defend our father. The funeral will be difficult, and you should not come unless I tell you to. My mother and Khalid will fight about the arrangements, and I must try to make peace, telling them that we can have both a quick Muslim burial of his body and the Javanese rites we women can perform to ensure his spirit is at peace. Khalid may not approve of those, but he does not have to come.'

'I must see you again. I want to stay with you.'

Hodges was still befuddled by what had happened, not keeping up with Sri. 'How can we meet?'

'Banten will not be safe for you now, and especially not if people see us together. And now I am without a father, Khalid will think it is his duty to marry me immediately to his influential Muslim friend. But when I explain that to my mother, she will take my side. She may even help me to escape. If we are to see each other again, we must leave here.'

'We? What? Where could we go? You cannot come on my ship. The general wants to leave as soon as possible. But I cannot stay in Banten.'

It did not take Sri long to brighten. 'Japara, of course. My mother has a brother there who would help us. That is close to the real Java, where the traditions of our ancestors are still practised.'

'Is that the home of the great king of Java? I have heard strange and wonderful stories about him, but none make much sense.'

'The king they call Kiai Gusti? Yes, but in the interior behind Japara. Nobody seems to know for sure. Some say he was killed by the Muslims, others that he fled to Bali, and others that he lives still and plots how to take all the Muslim ports back under his power. I have heard speak of a new kingdom of Mataram, but some say it is Muslim and others swear it upholds the old beliefs. Perhaps all are right, since there are many kings in Java. Banten is far from the greatest. At least one of them must be defending the old ways.'

'That might give me a chance,' Hodges was catching up now. 'If I desert the ship, I am a dead man as far as England is concerned. If I stay here I am also a dead man. But I can try to persuade my general that I am more use to the English in Java, on a mission to find this king and make him a friend of England.'

'That will be difficult and dangerous. You would need to be friends with both Muslims and old believers, foreign traders and Javanese. There is still fighting there, for the prize is all of Java. All sides would value a foreign friend with military skills, but also distrust him. You would need to be careful.'

'I would need a clever interpreter.'

'Ah yes, right again. Your bad Malay and not-so-bad Portuguese might help in Japara, but will be no use once away from the coast.'

'One who speaks Javanese well.'

Sri's smile was dazzling. 'Not a pompous official, not a devious Chinese, not some trader who will betray anyone for a profit. You need a female interpreter, who will threaten no one.'

'A young, pretty, giggly female interpreter, whom everyone will be charmed by, and no one will suspect of having a big brain?'

'Yes, truly – though older and uglier might be better. We Javanese often use women as mediators and interpreters. It is the same in the market. Men are too proud to claim they have no money. They know they are hopeless at bargaining, so they send their wives or daughters. Like my father.' She fell silent and tears began to fill her lovely eyes.

Hodges tried to bring her back. 'You would be the perfect translator, guide and negotiator, I have no doubt. But you do not look like my daughter – your nose is too small and delicate, your hair too straight and black, you are altogether too beautiful.'

'As … wife … then?' Sri said the words very slowly, looking searchingly into his eyes. 'I doubt my mother would let me go away without a protector. But the strict Muslims hate to see their women with the feringgi.'

Hodges was speechless. From grief, to hatred, to thoughts of marriage, all in a few hours, was too much. He felt poised between heaven and hell. Sri knew he had a wife in England already. Perhaps that did not bother her, but it would certainly bother his officers.

It was Sri who broke the stunned silence, 'This is all too much for me to think about now. I must attend to my poor father's funeral, and to my mother. But I need time and you need to get out of here. Please go back to your ship now where you are safe. Somehow I must send a message to you when you can return to pay your respects to my mother. I will prepare her for that as best I can.'

'It will be easy for me to think of tasks to take me to the market, where there will be other Englishmen and I will be safe.'

'Good. Do you remember the furniture seller in the market where we first met? She is a good friend, Saraswati. I can send a message to her, telling you when to come.'

'Then make it soon. My ship will leave as soon as we get permission, maybe in five or six days. I will come every morning to the market, and invent some furniture purchase to discuss.'

'And bring some money if you can,' she added as an afterthought as she pushed him out to the street.


'A mission to these heathens?' Pickering bellowed. 'They'll have you for breakfast! Don't expect us to come and rescue you. We sail for home in six days' time, thank god.'

'But the stakes are high, sir. The Portuguese are telling them we English are rebel bandits, and in league with the Muslims and Dutch against all kings. The Dutch side with the Muslims because they hate the Portuguese. They talk friendship with us, but their game is to take everything and drive all the other Europeans out. We need to show these Javanese we are neither Dutch nor Portuguese, and not interested in their quarrels – only fair trade. I know they want to hear that; they know they are finished if either the Portuguese or Dutch win here. Both are out to rule them – the

Dutch their trade and the Portuguese their souls. This Gusti in the interior is the real power here. He can open all the spices of the Indies to us.'

'I trust none of these thieving rogues. We are only safe on our ships, where we can defend ourselves. Now we have our cargo of pepper, and we will get some cloves and nutmeg too in Banda. Then we have only to reach Gravesend safely, and we will be heroes – if only the accursed Portuguese, the pirates or the pox don't get us first. You'll have your share too, Hodges, if you just keep out of scrapes till we get back. You have done well for us here. What chance do you have to get back to England if not with us?'

'There will be another ship next year, god willing, and I will be here to welcome it with the key to Java. If we leave the Dutch to worm their way in here, there will be nothing for the next ship to buy. England will have to go to Amsterdam to buy all the spices of these islands, and they'll charge more than the Portuguese ever did. I wish you well on the home voyage. If you make it, and there's a profit, please make sure my wife gets my share. I have written this letter to the Company with the request and her details. God alone knows what will happen to you in Banda or me in Java. I pray that you make it home safely next year, but I will take my chance for a bigger prize in the years after that.'

'You're a strange one, Hodges. I don't fancy your chances of getting out alive. Even the men we are leaving in Bantam to gather pepper had to be forced to stay in such a godforsaken place. Once out of sight of our ships, what is to stop any rogue from slitting your throat? But if you're fool enough to do it I won't stand in your way. The general might even like your addle-pated plan, since he has more time for these heathens than I do.'

Hodges had been only a couple of times into William Keeling's elaborate cabin at the rear of the *Red Dragon*, mostly to be tongue-lashed for something. But the general had a reputation for understanding these Orientals. He could speak enough Arabic and Portuguese to get along with them – or so he seemed to think. Hodges garnished his plan with as much tantalising detail as he could dream up to pique his interest.

'Well, you're an enterprising lad, Hodges, I'll grant you that. It sounds like you want to do another Hawkins, when he went off to Agra to meet the Great Mogul. That didn't do us much good in the end, but at least he showed those Moors that we were not the pirates the Portuguese told them about, nor the second-rate wool-peddlers the Dutch thought us. How's your lingo? I've not found many here in Bantam who can understand my Arabic.'

'No, sir. The better your Arabic is, the more it puts you in the Muslim traders' camp here, and the less the Javanese will trust you. Portuguese is more useful with the Chinese and Javanese traders. I have worked hard on my Malay, and that works with all the important people here in Bantam. But I am assured I can't do anything in the interior without Javanese. For that I'll need a good interpreter, but fortunately I know someone willing to do that job for a small return.'

'It's damned risky, Hodges, but worth a shot. If you can convince these Javanese that they have another option, people who only want honest trade, you will have done the Company and the country a great service. But I wouldn't put money on your coming out alive, and I don't want another death on my conscience. We have lost enough men already on this cursed trip. Let's say I won't stop you, but I will solemnly warn you against it. If you insist on going, I had better have a note from you swearing that this was your own choice.'

'I do insist, sir,' said Hodges, trying to conceal his joy, 'and I will write you a note.'

'Good – so what do you need? Some money for the translator, for your own survival, and for a little advance on next year's pepper? What about a gift for the grand panjandrum?'

'Thank you, general. I need something that can impress them with our abilities. They liked the telescope, and another would serve the purpose. They know we Europeans can make fine telescopes. But spectacles they do not know. It seems a marvel to them when I explain how these glasses can prolong the ability of learned men to read, and artists to draw. This would surely convince them what they could gain from trade. I am afraid that the larger gold and silver ornaments, or even clocks, would attract thieves and knaves. I need to travel light, and to be able to defend what little I have.'

'Very well then, Hodges – some Spanish reals, a couple of pairs of spectacles and one of the smaller telescopes. And you had better take one of my pistols to impress those who are not so old and learned, and might like the clink of your silver. That's all I can do for you, my boy. And may god be with you.'

Hodges went straight back to Pickering to explain that he needed to visit the market each day to prepare supplies for his adventure, and to pick up news about Java.

'Then make yourself useful while you're there, and get the best price you can for a couple of goats for our journey.'

Next morning he was in the market, and asked for Saraswati in the furniture shop.

'Not here today,' said a young man. 'Maybe later. How about these chairs, made just as you feringgi like them.'

Hodges feigned interest. 'Yes, but I talked to Saraswati about a particular letter-holder I fancied. I'll come back tomorrow and see if she has found it.'

Where the Chinese were selling their hardware he found Ah Pong, who wanted to know all about the fight and the death of Bintara. When he explained how he and Bintara had tried to stop the fight, Ah Pong seemed satisfied. 'You meant well, Hod, but I fear you have made some enemies. There are many stories about that fight, and none agree which side you were on. Some of the Muslims claim you sided with the Portuguese and should be punished for Bintara's death. Bintara was a wise head among the Muslims; his death makes everyone nervous. I doubt the truth will come out about Gomez. They will threaten to torture him to force him to confess, but if he has enough money to pay the judges he will be set free and they will look for some other scapegoat. If you get mixed up in that process, the sultan may not let you leave with the ship.'

'They will have to find me first. I'm going to be as careful as I can be until I can find a ship for Japara.'

Ah Pong was helpful with what he knew about the Chinese ship movements, and pointed Hodges to the riverside where some lighters were taking cargo out to the ocean-going vessels.

After making his discreet enquiries and his purchases, Hodges went back to the furniture shop to again find no sign of Saraswati. As he turned back to pretend interest in the chairs, the young man approached holding a kind of wooden rack. 'Is this what you were interested in, Tuan? Saraswati came in and found it. And here is a letter to show how it works.'

He showed how the Chinese paper could be supported on the rack while reading. Hodges eagerly thanked him, negotiated a price, and retired to a corner of the shop to devour Sri's fine Portuguese writing.

*We have little time, Thomas. My family has had many arguments. I believe I convinced Khalid that you and my father were together trying to stop the fighting, but the tragedy makes him even more Muslim. He thinks I must quickly agree to marry his Indian Muslim friend for our family to be safe again. I said I had other plans, to leave Banten once our father is buried, to visit my Javanese relatives and spend some time in prayer and meditation. My mother was angry with Khalid, but also worried for me. She does not want me to go alone to Japara, so I told her I had already chosen you as my husband and protector. She cried much, but she knows I am headstrong and would be miserable with Khalid's friend, or anyone I did not choose.*

*Fortunately my father also trusts you, even more after the fight that killed him. My mother and I were able to ask him what to do, with the help of the balian you already met at the palace. He said through the medium that he had worried about me, because he thought I was a bit wild (not true) and might be in danger without his protection. He sounded surprised when I told him about our plans, but he assured mother that you are a brave and good man and could be trusted. He explained about that stupid fight, and that it was really a crazy foreign Muslim who killed him. He even gave me his blessing. Perhaps you will believe now that the dead are not quite dead, and that we need their help.*

*My mother cannot let me go without some ritual to mark a marriage. We have agreed to arrange this quickly and quietly. Perhaps it will only be a pretend marriage for you, but necessary for my mother. If you agree to that, please send a message through Saraswati, and wait at her shop the day after tomorrow. And arrange a ship to Japara immediately after that.*

*Be quick, my love, and careful.*
*Sri*

# Blessing

At the appointed time Hodges waited anxiously in the furniture shop. Dusk came, and the hollow wooden drum of the mosque sounded the time for *maghrib* prayer. His fears rose with each stroke. Should he just go to the house? Several times he started out the door and came back thinking of the risks, until Saraswati brought him tea and reassurance. 'Sri is as reliable as she is beautiful. You are a lucky man, since she seems to like you. But she has much on her mind with her father's tragic death. Please be patient.'

Eventually the servant girl he had seen at Bintara's house appeared, muttered some greetings to Saraswati, and motioned to Hodges to follow quickly. They went through an unfamiliar route to Bintara's house, where Sri was waiting anxiously.

She whispered to him what he must do and say to Raden Ayu, whom he must now call respectfully as mother, *Diajeng*. She repeated one Javanese phrase until he got it, which she said would express his sorrow, apology and devotion all at once. He had rehearsed many times how he should commiserate with a grieving widow and ask to marry her daughter in the same conversation. But all this was somehow resolved once he had mumbled the words Sri suggested. Ayu seemed to be caught up in the excitement of Sri's planning, and adopted a surprisingly practical approach.

'So you want to marry my daughter?' she asked in Malay, keeping the language simple.

'Yes, Diajeng.'

'Will you protect her and look after her?'

'I will give my life for her.'

'Do you have a wife in England?'

Hodges mind raced back to Margaret, then to Sri. There was no point lying. Sri had known of his wife and dead child since the séance with the medium. Could the mother be as pragmatic as the daughter?

'Yes Diajeng, but I do not love her as I love Sri.'

'Nevertheless, she is of your own kind, and knows your ways as Sri cannot. Do you intend to go back to England?'

Did he? No ... yes. He had not faced this question in the upheavals of the last week. 'I don't know. England is far away and the voyage very difficult. If I went, I would want Sri to go with me.'

'No.' Raden Ayu was firm. She began lecturing him in Malay, then switched to Javanese and instructed Sri to explain it clearly.

'She says that if you leave Java, you must leave me, and any children we may have. That is our way here with foreign traders. What is foreign may leave; what is Javanese must remain. She says I could not live in your cold country, wear all those clothes, and fight with your English wife and relatives. She says I must stay here.'

'And you?' Hodges asked Sri, but she only bowed to her mother with a deferential smile.

'As you wish, Diajeng,' he said.

'I wanted a fine wedding for Sri, one that would have the best of the Muslim and Javanese rituals, and bring our family together.

This is not possible. It must be done secretly and quietly at my sister's house, where we have some things prepared. You will be dressed in a proper Javanese way. And do you have the marriage gift, the *mas kawin*?'

Hodges showed the bag of Spanish silver Commander Keeling had provided.

'Good. This gift is a sign of your respect for our family, and for Sri. It is the beginning, not the end, of your obligations to us. Half of it is for Sri, so she is not dependent on you, for men are not reliable in matters of money.'

'All that I have is hers.'

'When the ceremony is over you must hide again, until there is a ship for Japara. You and Sri should meet again only when you are safely on board.'

'I believe there is a Dutch rice boat leaving tomorrow, and a Chinese one the day after. The Dutch might be more comfortable, but I want to go with the Chinese. I don't want the people in Japara to think I'm a Dutchman, nor the Dutch to know about my mission.'

'Good. There are many Javanese and Malay boats also sailing the coast, but they are more likely to be my son's friends, and might give trouble to Sri. After some months Khalid will miss his sister and begin to accept that an Englishman can be a good husband. Then I will send a message through my brother that you can return to Banten. I need my daughter back here. If your mission is a success, perhaps you will return as a great man and it will not be so easy for someone to stab you in the back.'

'He will be a success, mother!' Sri could contain herself no longer. She slid on her knees to embrace Ayu and kiss her hand. She dragged Hodges to her side and placed her mother's hand on their heads. 'Please forgive us all our many failings, and give us your blessing.'

Tears running down her cheeks, Raden Ayu intoned a Javanese blessing, then a short one in Malay, and even managed *bênção* in Portuguese.

'What is your English word?' asked Sri.

'*Blessing.* I ask for your *blessing.*'

'That is hard to say, but you have my *beresing*,' said Ayu.

They were directed out the back door by two of the female servants, each carrying a cloth bundle of clothes and ornaments. At Sri's aunt's compound preparations had been made. A dozen people were gathered in a room, the entrance to which was decorated with palm leaves. Two old women immediately rose to take Sri in hand and prepare her, while one of the older men took Hodges into another room. He was stripped to his drawers, and carefully washed by ladling water over his shoulders with a coconut-shell while something was chanted in a language Hodges could not understand. It reminded him of the form of baptism he had seen some reformers use in England. His companion then showed him how to put on a richly brocaded sarong so that it would stay put, and placed a finely carved and sheathed kris at the back. He applied some glistening oil to Hodges' upper body, insisting this remain bare despite his obvious distaste for all the hair. Finally a tight-fitting cap went on the head. He was led back into the room where people were gathered, and presented with first a basket of fruits to give to Sri's aunt as hostess, with a few of his Spanish reals, and then a bouquet of leaves to give to Raden Ayu, with the rest of the gift for Sri.

What kind of weird ceremony was this? Though he had bristled at being stripped and manipulated, Hodges was relieved to be able to treat this strange ritual as an exotic charade to please Raden Ayu. The less it resembled his English wedding, the less guilty he felt. Thank god there were no wedding banns, no demand to declare "any impediment, why ye may not lawfully be joined together", no reminder of his promises to Margaret "to forsake all others, so long as you both shall live."

He gasped in wonder as Sri appeared. Clad in sumptuous Indian cloths, her slender shoulders were nevertheless delightfully bare, glistening with fragrant oils. She moved gracefully as though she was meant for this, a contrast with everything awkward about him. But her eyes remained steadily downcast, refusing to meet his stunned gaze. The pair were seated on a little platform, he clumsily cross-legged and Sri miraculously folded on her knees. Now it was the old people telling him what to do, while she refused even to look, let alone explain to him. With some difficulty he was made to understand that he had to crush a raw egg with his foot – why on earth? One of the old women then produced a bowl of water and led Sri to wash the messy foot, still without her ever meeting his eye. Then they were kneeling again in front of Raden Ayu, and offering betel and other things to her and some older guests. Only when they had to feed each other rice did he get a fleeting smile, quickly suppressed. Finally they were obliged to sit without talking, let alone touching those lovely shoulders, while the few guests enjoyed a meal.

He ached at having to leave without really talking to Sri. He couldn't wait to leave Banten and be able at last to be with her. Everything had changed so quickly. Was it a pretence, or a dream, or had he really acquired another wife – a Javanese, heathen, mystifying wife? He had made those promises to Ayu because it was what she wanted to hear, but the words came naturally – he *would* give his life for Sri. He longed to embrace her lovely brown skin again, but would that make him an adulterer and a bigamist, damned by his country and his god? And how would she now react?

Securing a boat required some hard bargaining at the docks with the only Chinese captain preparing to leave for Japara. Thank god Ah Pong had given him some idea of a fair price to aim at. He had to pay nearly double that to the burly Chinese whose Malay was as rough as his looks. The deal Hodges insisted on was that he and his "assistant" would have a bare, enclosed partition of the cargo hold to themselves. He did not specify the gender, knowing that Sri wanted to be as anonymous as possible. They had to bring their own food and supplies. Through Saraswati he sent a message that Sri should come to the ship in the morning dark before the departure, dressed as a male if possible, with all the food needed for the voyage.

Hodges spent an anxious night at the docks, getting a little sleep in the partition on top of the clothes he was taking. In the small hours he moved up on deck to await her, but was dozing when a figure in jacket and trousers awoke him, looking as much like a man as Sri was capable of. Her long black hair had disappeared into a turban, her slim figure bulked up in a

European-style tunic that was much too big for her.

They swiftly took her cloth-bound bags down to the partition. In their relief at being at last together and safe, they embraced as well as their costumes would allow, and talked softly about what had happened and what it meant.

Raden Ayu had still been crying when Sri had crept out of the house. Losing a husband and a daughter within a week was too much to bear. Sri had had to promise a hundred times to come back as soon as possible, and she wept a little herself as she related it. Nobody had wept at Hodges leaving the ship, but nor had anyone expected ever to see him again.

'Those were sweet words to my mother, about being ready to die for me. Did you mean it? What about staying alive with me?'

Hodges paused, and drew closer. 'I wasn't sure what to think then. Everything was changing so quickly I could hardly believe it. But once that had come out, and I thought about it, I knew I really wanted to stay with you and love you. So I did mean what I said.'

Sri looked deep into his eyes before responding. 'Thank god for that. I felt the same.'

Sri made clear that she couldn't wait to become a woman again, even though it meant that she must remain in the airless cabin for the three days' journey. He left her to make herself comfortable, and went on deck to watch how the vessel cast off in the dawn and hoisted those strange Chinese sails stiffened by half-a-dozen horizontal bamboos.

By the time thoughts of Sri overcame his interest in Chinese seamanship, the day's heat had obliged him to remove his shoes and tunic. The small stuffy partition he was sharing with Sri would be still less appropriate for his English clothes. He was eager to see her again as a woman, and the vision that awaited him did not disappoint …

Gone were the jacket, the trousers, the turban. She had found a way to sit elegantly on her folded legs in the effortless Java way, clad only in a short comfortable sarong and a bright scarf that served to adorn rather than conceal the rest of her lovely brown body. Now Hodges did not lower his eyes, nor she hers. 'Is this really to be mine?' he thought.

'Come here, husband. Let me help you out of those hot feringgi clothes.'

So the Javanese ceremony had not been just a pretence for her. Whatever it had been for Hodges and his practical Englishness no longer mattered. He knew now that he loved this woman. Her hands releasing his remaining clothes inflamed him. Hers simply fell away as he caressed her. Restraint gone, he flung himself on top of her and entered her immediately. The fine waist and the swelling beneath seemed too delicate to receive the urgent gift he was intent on bestowing, and indeed she cried out and spasmed as he entered. He lay there for a moment in alarm, but found her hips spreading wider to receive him, and her legs folding around him. He tried to feel every part of her against him, caressing her delicate shoulders, her neck, her hair, kissing her high cheeks, her closed eyes, her dainty little nose. Then without their willing it, their pelvises began to work as one. Deeper and deeper he drove into her, making each thrust carry all the love, the hate, the frustration he felt for this treacherous warm country. He could penetrate it, he would; she was Java and she was his.

Sri held him with her arms and legs, clutching with all her might to make him hers, to squeeze out the wild foreignness and the strange ghosts. They were one, they must be one. As he came further and further into her she concentrated everything on that place where she held him fully. *Come further, let me swallow you. I am enough for you.* She put her feet on the floor and pressed her body against him, arching her back and lifting her pelvis alternately with the rhythm of his thrusting. Now they could feel only each other, deep within. Hodges pushed his shoulders up to arch his back and try to drive her through the floor with his climax. Gratefully Sri accepted the weight of him, the pain of his bearing down. Then they were still.

# Japara, 1609

The three days' sail passed swiftly. Uncomfortable as the airless partition was, it became their world, their place of discovery. When they tired of lovemaking, there was so much to learn about each other. Sri had brought enough tasty snacks that their energy was renewed without need for cooking. There was the fermented soybean cake she called *tempeh*, sticky rice packets in coconut leaves, peanuts and some crunchy little fish. On the third day, Hodges ventured on deck to try his hand at cooking some rice, but the result was so hard and inedible that he quickly settled for buying a noodle dish from a pitying fellow-passenger.

'And where is the Englishman travelling? Will you buy rice in Japara, or travel on to the Spice Islands?'

'I have a mission from the English Company to meet the great king in the interior of Java. So I must find the means to travel inland, and send word ahead that I am coming in peace to arrange trade with him.'

'But that is very dangerous, Tuan. There are many wanting to be king now in Java. The Muslims were united for a time while they had a Shiva-worshipper to fight, but now they fight among themselves. You can offend them by what you wear, what you eat, before even talking of what god you worship. I keep quiet, agree with all, and wait to see who wins. We had a good queen in Japara for many years who kept the peace for all traders, but when she died they started fighting again, and the stern Muslims of Demak tried to take over. You must choose carefully who your friends are.'

'My Company wants to support the strongest, the one with the best chance to keep order and protect traders. Do you have any advice?'

'Not easy. Some say there is a new king in Mataram, towards the southern coast, who may be ruthless enough to get to the top. But there are many in Japara who oppose him, and say he is neither a proper Muslim nor a proper Javanese. Perhaps his men can protect you, if you can find them.'

Sri was comforting when Hodges shared the alarming news. 'We will talk to my uncle first. He knows many people. I have a message for him from my mother that should convince him to help us. It explains that we are properly married. But stricter Muslims will want to know whether I am one of them and, if so, why you are not. When we are in public I should keep my distance as just a translator, and a woman at that, so my religion is of no account. If we are among Muslims as man and wife it will go better if I do not tell them I am Muslim – *belum*, not yet, I will say; I stay with the Javanese beliefs of my ancestors.'

'Does your Allah not care if you deny him? In Europe many have died for their faith, reformed or papist, rather than deny it.'

'Does it really please your god to have so much blood shed in his name? There is only one truth, but only god knows what it is. What men fight about are only the names, the words men use about him. But these words cannot be god. I can find him only by being still, and listening to what is inside me.'

She took up a cross-legged position, closed her eyes and began breathing deeply and steadily. This was a vision of a different Sri, just as beautiful but in an inaccessible place of apparent peace. He tried to emulate her position.

'Teach me,' he said softly as he pushed his protesting legs into position. She opened her eyes, smiled, and went over to ease him into a correct position, softly urging him to breathe deep into his stomach. But her touch inflamed him again, and he pulled her to him.

'Later.'

Japara was a town divided. Near the river docks it looked like a smaller Banten, with Muslims and Chinese each in their fortified camps on opposite sides of the boat-filled Kali Weso. Sri's uncle, Raden Kajuron, lived in another collection of Javanese walled compounds behind the Muslim camp and its mosque. Sri thought it wise to cover up like a strict Muslim and walk far ahead of Hodges through the market and past the mosque. She passed silently while he, trying to keep her in view without appearing to look, was mobbed by curious children, some shouting *Belanda* or *Portugis*. 'No,' he shouted back in what was by now a practised pattern of Malay. 'Inggeris – friend, trader.'

He shook them off only by walking purposefully towards where Sri had disappeared around the back of the mosque. Only after following the path out of the Muslim camp up the river did he glimpse her again, talking to a woman fruit seller near a different set of houses, each with its walled compound and gateway, with a few steps up to the ornamented entrance and down the other side. Sri broke away and disappeared into an alley between the compounds, and Hodges thought it wise to take an interest in the fruit for a time. As he bargained over a couple of mangoes she asked as usual, 'Belanda?'

'No, English. We are new here, from a different faraway country. It is near to Holland but much bigger, stronger and better.'

Since she seemed friendly, with Malay as bad as his own, he ventured to ask, 'Do you know the house of Raden Kajuron?'

'Of course. Down this alley, the third compound. Is he having a feast? A young woman just asked me the same thing.'

'Perhaps. He didn't tell me.'

'You are lucky to find him. He is often away these days, in the interior. I think he doesn't like it as much here as in the old days of the queen. Nor do I, but I'm stuck here. Maybe you'd like to take me to your bigger, better country,' she cackled through her betel-stained teeth, handing him the mangoes. 'Anyway, while you're here, watch your back.'

Kajuron's compound was substantial. A young man took his shoes, sword and luggage as he entered and pointed with his thumb, bowing, towards the raised platform of the pendopo. Sri rushed to him and whispered, 'I think he will help us, though my father's death was a shock for him. He needs to know that you can be a good Javanese, so we must begin by asking his blessing.'

She reminded him of the Javanese phrase that had worked with her mother. 'I told him your customs are like ours, and that you seek his "beresing". Come, let's show him our respect.'

She glided across the floor in a crouch to where Kajuron sat cross-legged, motioning Hodges to follow. There was no way his legs could do that. He walked slowly, stooping for half the way, then got on his knees to crawl the rest. Kajuron was silent as Sri murmured her Javanese explanations in her low deferential voice. There was a long pause, so Hodges muttered his Javanese phrase. Another agonising wait followed before Kajuron extended his hand. Sri grasped it with relief and placed it on her forehead; Hodges shuffled forward and did likewise.

Now the Raden summoned the woman who was sitting a little behind him, presumably his wife. There was an anxious exchange with her, to which Sri added her pleading, nodding repeatedly to Hodges. Eventually she too extended her hand for a blessing. At last Kajuron began to speak, in Javanese but seemingly addressed to both of them. Sri whispered a short summary to him.

'I am very sad for my sister, your mother. Now that your father is gone she should return to the heartland where Javanese ways, *kejawen*, are still practised. There are too many foreigners in Banten, and now even in Japara, and their fighting about their gods or prophets is destroying our country. Most Javanese accepted Islam because the Muslims seemed the best of the foreigners, willing to learn also our wisdom here in Java. But now there are some who want to call people who do not agree with them *kafir*, unbelievers, and even to kill in the name of their religion. Your father did everything to become a good Muslim but it could never be enough for some of these newcomers.'

'Tuan Hod, Raden Ayu tells me you are a good man and will care for Sri, and so I bless you and your marriage. She is too spirited and too pretty to be safe without a father to protect her.

I have a small house in my compound where you may stay for a time. But what is your purpose here, and how long will you stay?'

Hodges spoke slowly and carefully in Portuguese, with time for Sri to translate. 'We thank you for your kindness and hospitality. We are very grateful to have a place we can be together after the problems in Banten. We English wish to trade with Java, and the islands hereabouts. In Banten, however, the Portuguese, Muslims and Dutch fought each other, and made it difficult for our message of peaceful trade to be heard. My commander has sent me here to contact the King of Java, and to make an agreement with him that we can trade fairly with all.'

'We have many kings now in Java, since the great king Gusti Pateh was defeated by the Muslims many years ago. The old kings were in touch with the old gods; some said they were themselves gods, and their power was not like that of ordinary men. There are still some in the east, and in Bali, who say they are the sacred descendants of Gusti. But they have little territory and no control over the trade. For a time it seemed that a new Muslim kingdom in Demak might unite the Javanese again, but their rulers were only men, not gods, and others resented their power. The stern Muslims of Demak with their Gujarati and Turkish friends would have none of the old ways, but they could not rule Java without them. There has been much fighting.

'It is true that a new kingdom is arising now at Mataram, in the part of Java south of the fire mountains. Their king says he is a Muslim too, but he protects the old sages and the holy places, so he gets the support of many Javanese. People here are tired of the fighting and want only a king who can stop it and impose some order. Perhaps he is your best chance. I believe no feringgi has been to his kingdom yet, for it is a difficult journey.'

'How could we reach there? Are the roads safe?'

'Roads? There are no roads, my friend, not since the days of the Gusti. Then they say there were roads that oxcarts could travel on, with bridges over the rivers. The bridges have all gone, and in many places there are only goat tracks through the hills. Travellers are not safe there unless they have a large group of guards. I think you should wait here until I can talk to the Mataram men here, and see if they will take you in one of the convoys. They need supplies from here – fish and salt from the sea, Indian cloth, Chinese tools, foreign weapons. But I doubt they would agree to take you unless they know you will be welcome in Mataram.'

Kajuron's wife broke in: 'Enough talking. Our guests must be exhausted from their journey. And on that ship for three days; no wonder they smell! It's time we let them bathe and rest, and enjoy some good Javanese food. I'm sure they could not eat properly in Banten.'

'Very well. And in a few days there will be a wedding at the house of our most prominent neighbour. Perhaps you will meet some people there who can help your cause.'

Now Hodges would experience the proper Javanese wedding Sri should have had. It seemed a big one. The dress was extraordinarily varied, with some Chinese in their best long tunics buttoned up high, but their women dressed much like the Javanese. These had all manner of beautiful cloths from India, competing with one another for the brightest colours and designs.

The soft sound of the gongs greeted them as they processed beneath palm fronds into the compound. Sri tugged him towards the musicians, behind a screen erected on a small stage. A man sat cross-legged immediately behind the screen, where he could reach a store of flat puppets, each attached to a rod of bone or horn, sharpened so it could be anchored in what looked like a banana-trunk to hold it steady.

'That is the *dalang* who moves the puppets and speaks their voices,' whispered Sri. 'Come, sit behind him so we can see what he and the musicians are doing. My uncle will have to sit on the other side and watch the shadows on the screen with the senior guests, but fortunately we are not important and can hide back here with the children.'

The dalang was resting and drinking cups of tea while the musicians played their varied gongs, dominated by a harsh female voice contrasting strangely with the soft diction of Sri and her friends. Sri glided in as smoothly and soundlessly as ever, but Hodges' clumsy attempts to follow drew all eyes to him, including those of the dalang. He quietly began moving the leather figures about.

'Are they puppets he is playing with?' Hodges whispered to Sri. 'Why are they so flat?'

'These are the kind of puppets most popular now in Japara and the other ports. Some of the foreign Muslims had disrupted our older plays and even beaten up the actors playing in masks, or puppeteers manipulating more realistic puppets. When asked why they should behave in this way, they said the Prophet Muhammad in his wisdom banned figures on the stage because people made gods out of them.'

'And did they?'

Sri puckered her sweet mouth. 'Well, perhaps. We do show gods like Krishna and Arjuna in our theatre. But of course they cannot be the ultimate god, Allah. The Muslims are right – he is too great to be imagined at all. These figures just make it easier for us to think about some quality we can emulate, like mercy or wisdom. Anyway, as I tell my brother who really likes the wayang stories though isn't sure he should, the shadows cannot be confused with reality. In more Muslim areas around the ports the shadow theatre is becoming the most popular way to tell the stories, since it doesn't offend any but the strictest foreign Muslims. Dalangs like this one started to be very popular for the way they could represent all the characters in the story, even female ones. The Muslims could sit on the front side of the screen, and know that they were seeing only shadows.'

The children behind them started to shriek with delight, bringing their focus back to the dalang. He had brought out some strangely shaped figures in black, and was projecting their voices as if in a Punch and Judy show at home, spicing their argument with kicks and punches to the delight of the children. As Hodges strained to understand what was going on, he caught some familiar words. They seemed to have switched to Malay, plus a Dutch *godverdomme* here, a Portuguese *merda* there. Some of the children were pointing at Hodges and laughing, and even Sri could not suppress a giggle. When one of the braver boys started to dance around Hodges imitating the clown, however, she gave him a murderous glare and a stream of Javanese that made him retreat in panic.

'What have I done now?'

'The puppets are showing the same characters you saw in the Banten palace. These are the clowns, the *punakawan*. They give the dalang a chance to forget the story and just entertain. The fellow with the round nose, Gareng, noticed that we have a special guest here, he thought a Dutchman, and he welcomed you. Petruk, the tall one, said you were his brother, and actually he was a Dutchman too. He could prove it with his long nose and his Dutch words.'

Now Hodges began to see the joke, though he didn't much like it. The Petruk figure was starting to roll around like a drunkard, amidst increasing blows and protests from the other character. Finally a third figure was introduced who seemed to quieten them down, and spoke more slowly. The children stopped their shrieking.

'This is Semar, the wise father. He is my favourite, not as silly as Petruk and Gareng, but he often makes sense of their pranks. Now he is saying that the feringgi do indeed look funny, smell funny and sound funny; so do the Chinese and the Indians in their different ways. Even Petruk and Gareng look and sound different. But they all have the same equipment on the inside. So they all see, hear, eat, shit and make love in the same way. Maybe God made us all different on the outside just so he didn't get bored with us.'

The dalang cleverly pinned down the clown puppets so that their shadows appeared on the screen to be humbly sitting. He introduced two new puppets, more delicate, and the voice he gave each one suggested they were a serious male and a female.

'Is this man and wife? It is hard to tell them apart.'

'Yes. On the right is the good king, Yudistira, and on the left is his wife Dewi Drupadi. My mother likes them because they are always faithful to each other, not like some gods and kings who set a bad example of womanising. But they speak a more difficult kind of Javanese with older philosophical words, hard for me to understand.'

She spoke to an older Javanese man nearby, who had been quietly conversing with an exotic-looking bearded man in a long cloak. The plot evidently took a lot of explaining, and meanwhile the bearded man moved to sit next to Hodges and said in good Portuguese, 'Welcome, stranger. We do not see many Europeans in Japara. Are you Portuguese or Dutch?'

'I am English – perhaps the first of my country to come here.'

'English! London, the Thames, Queen Elizabeth. I have not been there, but I have seen some English in Constantinople. I lived in Turkey for some years.'

'Are you Turkish?'

'Actually Jewish. But here I let them think I am a kind of Muslim, from *bangsa Nabi Musa* – the tribe of Moses. Don't tell them otherwise, please. They know and admire Moses, and Jacob – my name is Yakob. They know nothing of Jews, but some unkind things are said about us in the Muslim holy book.'

'Where did you learn your Portuguese? What brings you here?'

'My family was from Lisbon, and seem to have done quite well there in the spice business. Then King John turned against the Jews, insisting they convert or leave. They tried to fit in, being baptised into their Catholic faith, which I assume I do not need to be polite about if you are from England.'

'Papist tyranny!'

'Quite. But conversion didn't save my grandparents from all kinds of trouble, even before that terrible Inquisition came to Portugal. Some of the family fled to Constantinople and some to Amsterdam, and they kept their hands in the spice trade. Mine was the Turkish branch, but my parents told me you should never lose a language once you have it, especially one as useful in business as Portuguese. So they made me speak to them in Portuguese, even though we all spoke Turkish and Arabic in the streets. Eventually they sent me to Cairo to keep a closer watch on the spices. That was interesting, but I was curious to find where the Indian spices really came from. So I boarded the Muslim spice ships and ended up here. And what brings you to this far frontier?'

Hodges had hardly begun his explanation before Sri was beside him again. 'This is my wife, Sri.' He said it for the first time, with a great glow of pride. 'She is part of the reason I am here. This is Senhor Yakub, who is from everywhere, it seems.'

'*Encantada, senhor*,' said Sri. 'I hope you are enjoying the performance. This gentleman, Ki Sugino, has been educating me about it, since he has been a dalang himself.'

After polite Javanese introductions and bows, she continued in Portuguese to the two foreigners. 'Ki Sugino admires this dalang for his ability to mix old and new styles. All the dalangs know the stories of Yudistira and the other characters, but he manages to incorporate some of the new ideas the foreigners have brought – as you saw when he had some fun with my husband. Yudistira is the wise king, half-god, who has to defend his kingdom against the threatened enemy attack. He is a great warrior with various magic weapons, but he hates war. He always prefers not to kill. So he has been discussing with his wife how to use his powers to convince the enemy to find a solution without war. You can see that the puppeteer has managed to put a small book in his hand. That is the powerful new weapon he has invented for him, called the *kalimasada*, and he is explaining its powers.'

'But that must be the Muslim *Kalima Shahadat,*' Yakub interrupted. 'Except it is not a book, it is the minimal statement of their faith: "There is no god but Allah, and Muhammad is his prophet". What is that doing in the hands of a Javanese god?'

'You must be right, it does sound like that. I don't think Ki Sugino knows much about Islam, so he might not recognise it. But it fits with this dalang's novel tricks. I never saw a wayang figure holding a book before. Yudistira has been explaining that his kalimasada can open the eyes of the enemy to deeper truths. If he can trick the enemy king into reading it, then he will understand that one kingdom fighting another makes no sense, for all are fundamentally humans with the same needs. Probably the dalang made this new weapon in the form of a book because the Muslims' love of their holy book is new and strange to us Javanese. We have lots of holy writings of all kinds, but they are the palm leaves you have seen, Thomas. They are bundled together with only a string through the middle to hold them together. I have my own collection of old stories at home, but I often add another one or lend a few leaves to a friend. I don't think one version is holier than another. Could the dalang be saying that the Muslim book can end all the arguments and conflicts, because there is only one truth, mysteriously locked in it?'

'We too have such a book,' said Hodges. 'But it does not seem to end arguments.'

'We too, of course,' Yakub broke in, 'not so different from yours. But from what I hear, the mistake of the Christian reformers was to translate your Bible into German, Dutch and English so everyone can interpret it for himself. I met in Constantinople some reformers who had read the Bible so carefully in German that they became convinced there was nothing there about the Trinity. That made them such heretics that they had to flee to the Turks, who at least agreed that there was only one god.'

'So do we, so do we. Jesus is god, but part of god.'

'You will have trouble convincing these Muslims of that, my friend. If they know anything of your religion, it is that you have three gods. Few of them have read their Quran, and they seem to have no desire to translate or print it, but they do know the *Shahadat* – there is no god but god.'

Hodges turned to Sri to change the subject. 'Have you read this Quran, my dear?'

'Heavens, no! As Senhor Yakub says, it is only in Arabic, so only a few foreign Muslims can read it. For us Javanese, especially the women, it is enough to say the *Kalima Shahadat* and avoid pork. I like this dalang's idea of a magic weapon of unity. Look how people quarrel over religion, even you two, although it ought to bring us together. '

'I have read the Quran in Arabic,' said Yakub, 'and made a note of some of the kinder things it says about Jews. We share many stories about Adam, Abraham, Moses, David and Yakob. It comes in handy to quote some of its Arabic at the less tolerant Muslims, hardly any of whom can read it. Even your Jesus and Mary are there, Senhor Hodges.'

'Really?' Sri interrupted. 'I didn't know that. What does it say about them?'

'You may have heard of Nabi Isa, that is what they call him. That means "the Prophet Jesus", not a god, of course. On this I agree. He said some wonderful things, and I have no problem with him as a prophet; only you Christians have confused things by insisting he is god.'

Hodges reddened. 'But he rose from the dead, dammit, after your Jews killed him. How can he not be god?'

Sri calmed him with a hand on his arm. 'Please tell us, Senhor Yakub, what the Quran says about him. My father did talk about Nabi Isa, but I thought he had something to do with the end of the world.'

'To be honest,' Yakub lowered his voice, 'the Quran appears to have borrowed much from both the Jews and the Christians, though you cannot say that to the strict Muslims. They think it came straight from god. The Quran says that Jesus was also the messiah, *Isa al-Masih*. That must have come from the Christians, whereas we Jews are still waiting for a messiah. The Muslims don't appear to have a problem with prophets rising from the dead. Come to think of it, don't the Christians agree that Elijah went straight up to heaven without being a god? The Quran seems to say that Jesus will come back as a hero at the end of the world, to defeat what they call the *Dajjal* – a kind of evil version of himself.'

'And Mary?' asked Sri. 'I hope she plays some part in Islam. She seems very sweet in the pictures of the Portuguese.'

'Yes, they call her Maryam. She seems to be the most prominent woman in the Quran, with a whole chapter about her. My wife, who is a Javanese Muslim, was very pleased when I told her about Maryam. She thinks the Muslim teachers keep quiet about her just because the Portuguese are so enthusiastic – or maybe because they don't want their women to get ideas. I think the stories about her in the Quran must have come from the Christians, certainly not from the Jews. The Quran says she had no sin and was very pure, so that she somehow conceived the baby Jesus while remaining a virgin.'

'Well, I don't know why they should say that,' Sri protested. 'Isn't it by combining male and female,' she intertwined her slender fingers suggestively, 'that we get closest to the perfection of god?' Hodges spluttered, but there was no stopping her. 'The gods of the wayang are men and women like Yudistira and Drupadi here, who do what men and women do. Is Mary a real woman and mother if she doesn't?'

Heads turned back to the performance, where some other figures had joined the royal couple, and the dalang was intoning something from one of them in a deep voice. 'That one goes too far, though,' Sri complained. 'That is Arjuna, who is very wise and handsome, but has far too many wives.'

Hodges seized his chance. 'You call these puppets gods, but they have nothing to do with the true god, creator of the universe. They are as ridiculous as fairy tales or the Greek gods, seducing maidens and playing tricks.'

Sri started to protest, but needed reinforcements. She returned to Ki Sugino, whose explanation was slow and thoughtful, so the men went back to their arguing. Eventually Sri returned with what looked like a smile of triumph.

'Indeed there is only one god – we all seem to agree about that. But some of the foreign Muslims and Christians are wrong to think they know that this ultimate god is something like a human man, a father or a king. In reality our poor minds cannot comprehend what this god is like, except that he could not possibly be limited like you or me by size, strength, shape, sex, language, brainpower or whatever. These figures like Arjuna and Drupadi only point to an ultimate god because they are more than human, different from human, especially in their shadows.'

'*Brava, senhora,*' Yakub applauded. 'You should be the new queen of Japara, to bring back the peaceful days of the late queen.'

'But Sri, your people put offerings on trees, and make gods of elephants, tigers and crocodiles. They cannot know god at all if they worship these dumb creatures!'

'Why not? Did not god create them as well as us? Some say the crocodiles were here before humans and may be still here after we are gone. Why should they not also teach us something about the unknowable god?'

Hodges' outrage was fortunately interrupted before he exploded in a way he knew he would regret. A group of Javanese men were coming towards them, all dressed alike with beautiful sarongs, ornate krisses at the waist, long carefully oiled hair, but little other covering. They were shepherded towards Hodges by

Raden Kajuron, who introduced them to Hodges and Sri in Malay amidst much bowing. When all were seated, he spoke rapidly to Sri in Javanese. Eventually she turned to Hodges.

'These are the gentlemen my uncle hoped might be able to help you reach the great king in Mataram. Raden Pekik here is the most senior of them, and appears to be related to one of the queens of Mataram. My uncle has explained that you are English, not Dutch or Portuguese, but they do not understand what that means. They ask if you are on the side of the Muslims, the Chinese or the Portuguese. They want to know why you want to go to Mataram. Frankly, they seem suspicious that you must be a spy for somebody.'

'Please tell them that Europe is a place of many countries, and we do not all agree. England is not Portugal and not Holland. It is much greater than either of those countries, but they were the first to come to Asia because they had no resources other than commerce. England is the first of the great countries of Europe to come to Asia, and it wants to befriend the great countries here, not just the merchants as the Portuguese and Dutch have done. The Muslim and Portuguese traders may have religious motives in coming here to try to convert you to their religion. We have no such desire. We believe our religion is right for us, but we do not desire to impose it on anybody else. Our king wants only to know the other great kings of the world, to befriend them, and to exchange gifts and knowledge with them so that all can advance.'

He noted Sri's incredulous look. 'I can see it's not easy, but please try to make it clear that England is much bigger and more important than Portugal and Holland. It is – really.'

'Forgive me, my dear, but you don't look like the envoy of a mighty king, with no richly dressed followers. Perhaps I can explain that because you were misled by those commercial peoples, your king sent his big embassy with all its presents to Banten. Only when it was too late did they realise Mataram is the great kingdom, but lacks only the ships to make itself known across the seas.'

'Yes, yes – you're so clever. Do your best.'

The Javanese exchanges that followed were complex. Sri was always sweet and reasonable, but Raden Pekik sounded alternately angry, contemptuous and bemused. Raden Kajuron was appealed to at times, and made reassuring responses. Hodges was only consulted once more, when the Mataram people wanted to know the name and character of the English king, since the Portuguese had said other Europeans had no proper kings, but women or merchants.

'The illustrious King J-A–M-E-S.' Despite the difficulty of pronouncing this, he opted against using some equivalent like Portuguese Iago or Arabic Yakub. He wanted to show how different the English were. 'It is true we had a virtuous queen before him, like Japara I hear, but for six years now we have enjoyed this mightiest of English kings. For the first time he has united our whole great island, and even another great island called Ireland, as well as other lands across the seas. Perhaps he is like the great Mataram, uniting other kingdoms through his unprecedented grace and power.'

Sri smiled appreciatively. 'Now you're getting the idea. I like it.'

More discussion. Pekik gradually looked more cheerful, and evidently ended the conversation with a proposal.

'They are intrigued but not convinced,' Sri summarised. 'They propose that I go to the court of Mataram first in the company of the next convoy they have, and carry a letter and gift from you to explain the matter at the court. Meanwhile my uncle will look after you here.'

'No! That is far too dangerous. We must remain together.'

'Don't shout. I have told the Mataram people that I was the interpreter attached to you by the Banten court, and asked my uncle not to deny that. That makes your mission much more believable than as a runaway lover. Please don't reveal to these people that we are married.'

'I can't let you go, Sri. Think of some other plan. Perhaps we can go together to the capital, and there you can present my case first while I wait for judgment in their custody.'

More lengthy discussion. Then Sri again. 'This seems to be working. I told them that I had been commanded by the Banten queen not to leave you, since she felt responsible for your survival. They will arrange for us both to travel in a few weeks. But they still dare not allow you to enter the royal capital without the king's permission.'

'Very well. Please thank them for their hospitality.'

# The Road to Mataram

The weeks in Japara were busy as Hodges, Sri and Raden Kajuron sought to make the mission from a great king appear credible. Appropriate dress, gifts and retainers would all be a challenge. Kajuron offered a fine Javanese sarong, but Hodges was sure that he should look as different as possible from the Javanese. Brought into the scheme, Yakub offered a colourful woollen jacket and an imposing hat, possibly Swedish or German. 'The Javanese nobles accept many things as presents, but sell them to me once they have made themselves uncomfortable and ridiculous in them.'

A few exotic things were available in the market, and Sri did the bargaining for these. In the process she met a Chinese-Javanese lad with as many languages as herself, who showed great curiosity about England, but also about the Javanese interior. Hodges came to meet the young man, who answered to the name Buyung. He insisted that his Chinese father was one who knew the interior and could help. The father spoke in Chinese and heavily accented Malay. The son translated into Portuguese enthusiastically for Hodges.

'So you want to meet the great king, the Panembahan of Mataram, or whatever else he calls himself? That will be dangerous. I had a nice trade in Javanese rice for Indian cloth and Chinese ceramics in the days of the Japara queen, when Pajang was the strongest of the interior rulers. But these Mataram upstarts were savage. Most of my contacts were killed or fled in the wars with Mataram. I hear that things are quieter now, and there is plenty of rice for those who can organise to transport it safely. But I don't trust those fellows – too quick with the kris to do reliable business. How do you propose to protect yourself?'

Hodges explained his diplomatic mission from the English king, and the agreement of the Mataram representatives to accompany him. 'But because I am alone, they are suspicious that I may be a spy for their enemies rather than a real envoy.'

This sparked a vigorous exchange between father and son, with some obvious tension in the air. Finally Buyung turned again to Hodges with a look of triumph.

'My father thinks you may have more success than he, if you can really convince the Javanese that you are neither Dutch nor Portuguese. If you are as handy with guns as those other foreigners, the Javanese may hope to use you in their military ambitions. He feels he has risked enough in his young days, and now he has a family and a business to protect. He will not gamble everything on some adventure. But I told him I have nothing to lose. If I could become the first Chinese trader in Mataram, the rewards might be great. Above all,' speaking softly in Portuguese, 'it would give me a chance to escape from the old man and make my own life.'

'Would you be willing to act as my manservant? Kajuron tells me nobody can be respected if he carries his own gear on entering the palace. There must be some kind of procession, especially with the presents.'

'No problem, *senhor*,' Buyung bowed low with a cheeky grin. 'I can even dress like you in some funny clothes, and learn enough words of English to convince them I am from your strange country.'

'That would be splendid. And what do you need in exchange?'

'Just the freedom to change my tune once we are in Mataram and you have what you want. And the understanding that we will not betray each other to them, no matter what trouble they give us.'

'Agreed. Thank you Buyung; thank you sir.'

Hodges spent what time he could spare teaching Buyung some English phrases. 'Your pleasure, sire' and 'As your lordship commands' seemed likely to impress, with appropriate flourishes. Sri was an equally eager pupil, enjoying another language to make fun of him in.

An impressive letter was deemed essential. The royal letters Keeling had been given for the voyage had not been for Mataram, which no one in England had heard of. Hodges carried only his own seal, fortunately bearing the Crown of the East India Company. It would have to do. He bought the best available paper in the market, and carefully wrote out an English letter with many flourishes, full of honorific phrases from the King of England, Scotland and Ireland. A Javanese equivalent was the job of Sri, who exploited all the learned friends of Raden Kajuron in the city to find the right language to impress a proud Javanese king.

It was fortunate for them that the Mataram representatives delayed their convoy several times as they sought different luxuries to impress the king, negotiated with the troublesome cart men, and sought up-to-date information on the state of the roads.

Each rainy season brought chaos to the muddy tracks, while wars and floods damaged what remained of the bridges. Several times the message came from Raden Pekik that one route was the safest, only to be countermanded by news of a washed-out bridge or a threat from bandits.

Buyung had persuaded his father to part with a decent-looking horse, on condition Hodges signed a document in Malay that he would return the horse to Buyung when the mission was complete. Sri was to be provided with a sedan chair by the Mataram envoys, whom she had somehow convinced of her credentials. They travelled in the front of the convoy, with only a group of guards and their commander preceding them. Behind was a long tail of five carts pulled by oxen, in one of which was a bundle of cloths and other trade goods secretly consigned to Buyung to get his start in Mataram. The horse carried only the small parcels belonging to Hodges and Sri.

The first day's travel seemed absurdly slow as the road skirted around majestic Muria mountain. They had to cross numerous small streams flowing from it, two of which had washed out the simple wooden bridges laid over them. Hodges was grateful for the delays as the cart men coaxed their reluctant beasts through the rocky watercourses. It gave him a chance to call on Sri's translation to interrogate the captain of the Mataram military escort, whom she called simply Pangeran, about what lay ahead.

'We must reach Kudus tonight, however many streams we have to cross. That is a holy place, where pilgrims and travellers are respected. There are people in Demak who think our lord of Mataram is an infidel because he doesn't share their idea of

Islam. But they dare not attack us in Kudus, which is sacred to all Muslims and Javanese.'

'Kudus? Doesn't that mean "holy"?'

Sri knew the answer. 'Indeed it does. I think Kudus is named after a city above the winds, in your part of the world, which is sacred to the Muslims. I will ask.' She consulted Pangeran, who in turn consulted an older man dressed like a Kling.

'They say you must have heard of al-Quds because the Christians thought it so holy they fought the Muslims to control it, but were defeated by the great hero Saladin. The Muslims revere it because Muhammad flew there on his magic horse before he went up to heaven.'

'That sounds a load of nonsense. Could they mean Jerusalem? At least, that's what we call it – the place of Jesus. How strange, that there should be another Jerusalem in Java. I hope Christians are also welcome in this Jerusalem.'

The sun had set before they reached the gate of Kudus, and the guards looked increasingly nervous in the fading light. All relaxed once past the strange-looking Javanese gateway, like an ornamented cleft mountain of stone. Mataram evidently had its people in the town, who accommodated the convoy comfortably in a set of huts in one large compound. Buyung also had friends, and begged leave of Hodges.

'I might learn something from these Chinese traders. Their business forces them to be the best informed about peace and war, floods and damage on the roads.'

'Very well, but be back here at dawn for an early departure.'

'As your lordship commands,' he practised his English with

an exaggerated bow.

He returned as promised, having evidently slept little in the excitement of his first night in the holy city.

'Here's a deal, Buyung. You can catch up some sleep on the horse if you tell me what you learned.'

'Done.'

As they walked along a plain beautifully decorated with rice fields, Buyung fulfilled his side of the bargain.

'Where to begin. These were a strange kind of Chinese – even stranger than me,' noting Hodges' sceptical look. 'They speak my kind of Chinese, but they cut their hair and dress like Muslims, and don't eat pork at all. Even my mother, who says she is a good Muslim, doesn't mind some nice pork with her noodles. They say that they truly are Muslims, and if they weren't things would be difficult in that town.

'These Chinese do good business with the pilgrims to the holy tombs. They need shelter, food, and flowers and incense as offerings. Since they come from everywhere in Java, it's a great place for exchanging new goods and ideas. The current new fashion is chewing tobacco. These Chinese do their best business convincing the pilgrims that tobacco will cure all their ills, and controlling the market in it as the Javanese become addicted. Some are so impressed that they think the holy saints should have some too, and place it on the tombs.'

'What about the road ahead? Are we facing dangers?'

Buyung looked sombre. 'To be honest, they tried to persuade me not to go. Some of them had been to Mataram in times of peace, they say, but they would not go now. They tried to tell me

I could make my way better in Kudus, with just a few sacrifices of my pork and my foreskin. But the truth is they are old, established and contented. I told them I knew that when they were my age, and had nothing to lose, they themselves took plenty of risks. But now they are like my father, and don't want to risk their stock of goods and their nice houses and families.'

'What kind of risks? Is there a war on now?'

'If I understood them correctly, there are two kinds of war going on. First is the constant fighting between these Javanese princes. Each thinks he has a right to rule and will not submit to the others. Even brothers fight each other to succeed their father.

'But there is a deeper war between the Islam of the foreigners and the upholders of the old Javanese religion. That has been going on for a century or more. The Muslims won the big battles, because they have guns, determination, and a common purpose in fighting non-Muslims. But once there was no more infidel kingdom to attack, the princes who sided with the Muslims became just as divided as the others.'

'So who is on top now? Who do we have to look out for on the road?'

'It's not easy to be sure. The Mataram prince looks like the strongest, but those in Pajang or Karta are just waiting for a chance to take him down, and there are others further east who think they have a better claim to rule all Java. Then there are the Muslim militants, strongest in Demak. There is an Adipati who seems to lead the mosque community in Demak, but is now trying to unite the different Muslim armed groups so that they can destroy Mataram, just as Demak destroyed the old Buddhist kingdom a century ago. This Adipati does not accept that Mataram or Pajang are real Muslims, because they don't pray five times a day and know nothing of Arabic and their holy book. He hopes Demak can become a Muslim sultanate and rule all Java. Others seem to just like fighting in the name of Allah because of the loot they can get. And then there are bandits who profit from the general chaos.'

'How am I going to tell a bandit from a prince, Mataram from Pajang or Demak?'

'God knows. All I know is that men with short hair, like my Kudus friends, are trying to show they are good Muslims, and those with really long hair, like our guard here, are showing they are not. But most people are in between, so it's not so easy.'

'Great. Well you have your sleep now on the horse, and I will keep a sharp lookout.'

They travelled slowly up a river valley all that day, but Pangeran warned that the following day they would have to cross it at one place or another. There were a couple of ferry points which linked with the better and shorter roads, but each was likely to demand a heavy toll. The only bridge was further up the valley, and he would only resort to that as a bargaining threat to reduce the price of the ferry. Mataram and Demak both tried to control these toll-points, but the pickings were tempting for any armed band that could gain control. In fact, the Mataram ruler had appointed some bandits to run the tolls on one of the ferries, calculating it was easier to do so than to try to beat them. He hoped these people were still going to respect the royal status of the convoy, but he was sending a man ahead to check how things stood.

As he explained all this through the medium of Sri, Hodges could see how Pangeran enjoyed chatting with her. And why would this soldier not find her attractive, and seemingly unattached? Sri seemed to hold little back in chatting with him in Javanese, giggling over things that did not come through in her translation. He wanted to put this fellow firmly in his place, but realised that would not be easy to square with Sri's official role as court translator. He had to limit himself to demanding that she explain what they had been giggling about. The answer seemed always to be some fine point of Javanese wordplay that meant little to him.

As they neared the first of the ferry crossings, the scout reported back that the people in charge leaned toward the Demak side, or at least had little time for Mataram and would charge an arm and a leg to let the convoy cross. They gave this crossing a wide berth and hoped for better news at the second. Eventually it came – ambivalent, but promising enough for Pangeran to decide to risk it.

They arrived at dusk so the crossing was delayed until first light the next day. As usual, they made their separate camps. Sri was in one hut with the only other woman in the convoy, one of the Mataram courtiers on her way home; Hodges and Buyung stayed in a larger hut, together with the other Javanese notables of the convoy. As was his habit, Hodges made an excuse that he needed to talk to Pangeran to bring in Sri as translator. They had agreed that Buyung would pretend to have no Javanese in keeping with his exotic 'English' role, while ensuring that Sri would always be brought in to translate for Hodges.

'Be careful, Thomas,' she whispered. 'The word has got around that we have feringgi in the convoy, and you may become a pawn in somebody's ambitions. I will insist that you have powerful supporters, not just from the Inggeris and their ships, but from Banten. The Muslims who most distrust Mataram are the ones with most respect for Banten, so that might work. If they want to take you or me away, please do not fight, especially not for me. You cannot win here by fighting, and you must not give away our secret. Our best hope is to convince them that we have powerful protectors who would make them pay for any harm done.'

Hodges agreed, but kept his sword handy as he took his bath. As they finished eating, a group of armed men arrived, one of them on a horse, and began talking loudly to Pangeran. Eventually he heard Sri's sweet, reasonable voice trying to moderate the shouting, but had no idea what they were saying. He gestured to Buyung to come closer and whisper to him what was going on.

'Not good, sire.' Buyung said his new English words more loudly, before switching to whispered Portuguese. 'These men might be from Demak. Their leader looks to be the kind of Muslim who hates Portuguese Christians, and he thinks you are one of them. So we must avoid using Portuguese when they can hear.'

'What is Sri saying?'

'She is one smart lady. She is abusing them in the highest, most elegant Javanese – words I seldom hear. She is telling them that she is the official court translator for the King of Banten and his royal mother. She says she did not want to come on this terrible journey, but that the king commanded her because this mission is essential for his plans to defeat both the Portuguese and Dutch infidels. This mission is crucial to both Banten and Mataram, and anyone who interferes with it will have to answer to them both.'

'Good – but do they believe it?'

'Maybe not – look out!

Four of the armed men approached them and asked roughly in Malay: '*Siapa kamu* – who are you? Where are you from?'

'I am the ambassador of the great King of England, on a mission to the great King of Mataram.' Hodges had rehearsed this part of his speech in Malay.

'But we know you speak Portuguese. You are a spy for the Portuguese. What proof do you have about this King of Inggeris. If he is so great, why has nobody heard of him?'

Hodges tried to protest, but stumbled over the Malay words. Brusquely Buyung broke in with his new words of English. 'Buyung translate you, sire. You talk me English; I talk Malay.'

'And who are you? You do not look like him. Are you some slave of the Portuguese?'

Buyung must have prepared for this moment, for a fluent Malay story came out with no hesitation.

'Not at all sir. I was indeed born below the winds, from a Chinese father in Sumatra, so I speak Malay. But I am English too, since I was taken there as a young man and educated in their ways. Then, because I spoke Malay, I was asked to join this great embassy to Mataram, to help explain our mission to you Javanese. England is indeed a great country, I can attest. Its capital of London is far greater than any city below the winds, even Banten or Aceh, where I have been. But it is for my master, Tuan Hod, to speak. I will only translate.'

Impressed at what he could follow of this, Hodges decided to play along. Even if Buyung didn't understand his words, the lad probably knew better than he himself what should be said to convince these people.

'Please explain,' he therefore said in English, 'that I learned a little Portuguese because the Portuguese were the first people from Europe to come below the winds, so that theirs is the only language of Europe that is understood here. Your languages are not yet known above the winds. The Portuguese came first because they are closest, because they have nothing of their own so need to steal from others, and because they consider all Muslims their enemies. My country is far richer and greater, and has no need or desire to plunder the goods of others. We English have a different religion from the Portuguese, a religion of peace. We have never fought Muslims, but want only to trade with them. Indeed the Portuguese hate us as much as they hate Muslims, but they can do nothing against us because we are a mighty kingdom.'

Hodges paused long enough for Buyung to launch again into his fluent Malay speech, which seemed to have some connection with what Hodges had said because of the frequent spitting out of the word *Portugis*. This gave Hodges a chance to look for Sri, who was nowhere to be seen. Desperate, he interrupted Buyung's elaborate story.

'Tell them I must see the translator – *juru bahasa*.' This was a term for Sri he had practised in Malay, and even Javanese. 'She will explain. Where have they taken her?'

'You stay here,' the short-haired leader snapped, without waiting for a translation. Instinctively Hodges reached for his sword, but all four men pounced on him before he could get it free. They disarmed him and bound his feet so he could not move. Buyung was protesting, threatening the anger of the Banten sultan, but soon he was also bound and told to be quiet.

Prodded with spears, they were moved to a dark hut separate from the other travellers and left for the night, guarded by three men in turn as others slept. None would answer questions except with a poke of the spear: 'Diam! Quiet!'

At first light they heard the cries of the cartmen getting their oxen into harness and moving them cart by cart to the ferry. Hodges began shouting again about the juru bahasa, but received only blows and prods from the pikes. Eventually, as the sun was well up and the last of the carts was crossing, Pangeran appeared, closely watched by the leader of the Demak fighters, if that is what they were.

'Where is Sri?' Buyung had reminded him that revealing his involvement with Sri would only endanger her more, but he could not help himself.

Pangeran spoke first in Javanese, but Buyung was sticking to his role of not speaking the language and switched the conversation to Malay with his own more diplomatic questions. Pangeran's answer was chilling.

'Unfortunately these men do not believe your story about an English embassy to Mataram, and wish to detain you until they receive further instructions. They allow our convoy to continue to Mataram, where the translator may be able to make your case. Please be patient here. I have brought some clothes.' He placed their cloth-rolled bundles on the floor, but with no sign of the gifts and Buyung's trade goods.

Buyung was talking again in Malay, Hodges spluttering in English, but the Demak leader simply said, 'Wait,' as he turned and conducted Pangeran away. They were left to listen to the sounds of the last ferry making its crossing.

'God's blood,' shouted Hodges, as the English began again to come naturally. 'What have they done with her? Bring her back, you scoundrels!'

'Remember, sire, you are great ambassador from great king.' Buyung wriggled closer so that he could whisper in Portuguese. 'It is better she go to Mataram safely. She is a smart and elegant lady, and can better convince these Javanese bigheads than you or I that they should let us continue. Our job is to try to look the part, and not betray her by showing how weak we really are.'

'But she is alone, with no protection, while I rot here! I don't trust that Pangeran fellow one inch.'

'Patience, sire. She may be alone, but I wager she is safer than you or me. Now you owe it to her to stay alive by acting your part well.'

So they waited.

# Islam or death

'*Mana kafir ini?*' An authoritative new voice made itself heard in the hut to which they had been taken, asking for the infidels.

Days of uncertainty had passed. The guards had taken them an hour's walk from the ferry-point and put them in another hut, easier to guard since the walls were of wood with only one door. They had been alternatively harsh and talkative. Buyung had managed to befriend one of them he called Ahmad, as young as himself. He seemed to have little idea which prince his armed band supported. They were all Muslims, but some were from Sumatra, Makassar and Bima, so their common language was Malay. They had wrested control of this ferry point only some weeks before, and since then had lived well on the tolls they levied. It was the job of their boss, Hussain, to work out who they had to pay off to keep the money flowing, and who they had to fight.

The newcomer was better dressed, with an elegant kris at his waist. His armed followers wore smart green uniforms. As soon as he appeared in the hut, accompanied by Hussain and some of his guards, it was obvious he was in charge.

'What is your name, your country, your religion, and your purpose here?'

Hodges and Buyung had to repeat their performance in English and Malay, now embellished after they had agreed on some persuasive details.

'Are you a soldier? What weapons do you use?

Hodges was caught off balance, but insisted in his careful English that no, he was a sailor and diplomat, and left the fighting to others. 'England has many weapons and brave soldiers, and can defend itself against any state in the world. But in Java we have only peaceful intentions.'

Buyung's translation was much longer, and he appeared to warm to the task. His interrogator also showed much interest, and it was some time before Hodges was brought back into the conversation.

'I say English very smart with guns. They want to know which guns. Can you fix?'

'Would that help us?'

'Keep us alive.'

'Alright. I know guns.'

Again Buyung's Malay sounded both lengthy and enthusiastic.

One of the uniformed men unwrapped a musket and, on instructions from his commander, showed the firing mechanism to Hodges, without releasing his grip on the gun. Hodges recognised the type of snaphance Dutch soldiers commonly used. There was no spark when he pulled the trigger because the piece of steel, the frizzen, was jammed in a safety position. It needed some lubrication to enable it to move into the correct position for firing. When this was explained through various languages and gestures, some kind of oil from coconuts was produced. This did the trick. Hodges was able to position the frizzen correctly and generate a satisfactory spark.

Clearly impressed, the uniformed men withdrew. Shortly a meal was produced such as they had not seen since leaving Japara, and they fell upon the welcome chicken and fish. The commander returned and now introduced himself.

'I am Kiai Ibrahim, and I serve Adipati Suranata, the future king of Java. He has need of men such as you. You are fortunate that the Adipati is a great and generous man, and rewards well those in his employ. Here you are without friends, and you will not survive the dangerous times we are living through unless you find a protector. The Demak king is the richest and the ablest of the kings in Java, and he has many foreigners in his employ.'

'What kind of foreigners?'

'Makassar people, Gujaratis, Turks, Malays, and even a Portuguese who has accepted Islam. They help my master in planning the best fighting force in Java. The King of Mataram will not long be able to withstand him once his army is fully trained. You will be useful in Demak, but you would be a dead man in Mataram. Please join us.'

Hodges could get the gist of this even in Malay, but could not restrain himself from demanding from Buyung in Portuguese what was going on. In any case, the knowledge that they spoke Portuguese seemed to have leaked out.

'This is outrageous. I must find Sri and the way to Mataram.'

'If they think you are committed to the Mataram side, or to the Portuguese, these men will not hesitate to kill us. Do not believe his story about this Adipati in Demak. I know there is much division even among the strict Muslims, and his force cannot be as strong as Mataram. But we must keep them thinking we will cooperate at least until we can plan a way to escape.'

'Very well; ask them what they require of us.'

Ibrahim had his answer ready, as if it had been prepared.

'You must only become a Muslim, so that you are on the right path to your own salvation in heaven, as well as the right path for the future of Java. Then our king will treat you well, give you an honoured position training his artillerymen, with a house and a servant, as well as a wife if you wish.'

Hodges had time to compose a brave answer as the translation proceeded. 'I have my own religion of Jesus Christ. Tell him, Buyung, he cannot expect me to abandon that for his faith.'

The reply came back confidently. 'You may believe in Jesus. So do I. He is one of the great prophets, after Abraham, Moses and David. We all revere him as you do. But after Jesus came the last and greatest of the prophets, the Prophet Muhammad, who completed god's message for mankind. You are a modern man who understands guns and ships; you must also keep up with the revelation of god to us men. Islam does not contradict your religion, but only completes it.'

'I respect your religion, but it is not mine. Your master must know there are different religions in the world, and he cannot expect people to abandon their religion for his. What if I respectfully decline?'

'There is no reason for you to decline. Islam is the correct path for all men. If you stubbornly refuse my master's generous offer, he cannot trust you at all. Then you would be an enemy. Our faith tells us that those who reject the path of Islam after it is explained to them deserve to die. There is no alternative for you than death.'

Buyung trembled as he conveyed this last piece of information.

'These people are serious, Thomas. They kill people who will not submit to their faith, for they cannot trust what they call *kafir*, infidels. We must appear to cooperate, or they could simply kill us on the spot.'

Hodges remembered some words of scripture: *what shall it profit a man, if he gain the whole world, and lose his own soul?* He muttered something to Buyung about dying proudly being better than going to hell.

Buyung was not impressed. 'You Christians sound like the worst kind of Muslims, if you think god sends everybody to hell who is not in his chosen religion. Since Muslims and Christians have opposite ideas of who goes to hell, I doubt them both. If there is a mighty creator of everything he must have bigger ideas than to send most of us to hell.'

'What will you tell them about yourself?'

'I am young, and I want to live. I will say whatever they ask. But they are less interested in me, except perhaps as a way to you and your knowledge of guns.'

'You had better tell them that I am not stubborn, but I need time and more information. I know nothing about Islam.'

Ibrahim looked satisfied with whatever it was that Buyung told him.

'Very well. Tomorrow we will move to another place more accessible from Demak, and we will find people to educate you in the true faith.'

Their journey under guard appeared to be back in the direction of Kudus, but they stopped at a kind of school attached to a mosque, surrounded by rice fields rather than a town. There they were put in a small house, elevated on poles, with the guards taking turns sleeping underneath. They were alternately friendly and punitive. On good days they were able to walk around the school and watch boys of various ages learning to recite the Quran. Hodges took careful note on these occasions of possible escape routes if he were able to overpower a guard, but their captors appeared to have chosen well. The school and mosque offered no sympathetic faces, and around it rice fields stretched so far there were no hiding places.

On day three Buyung was taken away in the morning and did not return until dark. He was battered, with bloodied face and hands, and wanted only to sleep. Next morning he began to move his aching limbs, and with help from Hodges washed his wounds with the bucket for their morning bath.

'My god, what did they do to you?'

'Beat me, of course. I feared the worst, but thank god they seemed to prefer me alive.' Buyung winced with the pain, and could only tell his story in gasps, between cracked lips.

'They wanted to get a different story from what we have been telling them about the embassy, and thought they could beat it out of me. Especially they wanted to know who our real friends were in Japara and Banten, and kept on about the Portuguese. That was the worst, when a nasty big fellow with long hair kept pointing his spear all over my body. Finally he pressed it down on my hand, demanding the name of some Portuguese. I thought I had lost my hand, but finally I think it was obvious I didn't know anything, so I just got this wound.' He showed the deep gash in his bloodied hand.

'Did they force the truth out of you?'

'Don't worry. I kept repeating my story about the English embassy, though I had to make up more details about the ship that brought us from England, and some interesting details about my childhood in Sumatra. I said that in Banten the king and his mother made us welcome and gave us many honours. In Japara I kept repeating that we only contacted the people from Mataram, Raden Pekik and then Pangeran in the convoy. I thought it would be fatal to reveal any of my friends and relations in Japara, or of Sri's.'

'You're a hero, Buyung. Thank you. I'm not sure I could have done that.'

'You will soon have a chance to find out. They kept saying that there was no point in my serving you, since you were as good as a dead man. Either you must join them as a good Muslim, or you will be tortured and killed.'

'Just like that.'

'No, Thomas. The details were very colourful. You might be trampled by elephants, ripped apart by tigers, shot from a cannon, or slowly cut to pieces by the krisses of each of their soldiers.'

'So how did *you* escape this charming fate?'

'When they asked if I would become Muslim I didn't protest. Losing my foreskin seemed a small price compared with these other torments they were describing. I said the truth: that some of my Chinese friends and relatives have become Muslim. They have not complained about anything in their new religion except giving up pork. I only lied when I said that I never liked pork anyway, so that would not be a problem.'

The grisly options reminded Hodges of the *Book of Martyrs*

he had been encouraged to read at school, with its absorbing engravings of Tyndale's heroics before the butchers. Buyung's pragmatism hardly measured up.

'What about your own gods? Don't you fear their anger if you abandon them?'

'They do not seem to be jealous gods, like yours. If I feared anybody's anger it would be my dead grandfather's. He was a stern man who would hit me when I spoke Javanese instead of Chinese. I always make offerings to his shrine on the festival days so that his ghost doesn't punish me, but my Chinese friends who became Muslim do the same.'

'Do you believe they are serious about killing me?'

'They sounded really scary. But it is obvious they want your skill with guns, so they might be in trouble with their bosses if they just get rid of you. I guess you have a better chance than me of staying alive even if you resist, but I don't want your life on my conscience. You will have to make your own decision.'

He did not have to wait long. Hussain appeared in their hut and greeted them politely, carefully ignoring Buyung's injuries. He introduced the promised Islamic teacher, an older man who looked more Indian than Javanese, but spoke Malay well enough. 'This is Sheikh Saiful Alam, a learned scholar who can answer every question you have about Islam. He has even been to Mecca, and studied with the sages there. It is a great honour that he has agreed to come to instruct you, and you must show him every respect. I see that Buyung is well enough to translate anything you do not understand. And you need not pretend you do not speak Portuguese. We know all about you.'

Buyung intervened to explain. 'We speak Portuguese because it is a useful language between peoples, but we are not Portuguese. It is the same as us speaking Malay even though you may be Javanese and I a kind of Sumatran Chinese Englishman. You are most welcome, honoured teacher.'

The sheikh ignored him and turned to Hodges. 'Do you wish to become a Muslim, and join us on the path to heaven?'

Hodges was grateful to use Buyung to translate, since it gave him time to compose his thoughts. He didn't know whether he was ready for martyrdom. He was sure he wanted to delay the test as much as possible.

'I am content with my Christian faith, and believe that is what god intends for me. All men must follow god as they perceive and understand him. If you could convince me that god's intention was the Muslim way, then I would be obliged to follow my reason and conscience to accept it. But at present I know nothing to convince me of that.'

The sheikh looked grave. 'Islam is the path of reason as well as of god's word. The people here in Java believed in many gods and spirits, as do people in India where I was born. These spirits appealed to them when they were ignorant, like children, giving to animals and trees the veneration that only belongs to god. But god has gradually shown us through his prophets that there is only one creation and one almighty god who created it and us humans in it. Islam means simply acceptance; acceptance of this obvious fact.'

'I too believe this. There is only one god for all of us – Javanese, Chinese, Portuguese and English. But my way to understand this god is through Jesus, as he is explained in the gospels.'

'Jesus too preached that there is only one god, as did Abraham, Moses and David. But Allah had to reveal himself fully in his holy Quran through Muhammad, because the Christians had distorted the message of Jesus and other prophets. They made Jesus, his mother Mary, and many other people into gods to be worshipped. Islam had to be revealed as the true path of the one god.'

'There were indeed distortions of Christianity. There must also be distortions of Islam, because I see people here in Java who call themselves Muslim but who worship at the tombs of men, or even put offerings on trees. We English Christians have reformed our practice and condemned these distortions. I believe in only one almighty god.'

'People who are new to Islam find it hard give up all their bad habits at once. You too, when you accept the true path, may take time to understand its true beauty and rationality. Islam is an easy path so that all may join. You need only say the confession of faith, "There is no god but Allah, and Muhammad is his prophet." The rest can come slowly, as you learn that your past ways are not helpful.'

'You call this god "Allah," but that is an Arabic word. I call him "god" in English, or "deo" in Portuguese, because we each must understand him in our own way.'

'I prefer that you say Allah, because I do not know what may be meant by your "god". Perhaps that may also have other meanings of many gods.'

He rustled in a cloth bag he had brought, found what he wanted and thrust it before Hodges. It was an engraving, probably

Portuguese, of devotees adoring the Virgin Mary throned in glory.

'You say Christians believe in one god, but they use pictures like this in their teaching, which show the opposite. They are worshipping a woman here.'

'This is a Portuguese picture, depicting a distortion of Christianity. Mary, whom they are shown as worshipping, was a holy woman chosen by god to carry his son, Jesus, but she was not god and should not be worshipped.'

'You say Jesus was the son of god, and Mary was his mother. So was Mary the wife of god? These are already three gods – your famous trinity? If you really accepted only one god this could only be our one almighty Allah.'

'Mary was not god. She has nothing to do with the trinity. Jesus was a part of god, his human face, so that we could better know him. The father, son and holy spirit are three ways of perceiving god.'

Buyung was having obvious difficulty rendering this in Malay, and came back to Hodges several times. 'Can I say three people, three faces, or three gods?'

'No. Three in one. *Tiga dalam satu.*'

The sheikh smiled. 'I can see you have difficulty yourself in making sense of your god. You do not even agree with the Portuguese on these questions. That is why god gave his message to Muhammad, to end disputes, and make finally clear that god is one, and one only. You have only to accept that, and you are a Muslim.'

'Jesus rose from the dead, to be with his father. I believe therefore he too was god, and that he alone can save me. None of the prophets has the power to do that.'

'Then, Tuan Hod, you must die. God has decreed that those who stubbornly refuse to accept him, even when all is explained, have no right to live. What is more you will be an enemy of our sacred cause in Java. The Adipati will not be able to trust you, and must put you to death rather than let you serve our enemies. I am sorry for you.'

'I do not believe that religion can be forced on anyone, and certainly not on me. Perhaps in time you can persuade me that your path is the right one, and in that case I will follow my own conscience and accept Islam. But I cannot change the faith of my family and my people, the education of a lifetime, in a single day. Please give me time to learn more and reflect.'

Saiful Alam's demeanour changed: 'What need is there of time? The path of Allah is clear and easy. Why should the Adipati continue to feed you if you are stubbornly clinging to the side of god's enemies? I will ask him to give you two days before the execution, but I am not sure he will agree to such a useless waste of time.'

With this the sheikh stormed out. Hussain remained only long enough to add: 'You are not wise, Hod, to anger Sheikh Saiful Alam. He is the greatest teacher in the land, and your opportunity to have a good life here in Java. Unless you quickly change your mind, there is nothing but a painful death for you.'

Hodges was crushed. He had faced death many times, and believed he was sufficiently at peace with his maker to meet it bravely. But now he wanted to live. He must find Sri, he must feel her gentle touch again. If she had been killed, or worse still betrayed him with that wretched Pangeran, all was lost. He would willingly die. Better, indeed, if he could die as a Christian martyr rather than in some meaningless scuffle in a barbarous land. But he could not believe he would not see her sweet smile again. She felt so close. He must live.

Buyung was not happy. 'We have to get out of here, Thomas, and being stubborn about your religion will not help. Who knows whether god is one, or three, or many? If it makes them happy to seem to agree with their ideas, why not? We are no use to Sri, to England, or to anybody if we are dead. I do not think this group of Muslims is really as strong as they pretend. If we stay alive and they relax their guard, we will surely have a chance to escape.'

Hussain was back, this time with the big man with long hair at whose hands Buyung had suffered. He was armed with various fearsome weapons.

Now the language was tough.

'You say you reject the Portuguese worship of many gods. Now prove it.'

He threw down the Portuguese engraving of the adoration of the Virgin. 'Stamp your foot on this, if you think it is blasphemy. Prove you are not one of them!'

Hodges stepped back in alarm. 'I reject their blasphemy, yes, but one should not dishonour a holy person, even if she is not god.'

Suddenly he was on his knees, gasping with pain. It must have been a blow on his back from the club of the long-haired one.

'Stamp on it!'

Another hesitation as Hodges tried to speak, and now the

blows came one after another. Hodges curled into a ball, but before he passed out he managed to mutter, 'Alright. Stop, please.'

When he came to, the engraving was still there. Hussain was still looking stern; long-hair was menacing.

'Stamp on it!'

Hodges hobbled to his knees, and got one knee onto the engraving. Another blow. 'Your foot!'

Finally his foot was on the paper, and he wriggled it around feebly.

'Very well. It seems you are not a Portuguese in your belief; at least not a good one. So why do you not join the true path?'

'I fear god.'

Another blow sent him reeling. He could barely hear what Hussain was saying.

'If you simply accept you will be honoured as a soldier of Adipati Suranata, bathed, fed, clothed and provided some feminine comfort. If you should eventually die you will enjoy heaven as one of Allah's soldiers. If you are stubborn, you will not only suffer a miserable and painful death; you will suffer even greater punishments from god, rotting in hell for your refusal of his mercy.'

Hodges tried to focus on that picture of the heroic Tyndale. Instead he saw only the face of Sri, and she seemed to be entreating him to submit, to stay alive, to join her in donning this outer garment of Muslim identity.

'Alright. Yours is the right path. I am with you.'

'You have seen reason. Well done.'

Buyung sighed with relief as Hussain and his thug departed.

Hodges sank into oblivion, wondering what he had done. When he regained consciousness, it was to the tender touch of a woman, dressing his wounds and carefully massaging the bruises with some ointment. Sri had returned!

She spoke some soothing words of Javanese, but this was not Sri's voice. He sank back into unconsciousness. When he awoke again it was to another voice coaxing him to eat some rice porridge. Carefully he prised open one eye to see a woman trying to feed him. Another helped a cheerful Buyung to eat, his wounded hand already wrapped in leaves.

'Well done sire. I thought we were finished. You made the right decision.'

'I'm not sure. We shall see.'

After propping them both up on cushions, the two women vanished. It was Hussain who returned with the sheikh.

'God is merciful, and has opened your eyes to the true path. Now you need only recite the words as I tell you. First you,' turning to Buyung.

'There is no god but Allah; *La ilaha illa'llah.*' Buyung repeated the words confidently.

'Muhammad is the Prophet of Allah; *Mu ammad rasulu-llah.*'

Now it was Hodges' turn. His thoughts raced back to the shadow play, with an apparently Hindu character wielding this profession of faith, kalimasada, as a magic weapon in his armoury. So be it for me, he thought.

'There is no god but Allah; Muhammad is the Prophet of Allah.'

'Welcome to the path of god,' said the sheikh. 'You are now

Muslims and brothers in our struggle. There are young students here in the school who will instruct you how to pray, and how to behave, and gradually you will learn. There are two more things necessary, as outer signs that you are on the right path. First we will cut your hair, so others here may see that you are one of us, and not be hostile to you. Later we will arrange a feast to mark the cutting of your foreskin, the *khitan* of we Muslims. But this will be a public event, and we will wait until you are restored to health.'

For the first time Buyung looked alarmed. 'But that is a custom of people from above the winds, Indians and Arabs and even Jews, so I hear. We Chinese feel strongly about our penises. Some say that this is not necessary for those who do not have such traditions.'

Sheikh Saiful Alam was now genial again. 'I'm sure we all feel strongly about that part of our body. I have met other Chinese who feared the khitan, but later they were grateful. There is more feeling in the penis without that useless appendage, and more pleasure in the act of love. It is true that the Prophet himself, peace be upon him, seemed to take it for granted, and the holy book does not speak directly of it. But it is a strong and happy tradition. For those foreigners who join the faith, the feasting is especially joyful. It is essential because everybody will want to see you and congratulate you for your wise decision.'

'As for you, Tuan Hod, it should not be a problem. Even Jesus, whom only this morning you thought was some kind of god, was circumcised like every other Jew.'

The barber was sent in the next morning. He had little to do with Hodges' hair. In the heat of Java he liked it short, and was grateful for the trim of hair and beard. Buyung was a different matter, since he had not entirely abandoned the long hair of his ancestors. As he had explained it, it was a compromise between his mother's and father's ideas, but still reached his shoulders on the rare occasions he let it down. The barber seemed especially ruthless in ensuring a very short cut.

'My father will not be pleased. He seemed to think I could not honour grandfather and my other ancestors if I didn't share their long hair. For myself I am glad to be rid of it, if only he didn't cut it quite so short. Except with my father and his business cronies, I would rather be Javanese than Chinese.'

'The hair will grow back once we get out of this mess. Not so your fine prick.'

'My father's never going to see that! But we must have a plan to escape before that happens. What if we pretend our bruises are not healed yet, and we can't walk properly, so this great event gets postponed?

'I'm not sure that will work. These ladies who have been massaging us seem to know our bodies pretty well.'

As they healed and were given more freedom, Hodges saw more of the little community, while Buyung ingratiated himself with the young men to find out where they were. He had a new scheme every day for how they might escape, but since they were never allowed out of sight of the guards, none seemed feasible.

One day there was sudden turmoil in the camp. The guards became stern and confined them to their hut, but would say nothing about what was happening. After two distant sounds of gunshot and much shouting near at hand they leapt into action, bound the two captives by their hands and feet, and rushed away with weapons at the ready.

'This is our chance, Buyung. Try to undo these knots and get away. There must be a fight on.'

They rolled together and struggled to undo each other's fetters, as the sound of conflict seemed to grow closer. Hodges had only succeeded in liberating Buyung's hands before the hubbub subsided. Footsteps approached, but now slowly. At the doorway stood Hussain, but now it was *his* hands that were bound. With him was Pangeran and two spearmen.

'I am glad to see that you are alive. Otherwise I would have had to kill this rogue.' Pangeran waved his kris at Hussain.

Buyung replied with a torrent of grateful Malay as one of the guards produced a knife to cut first Hodges' fetters, then Buyung's. Shakily they stood, as one of the spearmen seized each of them. 'Can you walk? Come with us.'

Pangeran addressed some stern Javanese commands to Hussain and allowed him to be released. As he moved away Buyung muttered, 'There seems to be some kind of deal. Perhaps we are worth something to somebody.'

'Where is Sri, juru bahasa?' Hodges demanded.

'*Selamat juga* – also safe. Wait.'

His heart lifted. He may have lost his soul, but he had not lost Sri. They were both alive. Had she rescued him? At what price?'

Pangeran would answer no more questions as they were taken out of the small village and across the rice fields. Buyung had more success in Javanese, listening to the orders being shouted and trying to joke with his guard.

'It seems they are part of a strong force from Mataram. They outnumbered Hussain's men, who surrendered after a little fighting and accepted an agreement. Their job is to take us to Mataram. It sounds as though you have an unexpected friend there.'

'You mean Sri? Who else?'

'They only call him "Romo". I have no idea.'

They walked back to the ferry crossing, where the larger Mataram force assembled. Some were already busy returning their men and equipment to the other side. They were in a hurry to put their two hostages on the next crossing, and relaxed their guard once safely across. The two men were given rice, bananas and a coconut to drink. Soon they were on their way again, struggling to keep up with what seemed an advance guard of some twenty men. Their soft bare feet soon began to bleed as they stumbled along the track. Hodges could hardly ask for boots when the soldiers were barefoot.

After what seemed like hours of painful travel, they reached a small town in Javanese style. Each compound was surrounded by brick walls with stepped gateways, as he had seen in Japara. The soldiers headed for the largest compound with the most substantial buildings, but Pangeran led the two men down a lane to a smaller compound with a number of huts. There he surrendered them to a venerable Javanese man who welcomed them politely to his home. Buyung was led off to one hut, and Hodges to a larger one.

And there was Sri – a beautiful jewel in this ugly, aching, wretched world. Her composure, her joy at seeing him, put everything right. As soon as the venerable host had withdrawn, she was in his arms.

# Sri's Story

'Thank God you survived, Sri. How is it possible?'

'And you, but a bit battered. Poor Thomas. Look at your feet!'

'How did you manage all this? Why did they let me go? Did you get to the great king?'

'It's a long story. Let me get some water and herbs to deal with your body, and then I'll satisfy your impatient mind.

'I was terrified when they took you away, not for me but for you. I have heard stories of what these Muslim fighters have done to Portuguese they captured. But I knew it would make things worse for you, for us both, if they knew we were lovers. So I kept trying to play my official translator part, and to warn them of how angry the King of Mataram would be when he heard that an envoy to him from a great country beyond the seas had been interfered with.

'The Pangeran told me that he could not fight them – they were much stronger than his small group of guards, and a defeat would have lost everything. He could only bargain, by paying an outrageous toll on the freight the convoy carried and surrendering the two foreigners. Fortunately, he managed to protect your presents for the king.

'We had some more adventures on the road, but it gets easier as you approach Mataram. You will see tomorrow, when we go back by the same route. The real problems started when we got to Mataram. The king – they call him Panembahan Krapyak – was never there, off building palaces or fighting wars. His capital is nothing like Banten. It seems even more divided, but it's hardly a city yet. It is said Krapyak intends to build one of the great cities of the world, but for now it's like a collection of fortified compounds, with little to unify it.

'I told everybody I could my story about the noble envoy of the great country of England, but all told me to wait for the king; nothing could be done without him. The Panembahan has many brothers he does not trust – some say his father had a hundred children by his many wives. Each one I saw told me not to see the others. Dipati Mandaraka seemed a kind of minister, older and wiser than most. He was the one who first mentioned Romo. Perhaps he could help.'

'Romo?' interrupted Hodges. 'The one they said was my mysterious friend? What kind of name is that?'

'Romo is just the high Javanese word for father, but this one seems to have no children. Let me tell the story.

'Mandaraka said this Romo seemed to be some kind of feringgi, but he spoke like a Javanese and had great influence with the Panembahan. Then I began to ask others about him, and all had different ideas. Some said he was a Portuguese who had turned Muslim; others said Dutch, Turkish, or Jewish. One even said English, though he did not know what this meant. What they agreed about was that he was not a soldier like the other feringgi, who had turned Muslim and served the king in training his soldiers to use guns. There are a couple of those in

Mataram, but I didn't see them. This Romo seemed to be more like a Javanese *tapak*, with strange powers from his meditation. I heard different stories, hard to believe. He could heal the sick, or meditate for a week without eating, or even be in two places at the same time. I think you will say the Javanese in Mataram are even more superstitious than those you met in Japara.'

'He sounds like a trickster.'

'Perhaps. But he turned out to be the key. I finally got to see him a week ago. He is definitely a feringgi, a European, but I don't know what kind. He was dressed like an old-fashioned Javanese guru, with long robes and long hair. I first spoke Portuguese with him, and then tried out some of the English phrases you taught me. He seemed to understand everything but always replied in Javanese. It was very cultivated Javanese, like my mother's father used to speak, but formal, like a book. I could tell even if I closed my eyes that he was not really Javanese.

'I explained the diplomatic mission from the great King of England, but he interrupted me rudely and said, "I know about England – more than you, I suppose. I am more interested in Banten. Tell me about the king and his policies. Is he friends with the Gujaratis, the Dutch or the Portuguese? Does he go to the mosque every Friday, and make his court do the same? What kind of Islam does he favour, and who are his favourite teachers?"

'I told him what I know, mostly from the queen mother: that the Banten people are tired of the Christians fighting with each other and with the Muslims, and want only peace among all the traders so that Banten will prosper. Once he got onto religion, I felt my knowledge was not enough to satisfy him. All I know about the Muslim teachers in Banten is the craze my brother Khalid developed in his youth for some sheikh who, he said, was teaching the Qadiriyyah method of chanting.

'This chanting seemed like nonsense to me, but it was all I knew about Islamic teachers so I made the most of it. This got Romo quite excited, so that he went looking in the great pile of books and palm-leaf writings he had in the next room. He came out with one palm leaf he thought had something about the Qadiriyyah. I could see he had trouble reading it, more because of his old eyes than his Javanese, I think. Once he found out I could read it, he asked me to do the reading. As I read more, he began discussing what each difficult word really meant, sometimes checking the Malay and Portuguese equivalents with me. He said "I wish I had your young eyes. There is so much still to read, and so little time."

'After he went back for more palm leaves for me to read, I protested that he had to do something to rescue the great ambassador from the King of England. He obviously preferred to talk about the manuscripts, and pretended that the Panembahan never did what he advised anyway. I don't believe that. We agreed that I could come again the next day, give some time to reading manuscripts, and he would tell me what might be done with the king.

'Then I realised we had a weapon that might work with this book-lover. Fortunately, they had let me take charge of the goods that were said to belong to the English embassy. Buyung's cloths were useful. I had to sell some to enable me to keep up the royal performance. I found the spectacles among your presents and took them along the next day, carefully bound in cloth. After a little time humouring him with his palm-leaf manuscripts, I demanded he find a solution for the captive English ambassador. All he would say was that he would bring the matter to the king when he returned to the palace, which might be a week away.

'When he went back to his manuscripts, struggling to read, I said the clever English people had invented something that could help him. I showed him the spectacles and he fairly leapt at them, put them on his nose and began reading. He was like a small boy with a new toy, so excited that he forgot all about me. I said, "These are the property of the English ambassador. No doubt if he is released from the ruffians who are holding him he will present them to the king, or to some learned servant of the king like you."

'He was very curious where they were made and didn't believe that the English could have done it. When I insisted that he first find a way to release you he just repeated he could do nothing until the king returned. I demanded he give the spectacles back, and he simply said he would keep them safe for the ambassador, and meanwhile make use of them. I have to admit I stopped being a proper Javanese translator of the court and just dived on him, knocked him over and seized the glasses. Fortunately, he was old and a bit frail, and surprised that I suddenly turned into a tiger, so I got the better of him.'

'Brave girl. I know what a tiger you can be.'

'I told him he would not see the spectacles again until the English ambassador was free. When he had recovered from the shock, he looked hard at me and said, "Why do you care so much about this English envoy? If you are just a court translator you could go quietly back to Banten and explain what happened. Something else is going on here. I cannot help you unless you are honest with me."

'I tried to keep up the show for a while, but it obviously wasn't working. In the end I told him the truth. I said that though you were really English and with a mission from the English king, I was your wife. So he would have to kill me, or rescue you, if he ever wanted to see the spectacles again. He burst out laughing and called me Srikandi – a woman warrior. "We need to make a plan," he said, as if he were now on our side. "The king won't be as interested in these spectacles as I am – reading is not his greatest love. But you said your man was captured at a ferry crossing. Now that is something he cares about."

'I told him everything I knew about the Muslim gang who had captured you and levied an outrageous toll on the Mataram convoy. He started talking about the people he knew in the king's army, including a pair of Portuguese *renegados* who were not to his liking but could be useful. Of course, I told him you were also a military genius. You would be a precious ally but a dangerous enemy if these bandits had their way with you. My job was to find the Pangeran in charge of our convoy and bring him into the plan.'

'Why him? He's just a soldier, isn't he? Why do you turn to him for help all the time?'

Hodges' sharp reaction took Sri aback. She put a reassuring arm around him and looked her sweetest.

'Be calm, my dear one. He was the one who knew the ferry

crossing and could explain the Muslim force that had captured it. He could say that the gang were loyal to Adipati Suranata in Demak. That was the weapon Romo needed to convince the commanders, since the Adipati was seen as a big threat to Mataram. Romo convinced them that this river crossing was crucial to the struggle going on in Java. They would have to move immediately to retake it for Mataram, and get hold of you before you were either killed or moved out of reach.

'They did not want to bring me along, but I insisted that you knew no Javanese or Malay and might be very uncooperative if I could not explain what was going on. So they left me here at Salatiga to meet you. Thank god it all turned out without a serious fight. I was terribly afraid you would be killed in a battle. But it seemed that the Pangeran,' stroking his arm again as she saw his expression darken, 'was able to make a deal with Hussain's group. They would release you and Buyung, and accept Mataram authority over the crossing. Some of the Mataram soldiers would stay there to ensure that they did, while the foreign Muslims among the group would withdraw to Demak.

'You seem not to like our Pangeran,' she drew closer. 'But we have to thank him that you are still alive and we are together. He is an honest soldier, but too much a Javanese man for me. You are the only one I love, Thomas.

'Let me show you how.'

# Romo

Mataram was confusing. Banten had been full of foreigners, and even Japara was accustomed to them, but here everybody seemed Javanese. They looked at Hodges with wonderment at best, hostility at worst. Few understood his limited Malay, but he couldn't take Sri with him to snoop around the market without destroying her image as the official translator sent by Banten. Buyung was useful, but quickly grew impatient with this role as he saw the opportunities for his trade.

'This is amazing. Do you see how few Indian cloths there are? Everybody is wearing drab local cloths, with none of the lovely reds and yellows the Klings bring. And when I see them heaving their earthenware pots around I know they would love our Chinese wares. In fact, they have some at the mosque; did you see? Treated like decorations too precious to use. This is truly a land of opportunity!'

'For you perhaps, but I don't know where to start.'

Sri suggested Hodges first contact the Pangeran, whom she began to call Sanjata since there were too many Pangerans in the town. 'He is the one you know already, and he speaks Malay.'

'Not him. You're right that I don't trust him. Anyway, he is too young and unimportant. Didn't you say there was a wise older minister – Dipati something?'

'Ki Dipati Mandaraka. We can try, but he is old and will say this new king does not listen to him. He prefers the previous king.

But I will try to arrange it.'

While Hodges was feeling disoriented and depressed, Sri was taking an interest in everything. Sometimes she reported to him excitedly about some aspect of a 'pure' Java society such as she had dreamed of in Banten; at other times she was shocked at the apparent barbarity of life on this frontier. She learned that a *senenan* would soon be held, at which the Panembahan would show himself to his people.

'Senenan?' asked Hodges. 'Is that something to do with Monday?'

'Yes. Senen is Monday so senenan is the feast held on a Monday. But in practice the king only does it when he wants to make a show. He uses it especially to inspire his warriors with feats of bravery and skill. If it's like the ones they used to have in Banten, there can be horrible cruelty. Anyway, that is a time you could see him. Be ready for it.'

'But I need an introduction first, so that he accepts me as an envoy not some adventurer.'

'That would be better, but I'm not sure Mandaraka will act so fast, even to receive you. His men tried to put me off saying he was not well. I insisted, but still haven't heard anything more. Maybe you should try your luck with Romo. Then you don't need me; you can speak Portuguese, or maybe even English.'

Hodges was wary of this freakish European. Was he a renegade who had sold his soul to these heathens, or some kind of crazy truth-seeker? It was only the frustration at having nowhere to turn that finally drove him to call at Romo's Javanese-style small compound.

'*Boa tarde, senhor. Sou o enviado Inglês,*' he called out.

There was a shuffling inside, and an older man appeared, with long hair and beard, bare feet and a sarong, but no shirt.

'The English envoy?' The eventual reply came slowly and awkwardly, but with the unmistakable accent of the West Country. 'Then you must speak English. Come in, but take your boots off first; and your jacket too, if you want to be comfortable. This is a Javanese house. We have no chairs here, but you may sit on the cushion against the wall if you need support.'

'And you? You talk like a Cornishman but dress like some heathen savage. Were you born English? If so, what in god's name are you now?'

'I dress like a Javanese because I live in Java, just as I would expect a Javanese in London to dress like an Englishman. In fact, I believe my dress is closer to Our Lord's than yours is, Hodges. But dress is not important. I hope yours is not too uncomfortable in this heat.'

Hodges settled himself awkwardly against a wall and removed his doublet.

Romo continued, 'Am I English? It is true that I have not spoken this language for twenty years, and you must forgive me if it comes back a little slowly. I was born Cornish, Trevithic by name. I can still speak a few words of Cornish. *Keskerdh Kernow!* That was the plea of our ancestors, so they said, before they were massacred in 1497. But my family really tried to be English, and brought me up to think Henry VIII was a great king and defender of the faith. It was Archbishop Cranmer and the tyrant Somerset who would not let us be English and Cornish at the same time, let alone keep our holy faith. They forced their English prayerbook on us and killed all who resisted. When my father was killed in 1549, with those who still hoped that Cornwall could live in England and in the Church, my mother had had enough, bless her soul. She could not bear to see another of her men sacrificed for a lost cause. She made me go to the English school I hated, and do something positive for my faith and my people instead of getting killed. "Go to France," she said when I started to get into trouble. "Study more; become a priest if you wish. Write. Tell our story." I have not been back to England since then, fifty years ago.'

'So you're a papist, and a traitor. Or a renegade, and a double traitor!' Hodges kept his hand on his sword. Had this Romo been setting a trap to betray him to the Portuguese?

'Not a renegade, I hope. On the contrary, I have tried to be true to myself, my faith and my heritage, even here. You can call me a papist, no doubt, since I was ordained a priest in Rome, no less. Even more, I joined the Jesuits, inspired by Father Campion. After he went back to preach in England I desperately wanted to follow his great example. I suppose I had the young man's zeal for martyrdom. But god had other plans. After I boarded a Channel boat, the skipper somehow found out my mission and refused to let me land. If I had, no doubt I would soon have been discovered and executed like my brother Jesuits, and you would not have found an Englishman in Mataram.'

'A prince of traitors, indeed! You supported Guy Fawkes, and the Spanish king with his armada. Probably you still weave plots to restore tyranny and superstition!'

'I am in Java; and now so are you. Two Englishmen somehow

found their way to Mataram. What point is there in bringing our disagreements here? The Javanese already think we Europeans do nothing but fight among ourselves. If the only two English in a thousand miles start fighting, we hardly deserve their sympathy. Anyway, enough about me. Tell me the news of England and your new ruler. Is it true that he made peace with the new Spanish king? Could those religious wars be finally over?'

Hodges seethed. This was his first encounter with a real Jesuit, and it was clear he lived up to the reputation for sweet oily words and evil intentions. But even so, he was right. Squabbling with him would not advance Hodges' cause. He took a deep breath before responding.

'We were too strong by sea. The Spanish were bleeding from all the ships Drake and the others sank in the Spanish Main. Their new king, another Philip, needed peace, though of course he was as much a papist and tyrant as his father – some say worse. Our new king, James, was a gracious peacemaker who began his reign by trying to settle all the conflicts. He made peace with Spain, so we are no longer supposed to attack each other's ships. Spain promised to accept James as a rightful king, and abandon its attempts to bring back popery to England.'

'*Beati pacifici quoniam filii Dei vocabuntur.* How does your new English Bible translate that? "Blessed are the peacemakers who will be called children of God"?'

Hodges grunted an acknowledgement.

'I am happy to hear it. James' mother was the Scottish Catholic queen, was she not? He should be the right man to see that war cannot be the way to settle how to reform the church.

And did he allow Catholic priests and the Latin mass to function again in England?'

'Never! How could he trust those plotters? There is tolerance for different ideas, but not for papists who want to serve a foreign tyrant. The Spanish are just waiting for a chance to divide and overthrow us again. I hear they are trying to make peace with the Dutch too, as the Dutch ships are destroying their trade and their empire. But of course, they have not accepted that men can be free to read the gospel for themselves and find their own way to god. The Inquisition is there to prove that.'

Romo sighed, but his thoughts were disrupted by an old lady stumbling towards them with a tray of cups and sweetmeats. He exchanged some words with her in Javanese as he passed a steaming cup to Hodges.

'Has your Sri introduced you to *teh* – tea – yet? The Chinese have brought many things to Java, but this is the best. I noticed early on that those who drank it rather than ordinary water suffered less from problems in the gut, and it is the same with me. This is Lakshmi.'

He spoke again to the lady, who bowed to Hodges. 'She keeps me fed and tries to teach me how to be a true Javanese – *wong Jowo*. I try to teach her how to be a true Christian without ceasing to be Javanese.'

'That is not possible! The Javanese believe such nonsense, with gods, monsters and demons in every corner.'

'So do we, brother. How can I explain to my Javanese friends our habit of burning witches? Your reformers only seemed to make that worse. Our angels, saints, and the devil himself, are not so different from the spirits the Javanese see everywhere. We poor humans would be blinded by the truth of the one true god. Instead we make a little puppet-show to try to glimpse him in the shadows. I am sure you must have learned much already from Sri. She seemed wise beyond her years. The first thing I learned in Java was that we cannot serve god by fighting, killing and burning each other over how each understands some partial aspect of his truth. We can best approach the larger truth that is god in silence, prayerfulness and discipline. I do that through the rule of Ignatius, and the Javanese through their meditation in holy places. Torturing and killing those we call heretics only takes us further from the god of compassion and righteousness. It hardens us against the unexpected truth of the silences.'

'That is balderdash,' Hodges spluttered, 'not Christianity. The gospel of Jesus Christ is the word of truth.'

'Yes, Hodges, yes.' Romo closed his eyes and appeared to focus within. 'As close as words can be to truth. We fight about words in Latin, Greek or English; the Muslims about words in Arabic, Malay and Javanese. But these are still only words. We have seen in England that even the best translation does not end the argument. God is far beyond us. But enough of this. You did not come here to talk about theology. What do you hope to achieve with your mission?'

'I want to tell the Javanese that England is a strong and rich country, which desires to trade freely with the whole world.'

'And then? What do you desire of the Panembahan?'

'That he should promise us freedom of trade to his dominions, and not allow the Dutch or the Portuguese to exclude us.'

'Perhaps you could persuade him that you are less quarrelsome than the Portuguese. They had too many fights with the Muslims for his taste. But why should he prefer the English to the Dutch? They appear to have many ships, and claim like you to be here to trade, not fight. There was a Venetian here recently who told the king precisely that. He should ally with the Dutch, since they have the ships to keep the peace in the ports and deliver the arms the king needs. They are real traders like the Venetians, he said, not interested in conquering and dominating. What more could you offer him?'

'The Dutch lie. They may talk a sweeter talk than the Portuguese, but they demand of every king with a port that he exclude other Europeans. Why do they spend their wealth to build and arm so many ships every year to send east? Because they want to take all the spices, blockading every port that refuses them a monopoly. Then they can demand whatever prices they please in Europe. If Mataram wants to be free, it must refuse the Dutch demands and allow different buyers to compete for its rice and spices. England can help them fight such monstrous demands.'

'Very well. But then the Portuguese would seem a surer ally against the Dutch. England has been a friend of the Dutch, after all.'

'Portugal is finished as a power. Philip's famous empire is falling apart. It remains only as an excuse for tyranny and popish obscurantism. Now that James has united England, Scotland and Ireland, England and France are the great powers of Europe, and will eventually be strong also here in Asia.'

'When you have finished with "popish obscurantism", what

will your new English faith be? Having a unique religion for England might make you even more quarrelsome than the others. Now that your king is the religious authority in England, will he demand the same status elsewhere? Or is every king to make his own religion?'

Hodges struggled to control his anger. 'We English are a practical people, not fanatics like you Jesuits or the puritans of Geneva. Now that we are rid of the power of the church, we are at last free to read and understand our own English Bible and follow Jesus as we find him there. King James has allowed the Scots to follow some of the ideas of Calvin in Geneva, or even stranger things. We only stop those who want to bring back popery.'

'Well, let us not fight here in Java, where there is already too much fighting. I hope you are right that the English king will allow men to find their different ways to god. That is also what Java needs. I doubt either the English or the Javanese can have peace if they stop people using the old ways they love in the name of a new dogma. If you listen carefully to your Sri, you may find a way to talk a language the king appreciates.'

'I doubt that.' Reminded of his mission, Hodges switched to a milder tone; he needed this irritating man. 'So how can I meet him, and make my case?'

'Do not rush it, my son. The king can be a violent man, cruel to those he does not agree with. You must think carefully what to say to him, and what to offer him as a gift that may take his fancy. The spectacles Sri showed me are wonderful, but the Panembahan does not read books. Weaponry is more to his taste. If you have something new there, it may spark his interest.'

'Perhaps the pistols will interest him. But you have obviously found a way to earn his respect. Was that done by agreeing with his heathen ideas?'

'Astronomy was the key. It was fortunate that we Jesuits were trained in it by Christoph Clavius, the great authority in Italy though a bit conservative. Some of his younger colleagues supported the idea of Copernicus that the earth must move around the sun. Their debates got us students eager enough to spend many nights with the best telescopes we could find. We argued about whether Clavius' Ptolemaic system with the earth at the centre fitted the observations better or that of Copernicus. It was more exciting than Dominican philosophy, especially as we began to realise that the great Clavius must be wrong.

'All that astronomy served us well when we came to the east, for each of these countries has its own system of studying stars and fixing the calendar. When I was in Manila, before coming here, I could correspond with some of my brother Jesuits in China. Their observations also fitted better with Copernicus. Here in Java I may be the first astronomer from Europe to observe the heavens below the equator, where again it seems Copernicus wins. But I have not heard from my colleagues for many years. What do they teach in England now?'

Hodges forgot his fear of popery. This was exciting. 'When I learned navigation we were taught that the sun and moon go around the earth, and Copernicus was mentioned only to laugh at him. But there was talk of a book in English that showed him to be right. Our commander on the *Red Dragon* had a copy.'

'You mean Thomas Digges? One of my teachers in Rome got

a copy and asked me to translate some of it for him. He could not believe that anything serious could be written in English.'

'Yes, yes, that's it! When we had trouble with the different stars we saw as we rounded the southern end of Africa, our general told us about Digges' idea that there may be an infinity of stars far away, beyond the sun and moon.'

'Yes, he did propose that idea, but was not able to produce evidence. We who have seen the skies beyond Europe have the best chance to resolve this.'

Seeing that they shared an enthusiasm, Romo invited Hodges to his study where he did, after all, have two chairs where they could be more comfortable. They were surrounded by a mountain of books and palm-leaf manuscripts, a small globe and a telescope.

'I tried to do as the Javanese do, but my stiff English legs do not thank me for it. So I had a Javanese carpenter make these for me, like they make beds and tables, but with a back. It is hard for me to read sitting on the floor, especially with these old eyes. And talking of old eyes, did you bring the wonderful spectacles?'

'No! They are a present for the king.'

'Very well; but please do not give them to him until I have had a chance to explain to him how important they are. Do you know where they were made and how it was done? The Javanese goldsmiths are excellent at copying fine work, but how to make such fine glass is a problem.'

'I believe the best spectacles are made in Amsterdam or Cologne. We English are making fine telescopes, but the glass for spectacles has to be finer.'

'Indeed. Did you know that the greatest writer on optics was an Englishman, Roger Bacon, a Franciscan friar no less? The Greeks thought that the eye contained a sort of fire, which emitted beams that bounced back to the eye as sight of the objects they encountered. Bacon could see that the eye was no such thing, but that light itself was what was conveyed from the object to our eyes. When god said, "Let there be light," he must have intended us to study and understand this most remarkable and essential of his creations. I have managed to repeat some of Bacon's experiments using a glass of water to bend the light, which is what the spectacles do.'

Now Hodges was hooked. The two men spent hours bending over a candle in a box with a small hole, a glass of water in front to see how it refracted the light. When Hodges finally remembered that Sri was expecting him he began to make his excuses.

'Come back with the spectacles, and I will ask my favourite goldsmith to come and see how they work. He also needs magnification to do his fine work, so he will be excited to see them. We must work together to find some material that can bend the light in the same way as those spectacles.'

'And what of my mission?'

'Ah yes, your mission. I think you should meet the Panembahan's son, Pangeran Angalagga. He is only a lad, not yet twenty, but the only one around the king who is interested in the new knowledge. He also played a part in your release from the Muslims. Let us next meet on a day he is visiting me to talk of geography and astronomy. He may be interested enough to treat the spectacles with the care they deserve, and perhaps to use his royal goldsmith to make more. And he can arrange a proper time for you to present your case to Panembahan Krapyak, his father.'

'Thank you, Romo. At last I might get somewhere.'

'Meanwhile, may I borrow your Sri again to help me with some translation? She is a very clever young lady. Perhaps you could both come tomorrow, preferably with the spectacles. You might learn some Javanese yourself. I am trying to translate the Gospel of Mark into that difficult language. I must not let optics and astronomy divert me from this sacred duty. If you have an English translation, please bring it along. I have only the Latin of St Jerome to work from, but the new translators have used the Greek of the original gospels, so some passages may be better.'

'That will be very interesting – if you stick to god's truth and not your popish distortions. Yes, I always have with me the English gospels my mother gave me. I thought everything was lost when I was captured, but it should be still there in the baggage that Sri rescued. But why Mark? Why not start at the beginning, with Matthew?'

'Mark tells a simpler story in fewer words. To be honest I will be grateful if I can finish even one gospel, and Mark is the shortest. In every passage I have to think of new words in Javanese to express our ideas – sin, prayer, Pharisee, synagogue, disciple, Rabbi, even the right word for god. There are Muslim terms for some of these, and for Jesus and the Jewish prophets, but should I use their terms? But enough of this – until tomorrow.'

Hodges' head was spinning. God's truth was simply truth, in plain English. This papist Jesuit had too many languages and strange ideas for one day. He longed for Sri's good sense and reassuring touch.

# Anggalaga

Sri was relieved to hear that Hodges wanted to see Romo again, but puzzled by his distaste. "Why are you not overjoyed to find another Englishman here, able to speak your own language?'

'He is a papist, Sri. They opposed our rightful queen and supported our Spanish enemies. I still don't know whose side he is on.'

'You feringgi with your quarrels! You may be a fighter, Thomas, but I think he is not. He seems more like our holy men, except that he reads many books like some of the Muslim ulama.'

They returned together to help with Romo's translation. Sri was allowed to bury herself in the part of Mark's gospel Romo considered finished, while Hodges and Romo talked. She came back with endless questions. Some of Romo's words were simply wrong; others she had never heard of. Often they had to debate what the text was really trying to say, going back and forth between Javanese, Malay, Portuguese and for Romo, Latin, Greek and English. Hodges was content to hunt among Romo's eclectic collection for books on astronomy. He wished he had worked harder on his Latin. Sri's excitement about her new discoveries kept interrupting him.

'You never told me these lovely stories – Salome dancing for John's head, Jesus walking on the water and the farmer sowing seed in different places. These are like the *wayang* stories, pointing to something deeper. I think Romo should use the same word for these ... What do you call them?'

'Parables?' Hodges offered the English word.

'Yes. Use the same word for them as we do for a wayang story – *lakon*. People will like that. Romo is not convinced. What do you think?'

Sri was excited by how many women appeared in the stories. 'This god of yours seems not so male after all.'

As they came to chapter ten and debated how to translate adultery, Sri could see the dark depression coming over Hodges. She protested to Romo in Portuguese to make sure her man could understand.

'Joining to become one flesh, one body, is a beautiful idea. When Jesus says "Whoever divorces his wife and marries another commits adultery against her," he is obviously condemning those who disrupt marriages by yielding to their lust. No one expects traders and wanderers who depart for years, perhaps forever, to remain celibate.'

Hodges looked miserably into his English gospel. 'It means what it says, Sri.'

Romo looked from one to the other, and carefully said nothing.

Sri stroked Hodges' arm and changed tack. 'You should not use the Muslim word *zina* for adultery, Romo. We Javanese women do not like that term since some Muslim men use it only to punish us. Jesus seems to say the same to women as to men – you are one flesh, and must stay together. But,' turning to Hodges, 'you cannot be one flesh if you are separated by vast oceans.'

Hodges turned his anguish against Romo. If he was damned for denying his faith to the Muslims, and damned again for adultery, he had better try to achieve something in this world.

'Are you trying to convert the king to popery? I don't like your chance of succeeding, but if you did he would have to make a friend of the Portuguese. The Muslims, the Dutch and the English would all be against him, and probably his own people as well. What kind of Englishman would you be, to turn the Javanese against your own country?'

Romo made a visible effort to control his anger, as if calling back the words that risked escaping from his mouth. He closed his eyes and settled into a meditative pose. His voice was lower when he broke the silence. 'How shall we "sing the Lord's song in a strange land"? Not by joining in the conflicts of the Javanese, or by asking them to join in ours. We have wounded god enough already by slaughtering each other in his name. The Portuguese confused god's purpose with their own greed and ambition, and drove many into the arms of Islam to counter them. No, Thomas, enough. Jesus told Peter to put his sword away, "for all who draw the sword will die by the sword". If force were the answer, god himself could have forced people into one fold. But he left us free to find our own way to him. We must use our minds, our hearts, and what the Javanese call our *batin*.'

'What is that – more devilry?'

'Tell him, Sri.' Romo said gently.

Sri knitted her brows and looked long at Hodges before explaining. 'It is our inner being which we must care for by practising stillness, peace and harmony within.' She pointed to her stomach.

'I am not a good Javanese because I am too busy and curious, but I hope when I am older I will have the kind of peace that my mother has deep inside. In fact, she does not use the word *batin*. That word was found in Islam by some clever scholars to explain to foreign Muslims what we Javanese do. We have other words for it.'

Hodges felt himself falling into Sri's earnest gaze, but pulled himself together to confront Romo again.

'So what are you doing here, if not trying to convert the Javanese?'

Romo paused again before answering.

'It is true I once thought that my mission was to "convert the Javanese", or whichever people god placed me among. Now I know that the Javanese have as much to give us as we them. They must remain Javanese; but I believe they can be better Javanese if they learn from Jesus. They have already learned some good things from the Muslims, that there is only one god so all men are brothers – and sisters,' glancing at Sri. 'At their best, like Sri here, they are better for that. But in time the Muslims created boundaries and made enemies of those outside. My task is to find a place for Jesus in Java, and to make known his gospel of love in a way they can understand. The hardest and most important task is to spare this island becoming another battleground for Muslims, Buddhists, Catholics and Calvinists. War only creates hatred and resentment, and closes doors to learning new ideas. I hope I can show Java that Jesus is a gateway more sublime than Portuguese or Dutch, popes or preachers.'

'I like your idea,' said Sri quickly, before Hodges could protest. 'Do the great men of Mataram show any interest?'

'Not the Panembahan, I'm afraid, but I have more hope for his son. Sometimes it is the great *women* who are interested. Javanese marriages seem more harmonious than ours in Europe, but the greatest men are the exception. They take wives and concubines just to add to their status, and many of the noble women wish it were otherwise. When they look at foreign examples, they like the Christian idea better than the Muslim and Chinese ones.'

'This prince,' Hodges broke in. 'Have you found a time when I can make my case to him?'

'Anggalaga; yes indeed. I think you will find him interested in you. He especially likes to try to understand the shape of the world. He could not get over how the Spanish had sailed right around the globe and come back to Spain from the opposite direction. Do you have a globe, or a good new map?'

Hodges shook his head.

'Never mind. Since you navigated here from England you must have the maps in your head. Try to draw one of your own. If you have no paper I can give you one of these Chinese sheets. Show the new discoveries in America and Africa, and how England, Holland, Spain and Portugal sit in Europe. And of course make Java look big, not to disappoint him.'

They returned on the appointed day to find Pangeran Anggalaga already there, apparently busy discussing Romo's foreign books on mathematics and optics. Sri was more nervous than Hodges, as she had to prepare the right words for royalty. In Banten it was mostly noble women like the queen mother she had had to deal with, and men had finer gradations of status and were more prickly about them. There, Islam had simplified the complex levels of Javanese speech, and introduced new neutral words, but here there were so few foreigners that the old system seemed intact. It was crucial to address the Crown Prince in terms high enough to please him, but not so high that Mataram would appear to outrank the court of Banten, which she was claiming to represent.

She began with a rehearsed speech explaining her Banten role and apologising that it was a business-like place with few refinements of speech. Anggalaga rudely looked her up and down as she spoke, and then interrupted.

'I know Banten is a mongrel place. It is not your speech that bothers me, but what you are here for. What we expect from Banten is a proper acknowledgement that there is only one ruler of Java – that is Mataram. We leave you free to trade with whom you wish, and demand only a proper tribute, such as we expect from the other ports like Japara and Demak. Banten was nothing until it was colonised from Demak. Java must be one as we face these foreign infidels, and it is Mataram that is destined to unite it. If Pangeran Ratu of Banten wants good relations with us, he should begin by sending one of his family here, or coming himself, to seek proper installation as ruler of Banten.'

'Forgive me, Kanjeng, I am only a translator, and know nothing of these matters.' Sri was in shock at this assault, and struggled to get the discussion back on track. 'My job is only to express the words of this ambassador, Tuan Hodges, from Inggeris on the other side of the world. He has journeyed very far to meet you and your father, and to convey the respects of his King J-A-M-E-S. '

'Very well, Tuan Hod.' He turned to focus the same intense gaze on Hodges. 'We have heard of this Inggeris from Romo here, but did not expect an ambassador from such a small and faraway place. What brings you so far across the world? Has your king already heard of the greatness of Mataram?'

Sri hardly needed to translate this, nor Hodges to give his reply in Portuguese to her, since they had already rehearsed what he would say. But they went through the forms. Hodges summarised again how he thought he might impress this curious young man.

'We live in a new age. My grandfather never knew there was a China, India, America or Java. I imagine yours never knew there was an Africa, a Europe or an England. Most people thought the earth was flat and stayed in one place while the stars moved above it. Now we discover new things every year. Ships from Europe have gone around this world, proving it is like a ball, rotating and circling around the sun. My ship was sent halfway around the world from England to discover new places and kingdoms. My king wants to exchange greetings and build friendships with these great kingdoms, and to learn what new things they have which we can exchange with the things my country produces.'

Pangeran Anggalaga's interest was aroused, and soon they were poring over Hodges' map, which he bent into a hoop to show how Drake had rounded Cape Horn and sailed across the Pacific. 'He was the first Englishman to report the greatness of Java,' said Hodges. 'But up to now our ships have only visited its ports, especially Banten. Now my king wants to greet your king personally, and asked me to find the great King of Java, wherever he resided. This is the goal of my journey, to deliver my great king's letter to your great king.'

Hodges had drawn his Java in big letters, as Romo had suggested. Following some of the maps General Keeling had brought on the *Red Dragon*, he had made it part of the unknown great southland, *Terra Australis Incognita*, to balance the mass of Europe and Asia in the north. Sumatra was a separate island, he knew, since the *Red Dragon* had sailed down its west and south coasts. People from Bali said that theirs was a separate island too, but smaller, and he had shown it separate from the Southland. No one knew what lay to the south of Java, but he had filled it with mountains and rivers as if part of an enormous Javan realm.

Anggalaga looked carefully at this section of the map. 'This is not right. Do you not know that Java is an island? I have been often to the southern coast, only a day's travel from here. It is much rougher than the north coast where traders come. They say the southern ocean is filled with evil spirits, ruled by a powerful queen beneath the waves. Even so, there are brave fishermen who venture out onto these waters, and they say the southern ocean is vast, with no other land to be seen. Give me a pencil. '

He drew a line from the east near Bali to the Sunda Strait between Java and Sumatra, where Hodges had shown the *Dragon* passing, putting Mataram closer to this south coast than the north. Then he drew a conical mountain to the north of Mataram, and wrote something in Javanese script next to it. 'You must show the great mountain Merapi to the north of our capital, and the great ocean to its south. This is why we are mighty. God has placed Mataram between the sacred mountain and the mighty sea. Each can kill with their fire and their flood, unless tamed by the dynasty divinely ordained to rule Java. Only we have this sacred power.'

Sri obviously had trouble translating some of these Javanese words. Romo had listened carefully to what was said. He intruded apologetically in Javanese to offer to amplify, and then said in English to Hodges: 'Sri has been very diplomatic in translating *sang hyang* as god. I try to persuade the prince that it is the one true god that has created the marvel of Java, but he is not quite there yet. These sang hyang include the many spirits of Java, but also the gods of the Indians and perhaps the Allah of Islam, his official religion.'

Anggalaga looked suspiciously at Romo as he made this interjection, prompting Romo to offer further apologetic and deferential words of Javanese. The prince was clearly having none of this, and embarked on a lecture that Sri summarised softly to Hodges. 'He is giving his views on religion. Islam has introduced some necessary discipline, forbidding some of the bad habits of our Javanese subjects. But these foreign Muslims, and Christians like you, Romo, will never convince us Javanese that god favours some miserable place above the winds as the centre of holiness. They say that Mecca is only a desert, where nothing grows. Look around you. This is the land the gods favour, whatever we call them.'

Hodges did not like the direction this conversation was taking and tried to get his attention back to the English embassy. 'Your Highness, the English have no wish to interfere with your religion. You have your own beliefs, proper to your country, and we have ours, proper to England. But that should not stand in the way of your king and mine acting in friendship, and allowing their subjects to trade with one another.'

Anggalaga eventually agreed to advise the king to receive the 'royal' letter from England at his next senenan tournament, where the exotic visitors would add to the spectacle. He did not sound optimistic about the likely interest of the king in this rather unroyal-looking embassy. Hodges should make sure he had an interesting gift for the king, preferably something of military use.

While all this was being discussed, Hodges was painfully aware that the prince was showing much more interest in Sri than in himself. Before taking his leave, Anggalaga asked her what seemed an aggressive set of questions that obviously made her uncomfortable. Romo had to restrain Hodges from going to her aid.

'What is he pestering her about? I don't like his manner.'

'I am afraid the prince seems unconvinced by the story of her being a translator from the Banten court. But you can only make this worse by showing too much concern for her. You must leave it to Sri to make her case.'

When he had gone Hodges anxiously quizzed Sri about the conversation. There were tears in her eyes, and she needed a hug before she could begin to explain.

'He was horrible. He does not think a Javanese lady should be travelling alone with this foreigner. He has some things he wants to discuss with Banten, but expected someone with rank and proper credentials to be sent for that. I am afraid he may not let me return to Banten. I think we must tell him the truth about us before things get worse.'

'Yes, my sweet, we must. We must be very careful not to let

him separate us. But before we tell the truth about our marriage, let us try to impress the king at this tournament. If he agrees to send a letter to King James in reply to mine, then we will have a safe passage out of here, and I will be rewarded by the English.'

'And then you would go back and leave Java!' she shot at him.

'I ... I didn't mean that. I don't know. I could persuade the next ship to leave me as an English agent in Japara, for relations with Mataram. And we could live together in peace.' The new idea had popped out in self-defence, but he quickly warmed to it.

Romo intervened gently. 'This court is not much accustomed to diplomatic conventions. Some visitors fare badly; some they like but only when they see their utility. They truly think Java is the centre of the world, and that they have a right to use foreigners as it suits them. But I think Thomas is right. You should go to the senenan and make as public a spectacle as you can. That will make it harder for Anggalaga or his father to lock you away. They may like you, or find your military skills useful. That has its dangers but, like me, you may be able to exchange your usefulness for a certain amount of freedom.'

'So, what will happen at this tournament? How should we present ourselves?'

Sri intervened before Romo had organised his thoughts. 'We have these senenan in Banten too. Many people love them because of the spectacular costumes and the excitement of battle. When I was young and silly I too thought the men on horses were very handsome and brave. Then when one of the dashing young men was killed I realised how horrible the mock fights really are. More so if they bring in tigers to kill criminals. There must be blood, either of men or of animals, or the crowd is not satisfied. I have not been since.'

Romo was more encouraging. 'These contests were certainly bloody in the old days, as if their gods required blood, even human blood, as a sacrifice for human unworthiness. Here I am an ally of the Muslims, telling the Javanese that god desires only the sacrifice of our selfishness, not of our blood. It is rare these days for the king's young braves to kill each other in jousting. Their spears are blunted. But criminals are still torn apart by animals, and I'm afraid the crowd loves it, much as the Romans did.'

'If I am to be part of this spectacle, how will I get the king's attention?'

Sri had the answer. 'In Banten the foreigners are often invited, and people love it when they put on a show. Dress in your finest, with some handsome retainers. Dress up Buyung's horse too. Try to make a spectacular noise, with fireworks or trumpets.'

Romo was thinking practically. 'They do not have many foreigners here, but they do have a kind of master of ceremonies who organises the order of events and the hundreds of people and animals who have to be mobilised. You will have to go back to the prince or one of his followers to find the right time for an entrance.'

'I'm not going near him,' blurted out Sri. 'You can do that yourself. Now is the chance for Buyung to fulfil his part of the bargain. He can translate when you talk to the organisers. I will only play this "translator from Banten" part one more time, when you talk to the king. It is getting dangerous. I just want to be your wife.'

# Tournament

'Thomas, Thomas, help! Open up!' Hodges now dreamed uneasily when Sri was not by his side. Usually a woman was in trouble and he had to do something. As Sri's voice became clearer, he remembered where he was. This was not a dream.

He rushed to open the door of his small hut and embraced a trembling Sri.

'I'm afraid, Thomas. I cannot keep up this pretence anymore!'

He saw that she had two bundles of her possessions and quickly carried them inside. It was the first time Sri had entered his hut: until now, they had maintained the pretence of a purely professional relationship. Hodges had been able to visit her room in the home of a sympathetic local family only very discreetly.

Now she sobbed out the story in Hodges' reassuring arms. 'Anggalaga's people want me to move to the *kraton*, the palace. They said they would come for me today, because it was not right that a single lady, and a guest of Mataram, should live outside.'

'Never! How would we see each other?'

'Worse than that. The king has his pick of the women in the kraton. I could never get out.'

'The monster! Stay with me. That is all I want. You will be safe with me.'

He took her to his bed and held her until at last the sobbing ceased.

'Shall we leave here? There are other places in Java, where

foreigners are less conspicuous.'

'No, Thomas, you must fulfil your mission, and then we can be man and wife. But I will hide here with you until then. And we must both be careful.'

This plan proved difficult. It was impossible to conceal Sri's presence from the family who prepared Hodges' food. Sooner or later their secret would become known. Meanwhile Hodges leaned more on Buyung and Romo to prepare for his big moment.

Buyung had been busy making deals and alliances. He responded energetically to the challenge of putting on a good show at the senenan. His most valuable patron was Pangeran Purbaya, the brother of the Pangeran Pekik they had met in Japara. The two brothers worked together to supply the needs of the court for imported cloth, Chinese ceramics and exotic luxuries, and had the biggest share in the luggage trains between Japara and Mataram. Buyung had soon made himself indispensable as a contact with his father and the other Chinese traders in Japara, who managed to supply the goods they needed at half the prices Purbaya had been paying.

Purbaya always had his tent erected at the *alun-alun*, the field of ceremony to the north of the kraton, at the time of the senenan. Officially this was so he could play his part in glorifying the king, bringing his best horses, young horsemen and gamelan orchestra to support the spectacle. But business was also done here, and his tent was one of the busiest as the court elite inspected the latest imported finery on display there. Buyung introduced Hodges to his patron, who eventually agreed that Hodges could take his position there until his moment came, while Sri could be hidden amongst Purbaya's women until she accompanied the English envoy and his letter.

After some further bargaining, Buyung even persuaded Purbaya to allow his gamelan orchestra to play when Hodges entered the arena. His grandest gong, one of the largest in Mataram, could mark Hodges' obeisance with a sonorous boom. Buyung would dress in his most outlandish 'English' costume to carry the letter in procession, and organise four of his young friends to dance graciously as they followed behind. Buyung even had his contacts among Pangeran Angalagga's followers, from whom he eventually learned that the English ambassador would make his entrance immediately after the prince himself had played his climactic part in the jousting and made his own victorious obeisance to the king.

Hodges was anxious that there be something more plausibly English to mark his moment, and pestered Romo for a musical instrument that was not a Javanese gong.

'My prized possession is an Italian violin I was able to obtain in Manila. I believe I play it well enough to impress my Javanese friends in the privacy of a room. But I wouldn't dare risk it in the chaos of a senenan. In any case it would not be heard with all those gongs and shouting crowds.'

'I understand. But there must be something like a trumpet, even in this benighted place.'

'There is one, but it belongs to the man who seems to hate me most in Mataram, a Portuguese renegade who trains some of the king's artillerymen. Here he calls himself Abdullah, but until joining the Muslims he was Antonio. He wants nothing to do with Christians. I suppose we remind him of what he has lost.'

'What then? Must I be announced by a Javanese gong?'

'You might ask Buyung for a Chinese cymbal. I don't much like their tinny sound, but they are distinctly different from the Javanese gongs – louder and higher-pitched.'

Sure enough, Buyung had imported a couple of these without yet finding a buyer. They were easy enough to play, and he trained two of the young dancers to use them at the right moments.

It was all bustle around the alun-alun on the big day. Tents of the nobles were being erected on one side, the royal dais on another. Horses were being groomed and fed, and other animals dragged to their place in cages. The events did not begin until the late afternoon, but Sri preferred to leave the hut at dawn and make her preparations safely among Purbaya's ladies. They were busy preparing sweetmeats and trying out their finest cloths to make a show.

Hodges moved to Buyung's place to plan their entrance. Buyung's young friends were going through his most bizarre garments and textiles, under instructions to look as weirdly non-Javanese as possible.

They set off well ahead of the starting time, using the short walk to the alun-alun to practise their moves. Two young lads led the procession, each carrying a Chinese cymbal. With these they beat a kind of rhythm that was lost on Hodges but seemed to help the four dancers at the rear to stay in time. They, two lads and two pretty young women, had practised some slow Javanese dance steps where the key action seemed to be in the hands, dextrously turned this way and that. Hodges had insisted they add something more vigorous in the manner of an English Morris or country dance. They settled for jumping and spinning around every so often when the cymbals clashed louder. The young Javanese giggled much at this barbarism, but gradually began to enjoy it as they managed to tame the 'English' whirl to match their rhythms.

Buyung preceded Hodges in the middle of the procession, leading the horse on which the two versions of the English 'royal' letter were carefully placed in one of Buyung's best Chinese plates, on top of a Turkish cushion. Sri had insisted that the most honoured place in the procession had to be occupied by the letter, not the ambassador, since it symbolised the distant majesty from whom it was supposed to emanate.

Next came Hodges, followed by Buyung carrying the gifts for the Panembahan, carefully rolled in a silk cloth. As they approached the crowds converging on the alun-alun, Hodges tried to shrink inside his bizarre costume, feeling ridiculous with his weird outfit and weirder companions. Yet the bystanders took note, laughed a little, and even cheered. He might at last be doing something for his king and country. He began to strut proudly, doffing and waving his monstrous hat.

The scene in the alun-alun was all confusion. People were assembling around its edges, but aggressive jawara were hitting and threatening any who strayed too far to the centre. Outside the ring of important men and their numerous followers, eager spectators jostled with market women selling strange fruits, drinks, sweetmeats, and what appeared to be floral offerings. Fortunately, the leading youths with the cymbals appeared to know where to find Purbaya's tent. A few bangs on their cymbals would clear a path. Crowds miraculously parted to marvel at the exotic group.

Once they arrived, Hodges found an excuse to call for the translator, in order to question the eminences among whom he was placed. Sri was at her most deferential and demure, eyes downcast as she conveyed Hodges' questions about the tournament and the answers. When the royal dais was pointed out, the place where the king would receive their letter and gifts, she managed to slip in some words of warning without looking at him or changing her respectful tone. 'Don't let them separate me from you there. We must leave the royal presence together at any cost.'

Without any perceptible signal, the assemblages of gongs at each of the great men's tents suddenly began playing in unison. They reached a crescendo as the royal procession appeared and began to cross the square. It was led by some wild-looking warriors, evidently the fiercest of the king's troops, the Bugis. Then came scores of pikemen in ranks, followed by about twenty young women carrying spears and krisses, the female palace guard.

Horsemen followed, among whom was the king, Panembahan Krapyak (though they gave him numerous other impossible titles). He could be identified only by the way the front row of noble spectators fell on their knees as he passed, obliging Hodges to do the same. He took a good look nevertheless at the king, his nemesis or saviour. The smallness of his stature contrasted with the magnificence of his horse. His hair was long and black, not yet shorn in the Muslim fashion, his neck and arms resplendent with gold jewellery. Where his son had seemed curious about everything, Krapyak looked straight ahead, greeting no one, seemingly concerned to appear grave and god-like. After him came his women. Three queens, the principal one riding a horse awkwardly, were followed by a host of pretty young women, their charms displayed as they danced their way forward. Was this their idea of a place for Sri?

As soon as the king was settled on his dais, his women and followers seated on the ground behind him, a group of horsemen galloped onto the field and lowered their lances before him in deference. For a time they rode about displaying their horsemanship, one even standing on horseback as he rode. At another sound of the great gongs they began attacking each other.

Hodges could see no pattern in it, compared with the carefully orchestrated jousting that had been on display when King James was enthroned. Each horseman guided the horse with his legs, tucking the reins into his sarong so he could hold a lance in each hand. With one he attacked while the other defended him from those behind. One rider was unhorsed, amidst great cheering and shouting; then another. For Hodges it was impossible to tell which horseman had triumphed in the melee, but one did raise his lance in triumph and trotted over to the royal dais to make his obeisance and ensure the king had noticed his skill.

Another burst of gongs marked the entry of a larger horse, more handsomely costumed. There was a buzz around the spectators as they recognised Pangeran Anggalaga. He cantered quickly past his father, barely pausing to lower his lance before going on attack. He rode swiftly and purposefully, and carried both lances before him. He must know, thought Hodges, that no one dares attack him from behind. In no time one horseman was unseated, then another. Anggalaga cantered over to the dais, left his horse and lances for the servants to look after, and made his obeisance to the king.

As the prince mounted the dais amidst applause and greetings, the other horsemen departed the field. The moment for the English embassy had come. The cymbal-bangers were ready and scarcely waited for the others to take their places in the procession before attracting the crowd's attention with their high-pitched noise. They were off.

It was the longest three minutes of Hodges' life as their strange procession crossed the field with thousands of eyes upon them. Were they laughing, cheering, or jeering? Hodges tried not to look, but gravely focussed on the task ahead. The first time the dancers did their 'English' leap there was surely laughter, but gradually the crowd warmed to the strange sight and gave them a cheer.

At the foot of the dais, Buyung prostrated himself in the manner of the Javanese obeisance. Hodges knew the Dutch refused to do this, so he was damned if *he* would. He doffed his hat and bowed low. 'I bring greetings, Your Majesty, from King James of England. He wishes you long life and prosperity.'

He said these words in English, since Sri, kneeling just behind him, had already practised how to render his opening greeting. Her voice in Javanese sounded much more deferential than his, as she joined her hands together in homage.

The king's answer was long and sonorous. Before Sri could translate it for him, they were startled to hear an English voice.

Romo was there on the dais, just behind the king.

'His Illustrious Majesty Panembahan Krapyak thanks King James for his tribute. We are happy to see that our virtue has become known around the world, even as far as your cold country above the winds. And what does King James send to honour us?'

Why had Romo not told them he would be here? And what did he mean by this 'tribute'? Was it a warning to play the Javanese game, or a hint to put the king in his place? He switched to Portuguese to make sure Sri understood the tenor of his reply, even if she chose to ignore it in the translation.

'I have travelled far, Your Majesty, for many months and even years, over dangerous seas and lands infested with bandits. My king would have liked to prepare luxuries appropriate as gifts from one great king to a brother king of equal status. But many things were stolen along the way. I bring you this letter, in English with a Javanese translation, and some token gifts that may show the ingenuity of my countrymen.'

As Sri was rendering this, Buyung moved on his knees to the foot of the dais, holding above his head the cushion with the letters. A courtier carried them to the king in a more practised fluid crouch. The same procedure was followed with the gifts – one telescope, one pair of spectacles, and one pistol.

The king's reply came back in Romo's English as if Hodges' pitch for equality was being wilfully ignored. 'My people will be glad to know that even such distant kings acknowledge the greatness of Mataram. We forgive King James for the modesty of his gifts, for he lives in a barbarous land at the end of the world. It is enough that he understands our greatness.'

Now the gifts were being opened, giving Hodges a chance to remonstrate with Sri. 'Does he not understand that England is as great as Mataram? Greater, in fact.'

'Romo and I are protecting you, Thomas,' she whispered without altering her expressionless demeanour. 'It costs you nothing to play his game, but may save your life.'

Anggalaga was showing his father how the telescope worked, enabling him to see some attractive ladies on the other side of the square. He showed the king the spectacles with a few words, but seeing his lack of interest, passed them to Romo to demonstrate to the old man seated behind the king on the dais. Sri whispered that this was Ki Dipati Mandaraka, the wise old counsellor. Romo must have expected this moment, since he was able to produce a palm leaf of Javanese writing and show this venerable figure how he could read it. The old man's eyes lit up and he hooted with joy.

The king was most interested in the pistol. He fondled it, felt its weight, aimed it across the square and examined the doglock mechanism. He gave some instructions to Romo, who came down to escort Hodges onto the dais, with Sri following a discreet distance behind. 'The king wishes to see more of how the pistol works,' he explained. 'Please sit beside him during the next events, and demonstrate its workings.' And in a lower voice, 'You must humour his haughty language. It is his way to combat the threats he sees everywhere within the kingdom. But be very careful how this ends.'

The king motioned Hodges to sit next to him and explain the mechanism. Growing impatient with Romo's stumbling over Javanese military terms, he shouted for the Javanese translator. Sri advanced, eyes carefully downcast, but trembling with anxiety. She was quicker to understand Hodges' explanation of the doglock, and how the 'dog' held the cock in place to enable the pistol to be loaded safely.

While Sri was struggling to combine the strange foreign terms with the loftiest form of Javanese, Hodges was distracted by the scene being enacted on the field. A ring of spearmen had formed at its centre, into which was hauled a cage containing a tiger – a frightening creature Hodges had so far only heard about. The cage was opened by two men who quickly sprang back to safety, while at the same time a nearly naked man was thrust into the circle of spearmen to face the tiger. He was armed only with a short kris, but fortunately the tiger was more interested in escaping than attacking him. It tried several times to penetrate the ring of spearmen, who responded only by advancing in an ever-tighter circle. As the beast snarled at the advancing spearmen, the man seized his chance to spring onto its back, slashing at its neck with the kris.

The Panembahan could see that Hodges was distracted by this spectacle, while Sri was doing her best not to look at all. He barked a command to a courtier, who advanced without ever raising his body above the king's. He explained the tiger event to Sri, though it was all over before he could begin. The tiger had tossed the man off and turned to slash his stomach while biting at his neck.

'This man was accused of killing a guard and robbing precious cloths from a house at night, and then setting it on fire to cover his tracks. The judge declared him guilty, but he refused to admit his guilt. He is therefore permitted this means of execution. If he were truly not guilty, then he would be protected by god – he said by sang hyang.' Sri had remembered Romo's correction.

As the victim was dragged away, the king began barking commands to his followers, one of whom ran out to the ring of spearmen to convey his instructions. The spearmen pushed the wounded tiger back into its cage and dragged it into the centre of the field.

'Can the pistol fire that far?' the king asked Hodges.

'Not with any accuracy. It should be deadly at about half that distance.'

More commands followed, and the cage was brought closer.

One of the king's servants loaded the pistol on Hodges' instructions and handed it respectfully to the king. He aimed at the tiger, fired, and recoiled at the blast. The tiger was unhurt. Angrily he thrust the pistol to the servant, commanding that Hodges show whether it could kill the tiger.

Hodges knew that much was at stake. Fortunately, by the time he had reloaded the pistol the tiger had lain down, so he had a chance at the head. He took careful aim, fired, and was relieved to see the tiger slump down. The king immediately grabbed the pistol from him, stood up and held it aloft triumphantly to the cheers of the crowd. He sat down seemingly satisfied, and addressed some remarks to Hodges that Romo rendered into English in a low, steady tone that concealed the urgency of his own interpolations.

'This pistol is accepted as a tribute from your country, England. The king implies he was the one who shot the tiger with it, so I believe you must respond accordingly. At all costs do not contradict him. He asks when you will return to England. He needs some time to prepare a letter to King James.'

Sri came closer to Hodges, resisting an urge to calm his anger with a touch. 'Please be careful, Thomas.'

'Please tell him I will await his convenience. Then let me turn the conversation to what his letter will say. We live in a new age of many new inventions, of which these three gifts are examples. My countrymen are leaders of these new discoveries. We travel the whole world with our ships. We offer to exchange these new machines we make with the products of Java, the rice and spices. We hope the two great kings of Mataram and England will agree in their letters to allow their subjects to trade with one another. We ask only this.'

The king did not look pleased at hearing this translated. He looked sternly at Sri and then addressed what sounded like a series of commands to Romo.

'The Panembahan asked me to explain this in your own language. We require no trade from your country. Java has everything that is needed for a good society. It is enough that your king sends some gifts to me as tribute when he can. Pistols and other firearms would be welcome. In return we will treat his envoys well, and send tokens of our majesty to him. You, as the carrier of this tribute, are welcome to stay at my court for long enough to train my soldiers to shoot better. I will see that you are well treated in all things.'

Hodges turned to Sri in dismay. 'What are we to do? Does he mean me to be his servant, and help fight his wars? You must explain that my king does not allow me to serve another king, but only to carry his greetings to his esteemed brother king.'

'You must appear to cooperate, Thomas, until we find a way to depart safely. We must stick together. I am more worried about what he intends for me.'

Their conversation was sharply interrupted by the king, who issued commands to Sri. She approached quivering and answered his words deferentially, but with what sounded like increasing determination. Hodges looked around anxiously, and gestured to Romo to explain what was going on.

Romo directed Hodges' attention to the activity on the alun-alun rather than to Sri's predicament. 'Please do not watch the king, or his courtiers will grow suspicious. I will appear to be explaining this contest, but in truth we will need to be careful to get Sri safely out of here.'

Another tiger in a cage had been brought onto the field and released in the centre of the circle of spearmen. This time its antagonist was a large black buffalo, of the type seen everywhere pulling ploughs in the rice fields. The tiger was having the worst of it. Its claws made little impression on the thick hide of the stolid beast, which relentlessly tossed and crushed the tiger on its horns.

'Note how the crowds cheer the buffalo. They see it as a symbol of orderly Javanese society, while the tiger represents the wild enemies that threaten it. I am afraid they see us Europeans as fierce and uncivilised like the tiger, and it pleases them that the buffalo usually prevails.' Without changing his tone or the direction of his gaze, Romo continued, 'The king is telling Sri that she must come under his protection as a single woman far from home. She is explaining that she is married, but this does not seem enough for the king.'

Just then Sri leapt to Hodges' side and grasped his arm. 'I have told him that we were married along the road here, and that you will protect me,' she whispered.

Hodges addressed the king through Romo. 'Please tell His Majesty that Sri is indeed a skilled translator from Banten, but that we became attached to each other and married on the way here. I will protect her, and we must not be separated.'

The king seemed disturbed at this development, and consulted his son Anggalaga before giving his judgement. It was the prince who conveyed it to the anxious couple.

'You have deceived my father and myself, for which you deserve severe punishment. I have told my father that it is not proper to execute an envoy from a distant king who has come to offer tribute, even if he misbehaves. Besides, I believe you can be useful to our army. He graciously allows me to take responsibility for your good behaviour henceforth. A house will be prepared for you in the kraton, close to my own, where you may live together. You must thank His Majesty for his indulgence.'

Sri was weeping as she translated this, but did not hesitate to make her humble obeisance, and encouraged Hodges to do the same. She expressed some apology and hushed him when he sought to protest.

The tournament had ended. The royal procession reassembled to exit the alun-alun amidst another great clamour of gongs. Hodges and Sri were given a position a few rows behind the royal party, but it appeared they were being guarded by one of the royal pikemen. They were permitted to return to Hodges' hut together, but the guard took his place outside.

Sri required a lot of loving that night, after she explained all that had transpired. 'What the king said to me was not polite, and his son was little better. They spoke to me as though I were one of their subjects, to be disposed of as they pleased. It is not permitted to marry a foreigner, they said. I fear now for us both. They will probably keep you alive as long as you are useful to them, but they will find some way to send you on a military expedition, and then I will be just one of the palace women. The king spoke as though I should be honoured to be one of his favourites. He seems accustomed to having his way with women, married or not.'

# The Kraton, 1610

'It's happening, Sri, as you predicted.' Hodges trembled as he reported on his most difficult day yet.

'They demand that I go with the army to Pajang. They say it is not enough to train their riflemen here at home; they become disorganised in battle and need stronger discipline. Of course I refused. I insisted that my king would not allow me to fight for another, and that I would not go. Anggalaga came in a rage to ask why they should protect and feed us if we will not help the king. "If the English are our friends," he said, "they must support us in the field against the rebels and troublemakers of Pajang." Abdullah's relish in translating this to me was obvious. He may have added even more spite than the prince intended.'

Their first months within the kraton had been tense. Hodges was called each morning to help the artillerymen service their motley collection of muskets and arquebuses, and to train them in firing. At first Abdullah translated for him, but the Portuguese renegade took an instant dislike to Hodges and his knowledge of firearms. According to Romo, Abdullah had been a cook when he was Antonio, and only pretended skill with guns to have a secure place in Mataram. They quarrelled often, and it worked better for Pangeran Sanjata to translate for Hodges through their shared basic Malay. Hodges quickly learned the essential Javanese commands, while the technical artillery terms were Portuguese or Dutch anyway.

Sri became exceptionally wifely within the kraton, in a way she had never been before. She wanted everybody to know that her role there was simply as the wife of Tuan Hod, to prepare his meals and wash his clothes. This did not save her from other duties. Frequently she had to dress in the correct court attire to take part in some royal ritual or attend on the queen. However downcast her eyes, she could feel the king's eyes on her at every court appearance.

'We must act, Thomas, before it is too late. Yesterday a beautiful young woman at court was strangled to death for no other reason than that one of the young nobles was so infatuated with her that he asked the king's permission to marry her. He was exiled for his presumption in desiring something the king considered his. But she, being of ordinary birth like me, could just be disposed of. This king can do anything within his kraton.'

She crept inside his reassuring embrace before continuing. 'I have something else to worry about, Thomas, besides the king and Anggalaga. I believe I am going to have your baby.'

Hodges held her tighter as he absorbed this. Could they cope with this complication? Would this be a Javanese baby, or an English one? Would it bring them closer or force them apart? He had avoided thinking about the future, and having to choose between Sri and England.

'Will the baby be as beautiful as you, Sri?'

'Of course, but as strong as you.' She snuggled closer. 'When I first suspected it, I thought we could not have a baby with everything so insecure. When I dreamed of having a baby it was in our own home with you by my side, and my mother to ensure all the right preparations. But even if you survive the Panembahan, how long will you be in Java? I don't want to have a baby with no father. There are *dukun bayi* – what do you call them, midwives? – who know how to stop a pregnancy, even here in Mataram.'

'We must get away from here, Sri, to somewhere safe, where we can look after the baby together.' This came out of Hodges' mouth before he had any idea what it might mean. He'd always prized his common sense and planning, but from somewhere deeper came the conviction that he wanted this baby with Sri.

It was she who had a plan. 'If you really want to stay and have this baby with me, Thomas, it might help us to escape from here. I don't think the king will want to share his bed with a woman carrying another man's child. And a pregnant woman has certain needs, you know.'

Hodges was out of his depth here. He remembered only his wife's mood swings when she had been pregnant.

'What do you mean? Special foods?'

'Yes, many things, but especially cleansing the soul. Bringing a new life into the world is the most amazing thing humans can do, but it is very dangerous unless the sang hyang wish it to succeed. There must be rituals, and meditation, and pilgrimage to holy places where the sang hyang congregate. We must find someone the king trusts, to explain that I need to go to spend time meditating and purifying myself at a holy place outside the palace, so that the birth will be successful.'

'And for the father too?'

'That will not be so easy. Perhaps I could go a little crazy, and find a dukun, a healer, who will say that the problem is that the father needs healing too. But if we make too much trouble they might just get rid of us. Let's try one step at a time. You must tell Anggalaga that I am pregnant, and you are worried about my health. I will try to find out who has spiritual influence with the king.'

'Perhaps Romo will know such people. '

The opportunity to talk to Romo came sooner than expected. Hodges practised with Sri how to say the vital words to Anggalaga about the pregnancy. He was surprised at the prince's mild response. Evidently he thought Hodges' obvious enthusiasm for the child would make him likelier to stay and 'become Javanese'. But Anggalaga needed to summon Abdullah/Antonio to explain his further request.

'Romo pesters me to allow him to build a church for his Christians. The Muslim teachers oppose it. There are too many religions here, and they cannot all be right. I have decided to let them all speak, and debate with one another, and then my father and I will decide whom we should allow in the kingdom. When I told Romo this, he advised me to let you also make your case. He tells me there are now two kinds of Jesus-followers. He represents one, the Romawi, and you the new way that the Dutch also follow. He says if I want to understand why the Dutch and Portuguese are always fighting, I must hear both sides of this argument. Do you agree?'

Hodges was taken aback. He had never been much interested in the arguments of the theologians about who was saved and how the bread became the body of Christ. It seemed a lot of hocus-pocus. He was a practical man. He tried to live by the commandments, even if he had broken two of them recently. But he knew what he didn't like, and that was a pompous Italian pope thinking he could tell people in England what to believe and what monarch to follow. He was damned if he would let the Javanese think that that was Christianity.

'I am a plain man, sir, but I will do my best. You must allow Sri to translate for me. I do not trust either Romo or this Abdullah here. Neither of them understand the true reformed faith of Jesus Christ.'

He glared at Abdullah, who translated this with obvious disdain. But the essential message seemed to get through, and it was agreed that a date would be fixed for this event, and Hodges would not be sent to the war front before it.

Hodges had plenty of time to consider what he might say, and to help Sri to rehearse how she would say it convincingly in Javanese. But what was the question? He hoped Romo would speak before him, so that he could limit himself to correcting what he said. In truth he found it hard to imagine how to make the English Church he knew, whether of the puritans or the bishops, seem attractive to Javanese like Sri. What they needed was a dose of common sense, and release from all the spirits they saw everywhere.

On the day there appeared to be five men invited to explain their beliefs in the royal audience-hall, as well as a large audience. The king and Anggalaga sat on a raised dais. The pundits formed a square, with Romo and Hodges invited to sit at its base, and to their right an obviously Muslim figure in a fez. Opposite him, on their left, was a wilder-looking robed man with long hair and wispy beard. In front was a man in a flowing robe, also with long hair but carefully groomed, seemingly on good terms with the princes before whom he sat.

Hodges managed to convey his problems to Romo while the others were making their preparations. Was there a guru influential enough with the king to convince him that Sri should be allowed to leave the kraton?

'Kiai Wirajaya there is your best chance,' said Romo, inclining his head towards the man directly in front. 'He is knowledgeable about the stars and the calendar, as well as more arcane spiritual forces. He advises the king about favourable dates and times for action, and for court rituals. If he likes you after this debate, he may be able to help.'

The kiai seemed to be more than just a contestant in the debate. He began the proceedings after appropriate salutations to the king and prince. Sri whispered a summary to Hodges.

'He is explaining why this meeting is being held. The king desires harmony in the land and will not allow fighting over religion as has happened elsewhere. He perceives you have different interpretations of what god – sang hyang – requires of men,' Sri interpreted.

'Can all your beliefs be trusted to live together peacefully, or must the king select one and banish those who disagree? Or perhaps we can agree on a Javanese way that combines the best of what you each offer? Since the king already accepts Islam, we will ask Kiai Ustad Ahmad to begin.'

The Muslim leader began with his own elaborate tribute

to the king, and praise for the divine wisdom that led him and his father to recognise the universal truth of Islam. 'There is no need for other religions. They are relics of an older time, before god revealed his full intentions for man in the Quran. Whatever wisdom Buddha and Jesus brought was superseded by the greater truth of Islam. Now that the kingdom has accepted Islam, it is subject to the law of god. This law generously allows older places of different worship to continue for a time, for it may take several generations for all to accept the truth of the Quran. But the divine law does not allow new places of false worship, such as the feringgi or the Chinese may wish to establish here. To allow them would only confuse and divide your subjects. As Your Majesty and your successors set the noble example you have done, all must eventually come to this sacred truth.'

Next it was the turn of the long-haired ascetic to the left, whom Sri described as a *tapak,* famed for meditating in holy sites for long periods, and for his profound but often obscure utterances. She strained to understand what he was saying.

'He seems to mean that the last speaker showed ignorance of the wisdom of Java. The king's ancestors understood that there are many ways to represent the ultimate reality, including the way of Buddha, the way of Shiva, and his own higher way of the *resi*, ascetics. Even these new ideas of the Muslims and the Christians have some of the truth, but when they say they have the whole truth they must be mistaken, for they know nothing of the wisdom of Java. Ever since Aji Saka came here, long before these other new teachers of foreign ways, the gods (sang hyang again) have resided among us in Java. We know their profound teachings, including the wisdom of Arjuna taught in the wayang. If you depart from the beliefs of your ancestors to follow some foreign idea, the very soil of Java will show the gods' anger, volcanic eruptions and floods will swallow the earth, and your glorious dynasty will not prosper.'

Now it was Romo's turn. Sri had no trouble with his bookish Javanese vocabulary, and the slow, deliberate way he spoke.

'Like the first speaker, I worship one god alone, creator and sustainer of all that is. We may call him as we wish – Allah, or Dewata, or Gusti. But like the second, I have come to see that we cannot confine him in a single tradition, dogma, language or form of words. We Europeans have wounded him by fighting too much over how to define him and the way to him. God, who is beyond all definition, has punished us for the sin of killing one another in his name. We have learned from that sad experience, as Your Majesty has learned from the fighting between Muslims and Javanese. The path to god is not fighting, but rather forgiveness and humility. Now our great thinkers see that we need to learn from one another and not forbid any way that may lead to him. The first leader of our church after Jesus already understood that, "God has no favourites, but in every nation everyone who fears him and does what is right is acceptable to him".

'My Muslim friend is mistaken in thinking that you can or should exclude other paths once you accept Islam. Our world has become one. The paths to god practised in different places must now learn from each other, as I have learned in Java. They should not exclude each other and build walls between people. That can only lead to more misunderstanding and wars. The Europeans know little of Mohammad or Buddha; the Arabs know little except their Islam. If you allow me to build a church here and teach the way of Jesus, Java will know all the great ways to god, and can set an example to the world of learning from each other in peace. Jesus teaches the path of love, forgiveness and humility. Since god loves us enough to forgive our terrible sins, he shows us how to forgive one another.'

It was now Hodges' turn. He spoke quickly in Portuguese, knowing that Sri already had the Javanese words prepared.

'Romo and I share the teaching of Jesus, but not the way to govern that teaching. Despite his sweet words, the church Romo serves acts as though there is only one truth, which it seeks to enforce. England and Holland have rejected that tyranny, and as a result they have gained a new freedom to explore many new ideas. We have come to see that reason and careful observation are also paths to understand the glory of god through his creation. Every day we gain new knowledge of the stars, the earth, the human body, as well as mathematics, printing and logic. Your Majesty should allow the Christians to come to your kingdom and teach their own faith, because they will also teach many new things about the world. But please be careful not to allow one path to exclude the others, as Romo's church has done in many countries in Europe.'

Kiai Wirajaya now took charge of the discussion, allowing each speaker to rebut the criticisms of the others, while himself probing what the teachings were about. Hodges was surprised how far Romo went in admitting the mistakes of the Roman church, trying to show that wisdom came in learning from mistakes.

The sharpest exchanges were between the Muslim Ustad and the long-haired ascetic over the gods displayed in the *wayang* and the old temples of Java. The Ustad demanded that these be banished as the work of the devil, and Hodges found himself supporting this position. They belonged to a superstitious past. The tapak insisted that they were the essence of Javanese wisdom, and Romo made the same case more clearly than the ascetic himself.

'This wisdom has accumulated in Java for centuries, and is only found here. God's purpose could not be that you destroy this precious storehouse. You must treasure it, but complement and fulfil it with wisdom from elsewhere.'

There was a growl from the Panembahan. Wirajaya was quickly at his side, and conveyed his demands to the group.

'His Majesty wishes to know the place of the king in the paths that each of you uphold.'

Hodges was taken aback by being asked to go first, reversing the initial order. He hoped Sri could make his stumbling attempts to answer sound more coherent in Javanese.

'We pray for our king every time we assemble in church on Sundays. In other countries probably they should do the same. The king in England is the head of both the state and the church, placed there "by the grace of god".' He stopped there, not knowing how to apply the idea safely to Java.

Now the tables were turned. While the translations were taking place, Romo had time to consider how to dissent from Hodges' position.

'The Christian tradition, from which England has diverged,

is that god has ordained two kinds of authority, temporal and spiritual. Kings are ordained by god to defend and govern their realms, but the spiritual is a different domain, in which each individual must find his own way to god, aided by wise teachers. Because god is only one throughout the universe, Christians have sought to bring god's wisdom and revelation together, from many countries, into a universal church. But it is not yet truly universal, because we are only now learning the wisdom of Java, China, and elsewhere in Asia. The church has no power to judge or punish. Christians and their leaders may only advise the divinely ordained king, serve him and pray for him constantly.'

The tapak took a very different tack. Sri had trouble following his arcane language, and Hodges kept asking her if he could really be saying what it seemed.

'Like the great kings of Java before you, Airlangga, Jayabaya and Hayam Wuruk, you are divine. You are the lord of the great mountain, the consort of the queen of the southern sea. You are Arjuna, you are Shiva, and you may become also Buddha as you mature in your journey of meditation and asceticism. You hold the kingdom in your hands.'

Ustad Ahmad grew visibly uncomfortable as he also struggled to understand what the ascetic was saying. He responded slowly and soberly.

'Only Allah is god; we humans, even kings and the prophet himself, are all men. The king is "the shadow of god on earth". Your Majesty's power comes directly from god. Only you possess the *wahyu*, the divine inspiration that god bestows on Muslim rulers. Only Islam can unite your realm, because only Allah is god and he asks all to submit to him – that is Islam.'

The king had had enough. He walked out without further comment, followed by the prince. Kiai Wirajaya remained, thanked the participants for their words, and invited them to share in a meal in the kraton. Hodges was again placed next to Romo, but without Sri, who had been firmly escorted to the ladies' section.

Hodges immediately went on the attack. 'Why did you not tell them the truth: about your pope who tried to dethrone the rightful queen of England, about your Inquisition that burns anybody who disagrees. Your pope and his cardinals and Jesuits are the greatest enemy of your pretty picture of learning from each other. You know perfectly well that when the papists are strong, as in Spain, they torture and kill every different opinion – Jewish, Muslim, or Protestant.'

'Calm down, Thomas. Quarrelling will hurt us both. Let these people see what Our Lord taught us – "They will know you are my disciples if you have love for one another." I spoke as I did for the same reason you did not mention King Henry's wives or his destruction of the monasteries. We each profess what we *wish* our faith to be, and on that I see we are not so far apart.'

'If you spoke the same words in Rome, you would soon be in an *auto-da-fe* yourself!'

Romo sighed. 'Sooner or later I must face my superiors. Fortunately, it will start with my brother Jesuits, many of whom know what I know – that god's people are more interesting and various than was ever imagined at the Council of Trent. Our faith, our creeds, were developed when the world was small, Thomas, and the fathers of the church sought to unify it by reaching a consensus within the bounds of the Roman Empire. The Muslim conquests sealed us off from the rest of the world, and made war for the holy land seem to be the way of Christ – despite everything he said to the contrary. When challenged from within by the reformers, the church reacted only with tighter discipline to combat the corruption that Luther had denounced. Only now do we know that god has been worshipped for many centuries in countless ways beyond Europe. God has not been deaf to the Asians, Thomas. He has heard them as he heard us, blessed them and enabled them to flourish, even in ways beyond us quarrelling Christians.'

Stunned, Hodges wanted to say that Romo must have been touched by the Javanese sun. But Kiai Wirajaya was making his rounds of the guests as if he represented the king in this matter, and had come to them. He spoke at length with Romo in a manner that sounded surprisingly friendly. Finally Romo turned to Hodges.

'The learned kiai was pleased that we seemed less far apart than he had expected. Perhaps the English are less combative than the Portuguese and Dutch. He believes the king remains uncertain what to do about the Christians. He wants above all unity in his domain, but does not like the way Ustad Ahmad talks about a sole path, with little room for the wisdom of Java. Perhaps Christian teachers can help to maintain the necessary balance in the land, so long as they do not start fighting with the Muslims or with each other. Of the things you said, he thinks the king will like best your English idea, that the king rules both spiritual and temporal domains. Kiai Wirajaya rejects my argument that they are necessarily separate. A king, he says, is only a true king by his spiritual prowess. Without that he cannot rule.'

Hodges had trouble focussing on these matters, as he pondered how to involve the kiai in Sri's scheme. As Wirajaya appeared to be concluding, he pleaded with Romo. 'Please tell him that Sri needs to talk to him about a very important matter, about her pregnancy.'

Wirajaya looked grave as this was explained. He disappeared in the direction of the women's quarters, where Sri must have had a long and complex story for him. He eventually returned looking graver still.

'I will talk to the king,' is all he said, before moving off to see the other guests.

Hodges had to wait through interminable dances, refreshments, more dances and performances. Finally Wirajaya's departure meant that others might leave. He hurried home to hear Sri's account of what had happened.

'I only lied a little bit, Thomas. Fortunately, one of the palace women told me that there is a shrine on the slopes of the mountain two days' walk from here, which is frequented by pregnant ladies who want to be assured a safe birth. It seems to be the grave of a holy queen, Dewi Anggraeni. She gave birth to twelve healthy children, spending every pregnancy in meditation and prayer at a shrine to Sumbadra, the wife of Arjuna. So she was buried at the shrine, and women have never ceased to bring offerings to her grave. I made up a little story that my mother had much trouble with pregnancy. She was very sick; one baby was stillborn and another terribly malformed. Finally she found the wise old healer who had cured my grandmother by explaining that there was what she called a curse on the family.'

'What nonsense,' Hodges interrupted. 'Do you expect the king to believe that?'

'Yes, that is how we explain the body's functions. Perhaps you can try telling Anggalaga the same story in terms of your famous Greek philosophers. There could be something wrong with the balance of humours in our family. Would that do?'

'There is nothing wrong with your body, Sri. You are perfect. Only your imagination gets out of hand sometimes.'

She punched him playfully. 'Anyway, Kiai Wirajaya seemed to believe me. I said this healer had fixed my grandmother's problems, and it worked too for my mother. She just had to go to the famous shrine and devote herself to the goddess in meditation for half the pregnancy, until the *mitoni* ceremony that comes after seven months. Only then, thanks to Dewi Anggraeni, she could produce the marvel that is me – and my brother of course. '

'You are amazing, Sri. If I were the Panembahan I wouldn't believe a word of it.'

'Thank god you are not.'

# Escape

Following the meeting with Kiai Wirajaya, Sri's status appeared to change. She was no longer asked to dance for the king or wait on his queen. There were visits from midwives and various kinds of healers, attempting to authenticate and remedy her problem. Sri acted the part superbly, already showing signs of the imagined ailment. One spirit medium even made contact with her deceased grandmother, with results that were sufficiently unclear to seem to confirm her story, or at least not to contradict it. This gave Hodges the chance he had been hoping for.

'If you can fool the medium so easily, Sri, you must see that this business of contacting the dead is just a hoax. These mediums are making money out of telling people what they want to know.'

'No, Thomas. She *did* talk to my grandmother. She knew things about her that I did not tell her. But why should you doubt it? Do not Christians also believe that people live on after death? And you saw the balian in Banten who knew about your poor little son, when you hadn't even told *me* about him.'

Hodges had tried to suppress that disturbing memory. 'Yes, that was strange. It must have been a lucky guess. A lot of children die. If this woman today really contacted your grandmother, she would have known nothing of a curse and exposed you as a fraud.'

'Now why should she do that? I'm sure my grandmother loves me, even though she only knew me as a small child. She must know the trouble I am in here. I think she likes you too, and has even forgiven you your big nose.' She gave it a tweak, to underline the point.

It was eventually agreed that Sri must go to the shrine of Sumbadra and Dewi Anggraeni, but Hodges was not permitted to accompany her. She left with a guard headed again by Pangeran Sanjata, to ensure she reached there safely. Her only companion during the meditation was a young maid hoping to become pregnant through the intercession of the deities.

Hodges watched her go with something like desperation. All he had as a plan were the vague directions Sanjata provided him as to where the shrine was situated on the mountain, just above the highest village on a particular path. Somehow he had to find a way to get there.

Anggalaga had other ideas. The expedition to bring Pajang to heel having been concluded successfully while Hodges was otherwise engaged, the commercial lifeline to Japara was now secure. Now the prince was assembling a vast army to march against Surabaya, and Hodges was to go with the artillery. Again he protested. His job was to take an answer from the king back to England and inaugurate a period of friendly relations between the two countries.

'Where are your ships?' asked Anggalaga mockingly. 'We see the Dutch and Portuguese in our ports, and plenty of Gujaratis and Chinese, but none of yours. First make yourself useful, and if an English ship ever comes to Japara, we will talk about that letter.'

Buyung, whose business seemed to survive every setback, was the best source of information about the fortunes of the big ships. He had established some regular customers in the kraton for his foreign luxuries, and would brief Hodges there when he could. He met every caravan from Japara, and usually found a letter from his father or another business partner explaining what goods were arriving in the markets of Japara and Banten, and at what prices. He brought the news and gossip, and sometimes even a foreign treat that he knew Hodges would appreciate even if the Javanese didn't.

The Dutch fleets were growing ever stronger, Buyung reported, to the point where all the other foreign traders united to feed Javanese anxiety about them. Still they represented good business, taking large cargoes of rice in return for the cloth they brought from India. The men Keeling had left in Banten were the only pathetic English presence, dependent on Chinese or Dutch charity to stay alive. There were, however, reports of one mighty English ship further afield, sailing under a famous commander who Hodges guessed from Buyung's third-hand iteration could only be Sir Henry Middleton. His heart leapt at that news. Middleton had commanded the *Red Dragon* on its first voyage to the east, and some of Keeling's crew still remembered him as a bold and skilful leader.

'What of the English ship?' he pestered Buyung on his latest visit.

'The Gujaratis from Surat say it is stuck at Mocha. Your Englishmen got into a fight with the Muslims there, and the commander and many of his men were taken captive on shore. There doesn't seem much chance of it reaching Java, Thomas.'

'Then what am I to do? What is Anggalaga up to with this

vast army he is preparing for Surabaya? Their weapons may be pathetically outdated, but in sheer numbers they will overwhelm any opposition.'

'The king, it seems, never cared much about the ports on the north coast, full of troublesome foreigners like us. But his son is growing in influence as the king weakens, and he has different ideas. He sees the superiority of the European ships, and gets reports of how they are gaining influence at any port that will play their game. Surabaya seems the chief of them now. It claims to be the true heir of the old Javanese kingdoms, as well as custodian of the holiest Muslim shrines. It can defy Mataram so boldly because of the wealth it is getting from the spice trade to Maluku. They say its port is now much busier than Japara's, even for exporting Javanese rice. Anggalaga seems determined to crush Surabaya before the Dutch or Portuguese build a fort there that is too strong to take.'

'How will I ever find Sri if I am taken so far east. How far is it?'

Buyung drew a map in the dust of Hodges' small courtyard. 'People here can send rice there if they dare, down the river from Pajang. If warring bands do not block that route, they say it can be done in a week. But coming back upstream is a nightmare. It could take a month.'

'Then I must escape soon, before the army gets too far away. Tell no one my plans, Buyung.'

'You can trust me, Thomas. But won't they already suspect you of that? The prince will have his eye on you, especially if you seem reluctant to go. Perhaps you should find some way to reassure him.'

It made sense. Hodges began throwing himself into the preparations. He advised the prince how to use his modest artillery to best effect, and how to counter that of Surabaya, by now probably bolstered by new Portuguese and Dutch weapons. He joined the drinking sessions he had always turned down when Sri was awaiting him. The leading military nobles hosted such parties on important occasions. They seemed to regard drinking bouts as not just a necessary evil, like the taverns of England, but a means of reinforcing their control over their men.

Hodges attended one such party on some kind of anniversary of Raden Danupaja, the artillery commander. It involved a great deal of drinking, both rice wine and palm wine. The men were especially interested in the dancing girls, *ronggeng*, who sat demurely by the musicians as the food and wine were served. Eventually one rose and danced invitingly before the commander, who joined her inside the circle formed by the men. Another dancer rose to partner the second in command, and so down the line. The girls seemed to have mastered the hierarchy better than Hodges had.

His own turn came as the fifth girl rose and sinuously weaved her way towards him. He had no choice but to try to emulate her slow, graceful movements, clearly with little success. The watching men grew noisier at each step down the hierarchy, but a bedlam of cheers and guffaws erupted at his own clumsy attempts to dance. His partner sought strenuously to remain demure, allowing the merest of smiles when he fell trying to match her descent into an impossible bending of the knees.

Once the commander sat down Hodges saw he could do the same, collapsing gratefully into the circle of spectators. Now it was the turn of the men to rise one by one. Some seemed interested only in showing off their skill to their comrades, while others fell under the spell of one of the dancers. One officer had set an example by stuffing a coin into a dancer's breast-cloth. Some of the men tried to follow suit and were rebuffed. One or two others appeared to be welcomed, and to continue dancing more intimately thereafter.

The rules of this game seemed obscure to Hodges. He was grateful none of the crew of the *Dragon* were here. Grabbing the girls seemed out of bounds; one offender was dragged away in disgrace. He asked those near him what the men expected in return for their money. The Javanese words that came back were beyond his comprehension, but the smirks and shrugs made clear it was not altogether innocent. He made himself stay until the end, after the senior men had left. Those who remained longest appeared far gone in drink and lust. Hodges' escape plan began to form.

The massive army began its messy march eastward. For the first two days they skirted around Mount Merapi, which showed its symmetrical peak through the mist often enough for Hodges to scan the slopes for a hint of where Sri might be doing her meditation. A sea of humanity crossed the rice fields, spilling over the inadequate roadways. Hodges' artillery troops started each day early but finished it late, obliged to stay on the crowded roadway to haul two large gun carriages. Hodges had advised leaving the unwieldy monsters behind, since they were as likely to injure his own men as the enemy. The Javanese thought him crazy, insisting that these guns alone would turn the battle. They performed an elaborate ritual and killed a chicken over each gun before embarking. Yet it still took two buffaloes and twenty men to haul them out of some of the creeks they crossed.

In the outskirts of Pajang, with Merapi still reassuringly visible to the west, the army reassembled. Here they were joined by yet more local troops. The young ruler placed in charge of Pajang after Anggalaga's recent expedition was now on trial to show his loyalty to Mataram. This he did by a miracle of feeding tens of thousands of men, but also staging an elaborate feast for Anggalaga and his principal supporters. The artillery commander, Danupaja, brought Hodges and the Portuguese renegade Abdullah along, together with the captain of the foreign Muslim musketmen.

'This will show them the whole world is on our side,' he joked. 'They need to be reminded there is only one king in Java. Dress in your own strange costumes.'

This was the grandest such occasion Hodges had witnessed. Gamelan players and dancers greeted each guest who came in an endless procession. When Anggalaga and his retinue made their entrance, every gong sounded in an indescribable din. As the meal of countless courses progressed, there were more dancers, jugglers and musicians to entertain. Rice wine was constantly proffered by attractive young women. This time Hodges was careful, pretending to drink with the men but quietly pouring out the wine behind him to remain alert.

As the food was cleared away, the time came for the

honoured guests to dance. First to rise was Anggalaga, followed by his Pajang host. As they gracefully moved around the admiring circle, a great commotion arose behind Hodges. The girls shrieked and the nobles reached for their krisses as a group of men broke through the circle of guests. They seemed to be half-crazed, clad in white, stabbing indiscriminately at anyone in their path. Hodges was quicker than Danupaja to seize his sword and strike down the first to break through near them, as he made a lunge at the artillery commander.

'Cursed *amok* men, but whose?' muttered Danupaja, as he looked at his bloodied arm.

Three of the amok men had got into the circle of dancers. They were obviously heading for Anggalaga, who was protected only by his own kris and the one guard quick enough to spring forward. The first amok was too quick for the guard, striking him in the chest. The prince turned left to sink his kris into this attacker, as another lunged at his right. Instinctively Hodges leapt forward and ran the second attacker through before the kris reached Anggalaga's back. The prince turned quickly and acknowledged Hodges with surprise before they were separated in the surge of guards surrounding him. There were wounded men everywhere. The white-clad attackers appeared to be dead or dying, but the Mataram men who had been slow to protect their prince now showed their loyalty by attacking the Pajang men.

This was Hodges' chance. He fled through the confusion, pausing only to take a pistol from a dead guard and to wipe the blood from his sword at the first well. To the soldiers confronting him in the camp he pointed behind him saying, '*Tolong!* Help!

The prince is attacked.'

He walked through the night, always towards the mountain. By morning he had reached the edge of the rice fields and dense villages. Reaching a creek that appeared to be coming off the mountain, he followed it into the jungle, drank deeply and collapsed as dawn broke.

He woke about noon to the chatter of monkeys. It took some time to realise where he was – alone in a Javanese jungle, a place he had never experienced. The Javanese always spoke of it with fear. As he drank again and washed, it became obvious that he was not as alone as he had thought. The creek-bed was muddied by the comings and goings of animals. He had so far worried how to avoid people, and what plausible reason he might give to anyone he met for a weirdly dressed foreigner to be wandering the countryside. But the jungle was the place of the vicious tigers. He had little idea what the footprints and droppings of a tiger might look like, but his imagination made every mark seem probable.

What to fear – the people or the animals? He could not spend another night in the jungle. On clear mornings on the march he had noticed that the upper slopes of the mountain had neither rice fields nor jungle, but open country. He must push on upstream and get through the jungle by nightfall.

Hodges scrambled up through the streambed. He passed several clearings where the going was easier but the evidence of animal movements more obvious. He felt safer among the rocks, but this meant he had to climb through waterfalls and over huge boulders to make progress. Whenever he tried to walk around an obstacle in the stream, the jungle was terrifyingly impenetrable.

Dusk came with no sign of the jungle opening. He pushed on in the dark, but after falling for the third time, his legs scratched and bruised, his footwear sodden, he could go no further. Fortunately, it was some time since he had seen footprints by the stream. He paused, removed his soggy boots and listened carefully. Nothing.

He must have slept through sheer exhaustion. He could not tell when he awoke or what had woken him. There seemed to be rustling sounds, or was it the wind? Then there they were – two green feline eyes only a pike-length from him. He kept his eyes on them in case the tiger pounced, but felt everywhere for the pistol. There it was. He grasped it, fired. Nothing but a dull, damp thud. There was no way the powder had remained dry. The eyes were still there, but after an eternity of waiting, they moved in the direction of the stream and vanished. Had the tiger gone? He listened intently but heard nothing.

Sleep was now impossible. He scrambled onto a large rock and placed his back firmly against it, hand on sword, until at last the light began to penetrate the trees.

# Merapi

After the anxiety of the kraton, Sri enjoyed her first days of isolation at the shrine. As she meditated, a peace descended. She felt for the first time that this baby would be safe, and she would be a good mother.

But as a week went by, and then a second, there was still no husband. Surely he would find a way to escape, she had thought; he was so brave and resourceful. She could use her meditation to free herself from daily concerns, but worry about her man kept turning it into something more like a prayer: *please may he be safe and free*. She prayed to Allah, to the sang hyang, to Sumbadra and her consort Arjuna, to whom her small shrine was dedicated. Every day she placed flowers before the statue. But perhaps it was Jesus who would best know how to protect this English Christian? Or Mary. She looked very sweet in Romo's pictures, though a little anaemic beside the buxom Sumbadra. Jesus and Mary might not understand Javanese, so it was in Portuguese that she invoked their services to protect her man.

Sri had become accustomed to periodic earthquakes since being in Mataram, but the shaking that interrupted her meditation in the third week was of a different kind, lasting longer and accompanied by a roar. The locals said that the sacred mountain had something to say. They prepared special offerings to place on a stone slab dedicated to Merapi on the small hill above Sumbadra's shrine. On the second day there was a deafening crash and the mountain erupted. Red flames shot skywards, followed by a great column of ash. Within minutes rocks began to land nearby, and everybody rushed into the building with the strongest roof, a little prayer-hall used by visiting pilgrims.

The old lady who had spent a lifetime preparing food for pilgrims to the shrine had seen it all before. 'Next will come the ash,' she said. 'When it begins to fall, you should put a wet cloth over your face and breathe through it. And be sure to fill the water pots right now and cover them, and the well. The ash will poison everything, so we must not breathe it or drink it. I'm sure the mountain is not happy about those goatherds who took their animals nearly to the top, let alone those who tried to plant maize up there.' She waved at the green hillside above them. 'They will be punished for offending him.'

Sure enough, ash began to fall. A great cloud of it came rolling down the mountain towards them, as they saw some figures running down the mountain towards the village. The goats were faster, and passed quickly through the village on their way further down.

'Should we also run? The goats seem to know it is unsafe here.'

'No.' The old lady was the calmest among them. 'Sumbadra will protect us, as she always has. Make sure she knows that we honour her, as she honours her father, the holy mountain.'

Three young goatherders made it to the shrine and took shelter there, coughing and gasping. They feared as much for their goats, their livelihood, as for the older comrades they had outrun. Just as the cloud of ash seemed about to engulf all, it turned eastward, leaving the village intact but for a coating of ash.

Perhaps Hodges will use this disaster to escape, Sri began to hope. But could he survive alone on the mountain? May all the gods protect him.

A few days later, as the villagers began to feel secure enough to clean up, Sri was told there was a strange-looking man enquiring after her. Her heart leapt as she ran out to meet him; but it was only Romo. She failed to conceal her disappointment.

'Where is he? Where is he?'

'If he's not here, then perhaps he's somewhere else on the mountain. Everybody in Mataram is talking about him and Pangeran Anggalaga. He has become famous. Twice on the road here people thought I must be him, and started to make a fuss.'

'Why? What happened?'

Romo told her about the military expedition to Surabaya, and the bloody incident in Pajang. 'Once the prince was safe and the attackers dead, he wanted to know who had put them up to it. Rightly or not, he was convinced it must have been the new king of Pajang, though he of course denied everything. He was brought back to Mataram for execution, and one of the prince's men installed in his place. The march to Surabaya is called off for now.'

'But where is Thomas?'

'Nobody seems to know what happened to him after he killed that amok. He was definitely not among the dead of that bloody night. Some say he disappeared because he was not a man but a *jinn*, or an angel the gods sent to protect the prince. I am sure he took that chance to try to escape and find his way to you. Anggalaga's men interrogated some in the army who said they saw him passing through the camp, probably heading to the mountain. That would make sense as a way to reach here without detection.'

'But now the mountain is enraged! How will he survive this river of ash and the poisoned water?'

'We must hope he found shelter at one of the villages on the mountain. They know what to do. But if so, we need to find him before the prince's men do. Anggalaga now thinks Thomas is a wonder-worker sent by the gods to protect him. He wants him by his side, but as a loyal Javanese, not an Englishman. He takes this eruption of Mount Merapi, coming so soon after his narrow escape from death, to mean that his moment has come. He believes, or at least he wants his people to believe, that the gods are announcing his destiny to rule Java. The bloodbath at the feast has not helped his relation with his father, whom he suspects of protecting the King of Pajang. He has taken charge of an expedition to make the appropriate offerings to the mountain, and to read its omens for a new reign. In the process he means to collect you and bring you back to the palace, to make it surer that Thomas will return.'

'How will we ever get away from this man?'

'I have an idea, Sri, but we must find Thomas first. Let's ask everyone here.'

The youngest of the goatherds who had fled to the village had indeed seen something unusual before the eruption, as he climbed an outcrop to keep an eye on his charges. A figure far below had drawn his attention because he was following an unusual route around the mountain where there was no real track, keeping just above the treeline. Then the mountain erupted and the boy ran.

Sri was distraught. 'How could he survive it? Is there any

place near there where he could have sheltered?'

It turned out there was another village, perilously perched like theirs above another of the streams that began near the summit. The village of Deles, in a fertile valley to their east, had been wiped out in a previous flow of ash and lava many years before. When it came time to rebuild, the surviving villagers had erected their houses just below the ridge above it, despite the torment of dragging water up to their houses every day.

Sri found a lad willing for a small reward to lead them to Deles. She prepared a damp cloth for them to cover their heads as they picked their way through a thick carpet of ash along what had been a narrow goat track between villages. Frequently they lost the path and had to stop and clear away the layer of ash to find its turns. Here and there fires were still flickering where hot ash had ignited dry grass and twigs. Eventually they reached a ridge from which a small village was visible across another ravine.

'That is Deles,' announced the boy. He wanted to be home before dark, so they let him go and plunged on, trying to keep the village in view even when they lost the track. After they struggled across the last remaining creek and headed up the escarpment towards the village, Sri lost patience with the older man's breathless stumbling. She needed to find Thomas.

'Take your time. I'll go ahead,' she shouted as she disappeared up the slope.

Romo sat down gratefully. No doubt it was dangerous to be on the mountain alone, but he was done in. The sun had set before he staggered into the village, covered in ash, bleeding and dishevelled from his many falls.

This village had evidently been closer to the ash cloud and had taken some punishment. Several of the small huts at the highest points were burned, and other roofs had collapsed. People were crowded into the largest three houses that had survived.

'Where is my young lady friend?' Romo asked the first woman he saw.

She looked startled by his appearance but pointed to the largest of the houses. Romo stumbled on. A crowd of children were in one corner of the building, but parted in alarm as his ghostly figure approached. There was Sri, crouched over the body of Hodges, bathing his burned feet and legs.

'He is alive, *deo gratias*.' Sri had not used this expression before, but was willing to give some credit to her Portuguese prayers. 'They say he scrambled into one of the houses with his clothes smoking and burns on his hands and feet, choking on the poisoned air. They could understand nothing he said, and thought he might be some kind of ghost. But fortunately they gave him clean water and covered his burns.'

Hodges raised his head and gave Romo a weak smile. 'Thank you for coming. You look worse than me. There is water here.'

Romo drank gratefully, but refrained from washing since the clean water was so precious. Sri had sensibly brought some *tempeh*, soybean cakes, and was encouraging Hodges to eat these. She offered one to Romo.

'They have so little in the village. We should feed a sick man rice porridge, and wrap the burns in papaya leaves, but here they have no rice and the ash has destroyed the papaya trees. We must get out of here somehow.'

Romo produced some coins and spoke to one of the women nearby. She agreed to make some sago into a porridge that would keep them alive for a while.

'No Sri,' he said. 'That path out of here is not fit for a wounded man, an old man and a pregnant woman. You can be sure Anggalaga's men will find us soon enough. We cannot run from them now. What you need is a plan to keep your distance from the kraton.'

'You said you had an idea, Romo.'

He explained to Hodges how Anggalaga had reacted to the assassination attempt and the volcano. 'No doubt you could live well in the kraton now, well but dangerously. Anggalaga now wants you near him, but for that he needs your loyalty. He will want you to abandon your Englishness and "become Javanese" in a very public way. That would include Islam, but he will ask more of you than he did of Antonio/Abdullah, because he wants you closer than that. There is talk that he would marry you to his sister.'

Sri gasped. 'She is ugly … and stupid and vain!'

Hodges groaned. 'No, Romo. You must tell him Englishness is not so easy to give up.'

'It is not. Anggalaga is smart enough to know that he cannot force anybody, let alone a stubborn Englishman like you, to believe what he does not believe. He also knows that Islam is not the only way, or the whole way. He thinks of it more as a weapon to unify his subjects and discredit his enemies. You saw it at the debate in the palace. He was really closer to that Javanese ascetic than to the rest of us. He is closest of all to Kiai Wirajaya, who tells him to heed the wisdom of the Javanese sages, including Muslim mystics like Siti Jenar. He taught that the commands of Islam were only to guide those on the lowest steps of enlightenment, since for the wise only god exists.'

'Siti Jenar,' Sri murmured. 'Was he real? My mother loves him as the truest of Muslims, but my brother said he was an invention of the devil, and never really existed.'

'Perhaps he is just a story, Sri, but one that helps many good Javanese like your mother and Wirajaya to reconcile the new religion with the old. Anyway, my point is that there is a Javanese way to establish ultimate truth through meditation and looking within, especially at the holy places where ascetics have been seeking god for centuries. The king has permitted the Muslim teachers to threaten European captives like Antonio with ghastly punishments if they do not become Muslim, but I will tell Kiai Wirajaya that would not work with you. I will say that the Islam of Ustad Ahmad has no appeal to you, but with Sri's help you are beginning to appreciate the wisdom of Java. I think I can persuade Wirajaya to advise the prince to let you spend time meditating in sacred places and learning from the holiest teachers.'

This did little to lighten Hodges' growing despair, remembering his wretched captivity on the road to Mataram. 'But that is all Javanese hocus-pocus, Romo; you must know that. Besides, it would only postpone the time of reckoning.'

Sri leapt in eagerly. 'It would be precious time, Thomas, and we could be together. If we can stay away from the kraton until the baby is born, things might change. Your English ship might come. The prince might find some other jinn to protect him.'

Romo added gravely, 'Anggalaga doesn't believe it's hocus-pocus, Thomas, and nor do I. This is part of a much bigger contest for Java. He will soon be king, one way or another. He wants above all to be in control of his kingdom. I cannot believe he would opt for an Islam that put influence in Ustad Ahmad's hands, any more than a Christianity that put it in mine. I think there is another way, and that you may be able to help him find it.'

'Me? What do I know about all these Javanese gods? If he asked me, I'd tell him to throw them all out, along with that Ustad, and give his people some common sense.'

'No Thomas, you wouldn't,' Sri pleaded. 'You sound too much like my brother. Please do this, if only for me.'

Pangeran Sanjata and his men found them a few days later. His instructions were to bring them under guard down the mountain to a small hermitage the ash had not much affected. There Hodges and Sri were looked after so that they would be ready to join Anggalaga's procession. Hodges' burns were treated with various leaves and potions, and in a few days he was well enough to walk. Romo continued down the mountain to find the prince and Kiai Wirajaya, and make his case.

They met again some days later, when Hodges was brought to a house where Anggalaga's retinue had camped, two days' walk along another road up the mountain from Mataram. Hodges and Sri were brought to make their obeisance to the prince. He seemed already to be assuming some of the air of kingship, looking graver and speaking more slowly than he had before.

'You did well to kill that devil who attacked me,' Sri translated. 'But you should not have run away. If my soldiers flee the battlefield, they are captured and executed. But they are usually afraid, and you showed no fear. Why did you flee?'

They had rehearsed his answer.

'I could see that you were safe, and the amoks were dead. I thought whatever duty I had to you as a foreigner was complete. I had not seen my pregnant wife for many weeks. I feared for her safety, and the child's, if there was fighting in the land. I apologise to Your Majesty.'

Sri pushed his head down to make his penitence look more profound. Anggalaga did not look impressed.

'You are in our kingdom and you must do as I command. You showed more courage than my own men, and so you will not be executed. But it is time to forget about the English ships that never come. You are in Java, and you must become Javanese, and live by our rules.'

'England is very far, Your Majesty, but it is great and strong with many ships. They will sooner or later return, and I must answer to them. They will say it is treason to serve a foreign king.'

Hodges did not trust Sri to deliver this protest, so was venturing it directly in his confusing mixture of Malay and military Javanese. He was brought up sharp with a dig in the ribs from Sri. Noticing the prince's anger, she hastened to cover his coarse words with a flow of unusually deferential-sounding Javanese. Hodges understood he had gone too far for safety, without benefit of the delicate politeness that Sri's Javanese made possible.

'Your king is in England,' Anggalaga thundered. 'We are the king in Java and we decide what is treason!'

Hodges was not offered further translations in the lengthy

exchange that followed between Anggalaga's crisp commands and Sri's soothing, deferential words. At one point the prince summoned Kiai Wirajaya. While he discussed their fate with Anggalaga, Hodges hissed his demand to Sri to be told what was going on.

'Please say nothing, Thomas. He can have us killed in an instant. But I think Wirajaya may be on our side.'

More commands followed, with more polite responses from Sri that sounded to Hodges like simply acceptance of everything he said. Eventually it appeared they were dismissed, and when they were out of earshot Sri finally explained.

'He was not pleased, and talked about giving you the choice other condemned feringgi had experienced, between Islam and a horrible death from tigers or elephants. But it sounds as though Romo's idea appealed to Wirajaya, that Islam should not be the only test of being Javanese or loyal. He played up the disloyalty of some of the Muslims, including those crazy killers in Pajang who turned out to be part of some Muslim brotherhood. Anggalaga ended by giving Wirajaya the responsibility for your education.'

They were also expected to accompany Anggalaga's retinue up the mountain. Evidently the education process would begin with some ritual the prince planned. As they climbed, Kiai Wirajaya left his position near the prince to explain to Sri what was in store for them. There was again much bowing from Sri in agreement, and much frustration from Hodges that his fate was being decided without his agreement. Finally, Wirajaya left to resume his position. Sri stroked Hodges' arm reassuringly, and tried to calm him with her sweetest words.

'All is well, my dear. We will have time together, to work out how to live here with a child.'

'We cannot live here! The king will not stop wanting his way with you, nor Anggalaga sending me on his endless wars.'

'Well then, we will have time to plan some way to leave. Either way we are together. Kiai Wirajaya insists we should be part of this ceremony to the mountain, since you must understand how god himself speaks to men through this spectacular demonstration of his power.'

'Sang hyang again?'

'Yes, all right, sang hyang. Wirajaya believes that god does not speak to men only through prophets and holy books, as the Muslims and Christians say, but through his creation of the natural world, which still continues. I told him what you told me, that there are no fire mountains in England. He said no, and not in Arabia either. This is because Java is closer to the sang hyang; they watch over Java and give power to its kings.'

'It is a strange god who sends hot ash and gases to kill people!'

'That shows he is near. And afterwards, he said, the ash will make the land fertile, so that we can grow every crop useful to man. Anyway, after that we must go to a holy hill near here to learn from its holy men about the secrets not known to everyone. Wirajaya said that Romo has already been to this place and meditated there for many days. So he will ask Romo to accompany us there and to other holy places, until we have learned enough to become proper Javanese.'

Hodges snorted. 'What nonsense! This mountain seems closer to the devil than to god. I can never be a Javanese, not if it means believing this hocus-pocus.'

She gave him a squeeze. 'Maybe a different kind of Javanese, who knows? Be a little patient. You have already changed so much since I first met you and your smelly feringgi body. Nothing is impossible.'

The procession reached another ridge, seemingly the last place protected by its outcrop. Beyond, the upper slopes were covered in material spewed out by the mountain, with stumps of trees still burning here and there, and the fumes making breathing difficult. It reminded Hodges of pious depictions of hell.

The shrine had a tower with nine levels of thatched roof, one above the other. A stage before it had been decorated with white and yellow cloths and palm branches. There a man clothed in white was sitting, murmuring something.

Hodges was surprised to see Romo there, evidently sent by Wirajaya. He indicated where they were to sit.

'Evidently we foreigners have an honoured place here, to witness what Anggalaga thinks is his endorsement as king by the spirits of the mountain.'

'Do you believe this? I have never seen so dreadful a picture of death and destruction.'

'Well, Thomas, the ancients believed something the same. The Italians have these fire mountains too, like the Vesuvius eruption that Pliny described. They call it a "volcano" because the ancient Romans thought it was the chimney used by the fire god Vulcan at his forge. One of my Italian Jesuit brothers made a study of all the volcanoes mentioned by the Latin and Greek writers. He was excited by the idea that these eruptions were signs that god did not stop creating after the seven days of Genesis. He would have loved to see Java, to prove his thesis that god is as active as he ever was, gradually building islands like this. This scene around us is indeed a wasteland, and you experienced it at its most terrifying. But the Javanese know what Italian peasants around Naples also know: that the most fertile soil is near the volcano where this ash has fallen. I can understand that the Javanese feel closer to god because they are reminded by the constant earthquakes and eruptions of his power, and their own dependence.'

'Closer to god my arse! Closer to the demons and monsters they invent like children to explain things.'

'Well Thomas, it appears we have some time to explore these demons and monsters. Kiai Wirajaya has given me the job of guiding you to three holy places, in the hope perhaps of broadening your idea of god. Unfortunately, Pangeran Sanjata and a couple of his men will also accompany us, just in case you should be thinking of escaping. Tomorrow we will head westward. We will walk slowly, but with god's help we should be in a place called Borobudur in three or four days.'

They moved even slower than this. The volcano had wrought havoc to some of the roads and bridges, and the little party had to pick its way carefully across streams that had turned into rivers of mud and ash. At one village Romo evidently had friends, and persuaded Sri to feign some indisposition that required her to rest for a day. There Sri did not return as usual after her morning bath, and Hodges went looking for her in the village. He found her sitting cross-legged behind some villagers, on the veranda of a house. Romo was quietly speaking before a cross and a candle placed on a small table.

'What's going on?' he whispered to Sri, as he sat down beside her.

'I'm not sure. I heard people saying some prayers in Javanese, so I came to see. They sang a nice Javanese song, too, repeating the word "Alleluyah". Now I can't understand what Romo is saying, since he is talking in some other language.'

'Now we see his popery. He must be mumbling the Mass in Latin. I thought he had become so Javanese he had forgotten about it. Latin was a way to keep ordinary people ignorant, instead of speaking plainly in the language of the people as we now do in England.'

'Like the Muslims with their Arabic. But his chanting sounds sweet, as the Muslim call to prayer sometimes does even when we can't understand it. What is he doing now?'

Romo had shown the people something that looked like a piece of tempeh, then said some Latin over it as he broke it and ate one piece. Next he raised a Chinese bowl, made the sign of the cross over it, and drank from it.

'*Pax Domini sit semper vobiscum,*' he intoned.

One of the Javanese answered '*Et cum spiritu tuo.*' Romo brought the tempeh down to the people and placed a piece of it in the mouth of each of them. He looked expectantly at Hodges, who simply shook his head.

'What is that about?' Sri whispered. 'Should we join in?'

'It is the communion, where bread is blessed and broken. We Christians eat it as a sign of oneness with Jesus, since that is what he commanded us to do. But he never said anything about tempeh. If you ate the bread, or whatever, that would be a sign you had become a Christian, maybe a papist.'

'So why don't *you* eat it?'

Hodges said nothing. He was lost in remembrance of eucharists past, with his mother and with his wife, especially at their wedding. The memories brought gut-wrenching guilts. He could not begin to explain this to Sri, but moved closer to her manifestly real and warm presence.

Later, Romo introduced his small flock to a very curious Sri and a wary Hodges. While Sri chatted eagerly to them in Javanese, Romo explained to Hodges. 'I too have had my adventures on the way to Mataram, and once had to hide for a few months in this village. These dear friends not only protected me, but wanted to become Christians. I get here when I can, but that is seldom. Mostly they say their prayers on their own, and some have even learned a little Latin, as you saw.'

'That looked like tempeh you broke on the altar. What kind of eucharist is that?'

'When did you last see bread in Java? Or wine? Jesus used bread and wine because that was how the Jews gathered for a meal together – a sign of their communion with him and one another. If Jesus had celebrated his last supper in Java, perhaps he would have found some way to use rice. I can't go that far, since I must break it in the consecration, and in my hands that is always a mess.'

'And the wine?'

'I use *tuak*, the palm wine, since that is the closest in function and even in taste.'

'It sounds like another reason for the Inquisition to roast you, Romo.'

'I hope not, I hope not. If I believed only bread and red wine could represent Christ, I would have had to do without the mass now for many years, and that I could not do.'

'And what is this "Romo" you call yourself? Are you trying to show you are a real papist from Rome, neither a true Englishman nor a Javanese?'

'Calm down, Thomas. You may call me Edward if you like – it sounds better on an English tongue than a Javanese one. Romo is one of the Javanese words for father, but I am happy if people link it to Rome. Believe it or not, the memory of the old Roman Empire lives on in Java. What they call *Rum* is more than that though. It is the empire in the west that might be Rome, or Constantinople, or Alexander the Great or the Turkish Caliph of today. Romo is also the way the Javanese pronounce Rama, the hero of the Ramayana story. He slays demons like other wayang heroes, but he is unusually wise. I like best the way he gave up the kingdom of his birthright to go and live a pure life in the forest. It reminds me of why I gave up the distracting pleasures of the real Rome.'

'Rama? Isn't he the one who loses his lovely wife Sita to the monsters? Javanese tell me Sri is like Sita, and I think they mean I am the monster who carried her off. So where is your Sita?'

Romo grinned. 'Yes, I can see they might think you resemble Rawana, the demon king – reddish beard, big nose, big voice, big all around. People often ask me that same question. I say Java is my beautiful Sita. I am wedded to Java now, though in danger of losing her to others.'

# Pilgrimage

The destination appeared to be a small village on a hill overlooking a tributary of the Progo River that they had ascended for the last part of the journey. When they had rested and bathed, an elderly man in a yellow robe greeted them. Sri explained that he was apologising for not feeding them. It was the practice of his order of monks, called *biksu*, not to eat after midday. An adequate meal would be provided early next morning, to fortify them for the pilgrimage he proposed to take the group on. Romo, who had been here before and met the biksu, explained to Hodges and Sri that his was the way of Buddha, or Siddhartha Gautama. There must have been such monks throughout Java for centuries, though many had died, fled, or abandoned the strict way during the wars of recent times.

'Muslim warriors attacked our refuge twice,' the biksu intervened. 'They would have destroyed us if not for the protection of the lord Buddha.'

'What does that mean?' asked Hodges.

Sri, wide-eyed, rendered the answer that the monks had given a special mantra to some young men who had come on pilgrimage, and it made them invulnerable to the spears and knives of the attackers.

'What balderdash,' said Hodges. 'So these monks make war with their hocus-pocus, but it's still war?'

Another exchange followed, after which Sri reported

earnestly. 'He insists the way of Buddha is against all killing. Even a mosquito may have been a human in an earlier life, or may become one again on the long and winding road to Buddhahood. All living beings are related. If others use violence, the monks would only meditate, since a calm death would be a step on the right path. If his blessing proved useful to others, less advanced on the path, to defend the holy places, that was their affair.'

'Sounds like a typical monkish sophistry. If killing mosquitos is their measure of damnation, I fear I'm slipping ever further down the wrong path. Another half-dozen last night, with no let-up by the critters.'

'Poor Thomas.' She stroked his hairy chin. 'They must like your rich English blood enough to fight their way through all the hair.'

'Each to his own tastes. I don't see why they don't prefer yours,' he said, as he nuzzled her smooth shoulder.

The meal came before dawn, and they were on their way at first light. The old monk was surprisingly agile in following a narrow path through rocks, roots, and increasingly pieces of masonry. They passed one stone head on the ground, then another.

'Are these their gods?' Hodges asked Romo.

'I think they are all of Buddha. He seems to be venerated more than Jesus, Mary and all our saints together. My brother Jesuits who have been in Ceylon and Siam tell us that kings and people there still follow this path, and cover hundreds of these statues in gold.'

The biksu had now conducted them to a place where monks and others were meditating before a stone statue. He bowed low, seated himself cross-legged under a nearby tree, and invited them to rest.

'As you see, there were hundreds of statues of the Buddha here, but most have been broken or buried by earthquakes, eruptions of fire mountains, wars and storms. Our ancestors built many other temples, but none so vast as this. This statue has miraculously survived, and so we especially worship here.'

The biksu led them onwards, explaining that they were among the ruins of a vast temple, with carvings that taught the way of the Buddha to the many devotees of former days. They passed by broken walls, many carrying stone sculptures of kings, men and women, musicians, boats, cattle, horses and everyday scenes. The monk stopped here and there to explain a story, most of which seemed to Hodges fantastic children's tales of miraculous deeds.

'If these were your ancestors,' Hodges muttered to Sri, 'they carved well but believed a load of nonsense.'

The biksu led them finally to a series of stone carvings decorating a long wall. It appeared to have been cleared of accumulated debris so that pilgrims could examine it closely. There were three similar scenes side by side, each showing a man sitting cross-legged on a horse cart, surrounded by what appeared to be retainers, in different scenes. After much questioning, Romo believed he understood why the biksu thought this important.

'The Buddha began his life on earth as a prince, Siddhartha, and so each scene shows him in the centre with many followers and servants. This series explains what we might call his conversion, though our friend sees it more like a step of knowledge. The panels show his meeting a helpless old man, an emaciated sick man, and a dead man being prepared for cremation. He lost his pride in his youth and strength. When he saw the dead man he understood that life itself, or perhaps the attachment to life, was a worthless illusion. He then abandoned his royal status and became an ascetic. Eventually he meditated for so long that he attained enlightenment and began teaching it to others.'

Hodges was unimpressed. 'So do these monks hold that the only way to salvation is to become a monk and spend your life meditating? I can see why the Javanese kings might have chosen Islam instead.'

'Let's ask him. This won't be easy.'

As this next discussion evolved, Sri became gradually more involved than Romo, and the guards and some other pilgrims gathered to listen. The monk seemed to be having such trouble with Sri that Romo became the mediator.

When Hodges managed to get Sri's attention, she seemed exasperated. 'He was trying to say it's a long process and takes many lives to reach what he calls *nirvana*. A woman seems to have not much better chance than his famous mosquito. First I would have to be reincarnated as a man, so that then I could become a monk, and finally make some progress. I don't think he knows what he is talking about.'

Romo was more sympathetic. 'This nirvana he talks about seems to be not so much our idea of heavenly bliss as detachment from earthly desires. Of course for male celibates like him or me, women are the greatest such desire. We can be tempted to put the blame on them. If he identifies women with the world of desire he is trying to escape from, let's not blame the Buddha for that.'

They had some weeks to debate these issues with the monks and each other since Kiai Wirajaya had instructed that Hodges must learn meditation and self-cultivation. He had little patience for that, but was happy to be away from Mataram as long as possible. Romo had more success interesting Hodges in how and why this huge temple structure had been built. They walked over the whole site, attempting to measure its dimensions and understand what it would have looked like in its glory. It appeared to have been a vast stone square, larger than the great cathedrals either of them had seen in Europe. Each side was more than a hundred paces in length. But they could find no entrance. It seemed to be constructed of a series of stone terraces narrowing towards a summit covered in Buddha statues. The monks themselves seemed confused about it. Some thought it contained holy relics; some that it was a sacred mountain made by gods at the centre of the world; and some that it was a place for teaching the message of the Buddha.

Hodges was baffled by the contrast between this vast place and everything else he had seen in Java. 'These Javanese have a lot of primitive, magical ideas; they build mostly in wood and bamboo. And yet somebody put as much skill and effort into building this place as the Christians who built the great cathedrals. Maybe it was a different people who built this monument.'

'No Thomas. These carvings are amazing, but they don't look very different from the kind of faces and costumes the stonemasons of Mataram still carve. Kiai Wirajaya is very proud of this place as the finest example of how Javanese aspire to divinity – that's why he insisted you come here. How many people must have laboured to build it? With today's population of Mataram, even if everybody spent the whole dry season hauling stones, it would have taken forever.'

'Maybe they had greater cities in the past, wiped out by one of these fire mountains. If they were so capable and numerous, why did they waste their effort on this temple instead of the roads, bridges and aqueducts that would have given them a decent life, like the Romans?'

'Waste?' Romo protested. 'Were they not worshipping god in their way, as our ancestors who built Canterbury Cathedral were in theirs? Would not god have heard them and sustained them, as he did us? Roads and bridges do not give meaning to life, and hope to the soul.'

When the time came to move, they started back eastward and again stopped at the village with the small Christian community. Again Sri provided the pretext and again Romo said his morning Mass. Sri wanted to hear the whole thing, and bullied Hodges into sitting with her at the back.

'I'll tell you what he is saying in Javanese if you tell me what the Latin is all about.'

Sri fulfilled her part of the bargain readily enough, since Romo's Javanese was slow and straightforward. He welcomed his small group, and thanked and congratulated them for giving an example of Christian living in Java. As Sri translated his sermon, Hodges realised he was using the story of the good Samaritan as his text.

'He says it means that god is for everybody. Those who believe they are his special people may not serve him or even understand him best. It is often outsiders like this small community of Javanese who best understand his command to love one's neighbour as one loves oneself.'

Hodges was less able to catch the Latin that Romo mumbled very quickly, but he knew the order of prayers well enough to guess what was the confession of sins, the creed, the *sanctus* and the *agnus dei*. During the consecration he said the words clearly enough as he raised the tempeh: '*Hoc est enim corpus meum.*'

'What is he saying?' Sri was insistent now.

'He is saying, "This is my body".'

'Romo's body?"

'No, Jesus' body. This is where the papists really got it wrong. Jesus said these words at his last meal with his followers and asked them to remember him by it. So they say the bread magically becomes Jesus' body, and that we are really swallowing flesh, not bread.'

'Arrgh! They say there are people in Sumatra who like to eat human flesh. I didn't know the feringgi did that!'

'It's a nonsense, Sri. But I'm afraid it's a nonsense that has caused too much fighting, even among the English. Some of my relatives won't speak to others because they disagree so much about this.'

'So what do you think it means, Thomas?'

Now Romo was distributing the tempeh, and again Thomas shook his head, and restrained Sri from going forward in curiosity. 'I won't take his tempeh, and he probably wouldn't want me to, because I believe it is just tempeh. We should get rid of all that magic, that hocus-pocus, if we want to progress. Jesus must have meant his breaking of bread as a sign of his promise to be with us as we gather to eat.'

Their journey took them past numerous other stone temple ruins, some of which they paused to examine. Kiai Wirajaya had, however, insisted they made a longer stop at a village called Brambanan to study the nearby ruins. Wirajaya himself honoured the village with a visit after they had been there a few days. The villagers and some of the guards showed him great reverence and asked him for blessings. Hodges and Romo had wandered over the vast temple site, and were glad to have someone to ask about its perplexing structure.

There seemed to be stones everywhere, in a huge square at least four hundred paces on each side. Rather than the single ruined building they had seen in Borobudur, this comprised hundreds of small stone shrines, some of which still had a statue discernable of man, beast or god. Here the ravages of earthquake and forest appeared to have done most of the damage, though some statues looked to have been deliberately defaced by zealots. Many of the square stone building blocks must have been taken away for other purposes, for they had seen fine stone foundations of otherwise flimsy houses in the village. Trees had grown over the ruins everywhere, but there was one cleared cart track through it to a collection of little shrines being cleared by an enterprising villager with his oxcart. The building blocks could be had for almost nothing, he told Romo, provided you hired the services of his cart to bring them where you wanted them.

Another path led to what appeared to be the centre of the

vast complex, and this was used by devotees. Romo and Hodges followed them one morning and found the most extensive cult was devoted to a statue of a female god with many arms, standing on a bull. She seemed less prominent but more honoured than a male figure on the other side of the large ruin. Some of the worshippers told Romo she was a powerful god herself, or the consort of the male god on the other side. More seemed to think she was a beautiful princess named Lara Jonggrang, which Romo understood simply to mean 'slender maiden.' An evil usurper had killed her father and conquered his kingdom, and insisted on taking her as his wife. She used trickery to resist him successfully, and in revenge he turned her to stone. Most of the worshippers placing flowers there were women, who appeared to think the princess could help them in their battles with men.

Hodges dismissed all this as ludicrous Javanese make-believe, the women competing for the most fantastic story. Far from encouraging him to "become Javanese", this visit was driving him away from Java and from Sri. But Romo was convinced the massive complex must be a key to understanding Java, and could not wait to ask Kiai Wirajaya about it.

This was not to be so easy. In response to their questions, the kiai simply said, 'The way to knowledge is not to ask, but to wait in stillness.'

He agreed to conduct them to the monument the following day, but only after they had meditated in a particular spot from before dawn. Hodges' heart sank, but before he could protest Sri had already agreed on his behalf. They were woken in the dark, and Wirajaya led them to the foundations of a former shrine from which they could see the larger temples outlined against the silhouette of Merapi to their north. The dawn was indeed beautiful, but did little to assuage Hodges' feeling of being in the wrong place. Romo hardly helped by suggesting that he repeat some mantra to stop his thoughts wandering. He added with a mischievous grin, 'Try the rosary, Thomas, if you can't remember something in the Book of Common Prayer.'

Finally the ordeal was over, and Wirajaya led them along the pilgrims' path to the largest shrines in the centre of the complex. He sat to the east of the largest pile of ruins, the risen sun behind him, obliging his guests to do likewise. Eventually he spoke in a low voice to Romo, who was now permitted to ask questions. Sri crawled forward to be within earshot behind the pair, motioning to Hodges to follow so that she could explain the conversation to him.

'You have seen the way of the Buddha at Borobudur. These buildings represent the way of Shiva. Both came to Java from above the winds, in India, at the time of Aji Saka.'

'Do you mean the one from whom you began your Saka dating system? That should be 1534 years ago. But why would he bring two different faiths?'

'As you say, a long time ago, before the time of Mohammad. I did not say he brought these pathways. The devotees of Buddha say that Gautama himself came to Java; those of Shiva say he and the other gods were banished from India because Shiva presumed to be himself the ultimate divine truth, rather than an avatar. There are many stories, but they agree that at the time of Aji Saka Java became the home of both these faiths. These and the many other temples you see around you were built at that time when Java was the centre of the world, before the great disaster.'

'What disaster was that?'

'Some say plague, some earthquake or flood, but the oldest writings tell of a great eruption of a fire mountain, that covered the whole of Java with its ash and mud so that no rice could grow for many years. I believe this story, since the ploughs of our farmers sometimes strike in their fields the tops of temples that have been buried.'

'Do you mean that Merapi exploded, as we just experienced?'

'Some think so, but I do not. Merapi is the protector of Mataram, and we know its ways. There are many fire mountains in Java, and those in the west and the east are less benevolent than our Merapi, at the world's centre.'

'Most countries have only one faith, and barely tolerate others. Why did Java have two?'

The kiai paused for some time before answering this, closing his eyes as if in meditation. Hodges wanted Sri to press the question but she restrained him with a firm squeeze of his hand. Eventually the response came.

'Since ancient times we Javanese have understood that the universe requires balance. There are male and female; heavens and earth; mountain and ocean. We humans only survive by uniting in marriage. Families must combine with others in a village to manage the water channels, while even our villages know that they are bound to other villages for the cycle of rituals and markets. We call it *monchapat*, the union of four. The wayang stories are mostly about the eternal conflict between the Pendawas and the Kurawas. Most people favour the Pendawas and identify with them, but the Kurawas could never be destroyed, for that would mean the end of the world. People fight, but harmony must nevertheless be maintained between them.'

'I understand the wisdom in this, Kiai,' Romo intruded gently. 'But the devotees of Buddha and those of Shiva both think their way is the sole truth, do they not?'

'This is the mistake of you foreigners. Christians and Muslims fight each other because you believe there is only one truth. You think you have it and the others must be destroyed. But god the one, the ultimate, has created a world of surface differences. If he had wanted all to be Christians he would have made that clear to us Javanese from the beginning, as well as to the Arabs and Chinese. This is the truth you must learn from this place, Romo, as well as your English friend. The followers of Shiva knew that his image is not the whole. Truth is one, yes, but each imagines it differently. While Shiva is here facing us in the major shrine, his consort Durga faces north to the mountain. You see she is much more popular with the women. On the other two sides of this central temple you will see other avatars or aspects of Shiva, the elephant-god Ganesha and Agastya.'

'What about these other temples to the left and right of the main one?'

'Shiva is always balanced by two other gods to make the *trimurti* which better represents the totality of the ultimate. Brahma is the creator and Vishnu the sustainer. That leaves Shiva as the destroyer, or rather the one who changes the order, making him popular with kings.'

Romo was listening carefully to Wirajaya's low voice, and appeared to Hodges to be nodding. How could he call himself a Christian and tolerate this riot of pagan idols with many arms, this half-naked goddess to whom the poor benighted Javanese were offering their flowers and betel nuts? But Sri too was now listening carefully to what Romo was saying.

'The kiai is wise in understanding that god is unknowable, so that different paths to the ultimate truth must be treasured. Your ancestors knew the path of Buddha and the path of Shiva, and used them both to grow in knowledge and understanding. But now your world is bigger, since people from the whole world are coming to Java. Above the winds people practise the path of Jesus and the path of Mohammad, and these too have been sources of wisdom and signs of the ultimate truth for many centuries. Can they also be held together in the harmony you seek for Java?'

Once Sri translated this question Hodges began to see where Romo was heading. Wirajaya was slow to answer, again closing his eyes in meditation. Hodges had time to whisper to Sri, 'Is he just playing a crafty game to get his church built in Mataram? I don't see how he can believe what he is saying about these "many paths".'

'He sounds to me like a real Javanese who understands better than most. Maybe in English you have not the right words to make this harmony seem right?'

She hushed him then, since Wirajaya's answer was finally coming.

'Your question is the most important one, Romo. I think about it daily, and it is the question the king and the prince most want my advice on. I still do not have the answer. It is true that there is a unity in two, like Shiva and Buddha, a unity in three, like *trimurti*, and a unity in four, like the *monchapat*. Perhaps the four paths you speak of could represent the harmony and unity we seek. But these new beliefs from above the winds speak in different, contradictory ways. The Portuguese and Dutch do not even tolerate each other. Some Muslims speak like you, others like Ustad Ahmad who sees only one way. That is why you must learn from a third holy place, at Bayat, whether the foreign ways can become truly Javanese.'

Romo continued to make his plea that the way of Jesus was the fourth path that Java needed, because it was the path of love, self-sacrifice and service as well as contemplation. Shutting doors to it would end by making Java isolated. But Hodges' legs were aching, and his head spinning. He needed to stretch his body and relax his mind.

They spent weeks more at this village. Romo kept hearing about other temple complexes nearby, and wanted to check each one to try to understand which was devoted to Buddha and which to Shiva or some other god. Did one come before the other, or were they built by the same society? There must have been hundreds of shrines in the central complex they had admired first, but just to the south was another complex called *chandi sewu* – thousand temples. An hour's walk north was another ruin that Romo declared must be devoted to Buddha. He became excited about the treatise he must write in Latin for the learned men of Europe, explaining how Java had held the great religions of the east in balance. After much pestering, Kiai Wirajaya lent him a palm-leaf manuscript he said was ancient and precious, which would explain the mystery of unity and plurality. Romo required much of Sri's time poring over these fragile leaves, leaving Hodges to walk further afield. He had more energy than Romo, and more interest in how the buildings were built than making sense of their absurd gods.

Sri shared some of Hodges' impatience with the arcane words that seemed to cover up contradiction. One evening she was exhausted after spending the whole day on a single leaf. It had so excited Romo that he had insisted on translating the whole thing into Latin for his learned treatise. They had finally agreed to render the key sentence as: 'The truth of Buddha and the truth of Shiva are indeed different, but they remain one, as there is no duality in truth.'

Hodges refused to be impressed. 'All that effort, and in the end all it says is a nonsense. Either it is one or two. It cannot be both.'

Sri conceded. 'Perhaps you're right, Thomas, unless I missed something. But it does sound a bit like you trying to explain the trinity.'

Hodges did not reply. He hated this theological hair-splitting, whether by Javanese or Christians. The idea that his fate in Java should depend on it drove him to despair. But on a walk to another temple, he took it up with Romo, whom he knew would have found some way to explain the trinity to his Javanese friends.

'I have had many arguments with Muslims about this, Thomas. I have come to accept that god may have intended Islam as a corrective to the endless squabbling of the early Christians about whether Jesus was half god or wholly god, with one essence or two. But the Muslims, like later Calvinists, erred in the other extreme. By rejecting all appearance of plurality, even imagery and music, as idolatry from the devil, they gained a simple rationality, but lost that humility before an unknowable god that leads to acceptance of our human limitations. Javanese feel that loss strongly, and I have come to agree with them. The trinity and the cult of saints may be hard to explain rationally, but they bring us closer to understanding how Javanese approach the divine.'

# Mysticism

The last stop of this strange pilgrimage was Bayat, another few days' walk eastwards. The progress was slower, as Sri was beginning to need more rest. There were ample opportunities for Romo to explain to a sceptical Hodges and a curious Sri what he knew of this place. He had already been taken there by Kiai Wirajaya, who now entrusted Romo to explain its importance to Hodges. It was not, he admitted, an easy task.

'Kiai Wirajaya believes that this site is essential to understanding how Islam connects with the older tradition of Javaneseness, *kejawen*. For the rulers of Mataram, it is also part of the justification of their rule. It may be easier for Sri to understand these stories than for you or me. We no longer expect miracles to happen around us. Maybe we love the new Greek science too much to accept that. The Javanese are much closer to the supernatural.'

'Do you mean it's not just my pig-headed husband who rejects everything that he can't see? Do all you Europeans have this problem?'

'Problem?' Hodges protested. 'You mean we are finally freeing ourselves from superstition, and beginning to understand how the world works. I'm not sure about you papists though. You still to go on about holy relics and miraculous apparitions.'

'Not like our ancestors though, Thomas. The earlier Christians loved stories about miracle-working saints. When he gets stubborn, Sri, ask your husband to explain the patron saint of England, whose flag his ship still flies. St George was as good at killing dragons as your Bima.'

'That was long ago, Romo. But Sri is here now, a modern woman, and still believes such things! Anyway, what nonsense are we expected to believe about this Bayat?'

'Very well. Bayat, or Tembayat, is a small hill surmounted by the tomb of one holy man named Pandanarang. After many adventures in search of wisdom, he settled, built a mosque and taught his message on this hill. He is now honoured by most Javanese Muslims as Sunan Bayat, after the place where he is buried. They see him as the apostle, or *wali* as they call it, of this Mataram area.'

'Was he a real person?'

'I think there must have been a real person buried here perhaps a century ago, who was admired for his spiritual powers as a Muslim and a Javanese. But the stories about him are more fantastic than Jonah and the whale. It is plausible that he was a convert from the old religions to a mystical, esoteric form of Islam, and that he took over a place that had been holy to the Javanese for centuries earlier.'

'Does Wirajaya expect us to believe the fantastic stories?'

'Perhaps not. What he wants is for us to see how Javanese ideas can absorb even a foreign faith like Islam. They say that Pandanarang began life as a prince from the coastal commercial area, or some say a guru or ascetic within the old Javanese belief system. He was converted by the most famous miracle-working *wali*, Sunan Kalijaga, who is credited with many ways of reconciling

Islam with Javanese culture, including the shadow puppets. The stories are many about how he convinced Pandanarang about the Javanese idea that outward appearance and inner reality, or man and god, are opposite yet ultimately one. It's called *jatimurti*. When I talk with the sages here, I compare it with our theology of the incarnation. Kalijaga appeared to Pandanarang as different people, first a fabulously rich prince, then a poor beggar, demonstrating how appearances are untrustworthy.'

'It is so bizarre. So we can believe everything, or nothing.'

'Precisely. The second test Wirajaya put for us is more political, but won't be easy for you either. The rulers of Mataram insist that they are the rightful successors of the kings of Java. The truth seems to be that the old kings were far to the east, and that this area was a wasteland until Senopati, the king before the present one, brought some followers here, found the land fertile, and began to conquer other settlements and bring their people here. Islam gave him well-armed allies, and a pretext for conquest. For the Javanese, however, kings only have power and credibility as part of the divine order. That is why Anggalaga had to have his ceremony before the volcano. Bayat must have been a holy place for the old religion, where the ascetics used their supernatural powers to resist the Muslims. They say Pandanarang's powers were even greater because he was a reincarnation of the old kings of Java. When he prevailed, Bayat became the sacred centre of his kind of very Javanese Islam. Kiai Wirajaya tells me the king believes that it is through Pandanarang and Bayat that he has assumed the supernatural right to rule Java.'

'Does Anggalaga believe this nonsense? Sri hears rumours he

is getting stronger by the day.'

'He is more practical than most Javanese princes. He knows he needs skilled men and guns to expand his power, but also the support of the people. I think he really believes he is divinely destined to unite all Java again. He seems willing to use any of the rival ideas that will convince others to believe it – Islam, jatimurti, the volcano, or a reincarnation of former kings.'

'But not popery, I warrant. You'll never convince such people to submit to an Italian pope half way on the other side of the world.'

'You're right about that, Thomas. Long before King Henry and Elizabeth made the case for England, Javanese believed their island and their king were uniquely favoured by god. I believe my task is to support those who want to keep their door open to all the paths to god, not to close them as some of the Muslims would like.'

As their small procession led by the Mataram soldiers crossed the rice fields below Bayat, the traffic coming the other way was obliged to stand aside. Many of the women carried a brown pot of water on their heads or in a cloth slung over their backs. Sri chatted with some of them as they rested beside the path, she too needing rest as she grew heavier. She discovered that the water of Bayat was considered both holy and healthy. Mothers would have their children drink it so that they would grow up strong as well as pious. The extra burden on the journey back from the pilgrimage was justified by the value of the pot itself.

Once installed in the house appointed for them in the village, it appeared that its business was more pots than holiness. The woman of the house interrupted her work on the potting wheel only to greet her visitors. She then left them to her husband so she could get back to her pot before the clay hardened. Hodges was intrigued.

'Are other potters women?' he asked Sri. 'That looks like heavy work.'

'Of course, always women. Is that not the case in England? Women have more dextrous hands, I suppose, and especially more sense about how to make some extra money this way for the family. The men probably dig out the clay.'

Early next morning they joined the pilgrims on a winding path up the small hill. Three times they seemed to reach the sacred place marked by a *gapura* gate. They were instructed to bow low as they reached the open gate after climbing six steps, and then to go down the other side without raising their eyes. After the first gate they reached a yard with a well, a washing place and many people washing their feet, hands and heads. After the second, there were stalls selling floral offerings and lucky charms of palm leaf and stone. The big surprise that awaited them here was Buyung, who greeted them eagerly.

'Have you become a pious Javanese yet, Thomas? There are rumours in the city about your being a worshipper of Buddha or Shiva now, as well as a Muslim.'

'*Ndhasmu! Aku ora bakal!*' Hodges hoped his primitive Javanese was up to abusing Buyung and his flippant suggestions. 'I had no choice in coming here. What on earth is your excuse?'

'Just to keep an eye on you, Thomas! I heard that this was

your next stop. But to tell the truth, once I started asking about this place I thought it might have some potential. The Javanese like to buy our Chinese wares, but some of the pious Muslims fear they might be damned to a piggy hell for doing so. So I brought some nice colourful porcelain and told them it was a priceless tribute from the King of China to this holy place. They were flattered, and I think they will put it in the wall. As you can see, somebody already had that idea before me.'

He pointed to two Chinese plates recessed into the third gate. 'It's a cheap way to show that I am one of them, and that my wares have the blessings of god himself.'

'What news of Mataram, and of the English ships?'

'Not good, Thomas. The king grows weaker, Anggalaga more impatient. The king's brothers and nephews are looking to make trouble for the young prince. He wants to lead his army again against Surabaya, but fears one of his uncles would make a move for the throne in his absence. You are now seen as an ally of the prince. Were you in the capital, someone would surely have tried poison or a kris in the back to get you out of the way. Stay away as long as you can, until this business is settled.'

'And the English?'

'No sign of another ship. My father had word from Banten that half the English left there are sick or dead, and the rest desperate for food. It is the Dutch who are ever stronger, with ships always in the harbour.'

'Damn this cursed place. Nowhere is safe.'

'Things should improve here once Pangeran Anggalaga takes charge, as I'm sure he will. He is sensible, and he likes you. You will need some stability once you have a family – Sri's time must be close now.'

'Stability? Mataram is hardly the place I imagined bringing up a child. Who can I trust there? If I were to throw in my lot with the prince, I would never see England again. My child would be a foreigner to me.'

'Not really, Thomas. Look at me! I'm a good son of my Javanese mother as well as my Chinese father, even if he doesn't always think so. There are advantages in having a foot in both camps. Somebody needs to help them talk to each other.'

Hodges was preoccupied as the group was eventually led into the sacred uppermost space, where they joined pilgrims sitting cross-legged around a tomb. The thought of England added to his anxiety. If Sri were not there, how could England be home? But how could he get her there? An English Company ship would not take her, even if she could be persuaded to go. If he could somehow sneak her home on a Dutch ship, what was the punishment for a man with two wives?

The tomb seemed drab after the incredible stonework of Borobudur and Brambanan. Yet there were more people here, some meditating and some muttering repetitive phrases in unison. Their credulousness underlined how alien this place was, and how bleak his choice.

Sri had fallen naturally into her trance-like meditative pose. Romo was chanting like the Javanese, but in Latin. Hodges let them be. He had no taste for this mindless repetition, even as a charade to impress Wirajaya. He only knew he needed to be with Sri, to be a good father to the baby she was carrying. She was in no shape to attempt an escape, even were that conceivable. Yet Bayat served only to make Java less palatable.

Eventually he asked Sri if she really understood why they were there. 'If they want to convince me to become Javanese, why bring me to this shoddy place, where even *you* can't understand the hocus-pocus?'

'I like you as an Englishman, Thomas, even with your stubborn head. But the king and the prince probably feel they need to make you enough of a Javanese to trust you. You had better talk to Romo about what that means.'

Hodges was not in a hurry to do that. He liked things as they were, and hated the memory of his wrestling between 'Islam or death'. It was Romo who eventually raised the subject, after he had received a message from the court.

'We are running out of time, Thomas. The prince wants you in Mataram. He thinks you have had enough time to decide whether you will "become a Javanese".'

'How can I, Romo? Sri keeps reminding me I don't smell Javanese, I don't look Javanese, I can't sit Javanese and I can't speak proper Javanese. Even you don't seem to pass the test after ten years.'

'That's not it, Thomas. Anggalaga already has some strange people he trusts, and plenty of real Javanese he doesn't. I think what he has in mind is that you must make some public sign that you reject your Englishness. I'm afraid he still can't get past the idea that becoming a Muslim is the only thing that would do it. That seems to have worked for some of the Portuguese, meaning they can't be trusted any more by their own kind.'

'What about you, then? You seem to have been accepted at the court for years.'

'I'm afraid it's changing, Thomas. The old king did not take us Europeans too seriously. I was just an exotic decoration for the court, like the dwarfs and clowns. But Anggalaga has noticed that you shoot straighter than his men, and that the Portuguese and Dutch are hard to dislodge once they get a foothold somewhere. He wants to be able to trust you to show him how to fight these feringgi when he has to. Otherwise he doesn't want you at all.'

'Doesn't he now? I don't like the choice.'

'Nor do I, Thomas; nor do I.'

'And what has this place, Bayat, got to do with the damned choice? If it is meant to impress me with the virtues of Islam, it's not working.'

'I see that. I am guessing that he is trying to show you what accepting Islam means for him. At least for Kiai Wirajaya, Bayat shows that Islam can be added to *kejawen*, Javaneseness, without destroying it. This was a holy place before Islam, as you can see from the gapura gates and some springs that still have statues of the Indian gods. This Pandanarang fellow showed that by adding some Islamic coating to the Javanese idea of sacred power he could become even more powerful. Wirajaya seems to see Islam as a more powerful kejawen, that adds another dimension to the practices they already hold dear. Perhaps he thinks you and I can see it as a more powerful Christianity as well, that can incorporate some Muslim outer forms with more gain than loss.'

'Not me, Romo. How about you? Some of this mumbling in Arabic they don't understand seems like super-popery to me.'

'No. Jesus is "the way, the truth and the life". I would love to turn it around, and show Jesus as the fulfilment they are looking for, of Islam and of Javanism. But the behaviour of the European ships gives the lie to any such fantasy I might construct. The best I can hope is that Mataram does not close the door to the good we have to offer.'

'Buyung thinks life will be easier under Anggalaga if he comes to power.'

'For him perhaps, since he will accept whatever token formula they require. Not for me, unless I can change the prince's mind. First we must talk to one of the so-called saints of Bayat. I have promised Wirajaya that I will explain accurately to you what he has to say. We had better have Sri with us, since the language they use is often very strange. How is she?'

'She seems strong, given the weight she is carrying. But she wants more female company for the big day as it gets closer. I'm afraid she wants to return to Mataram.'

It was not only the language of the Ki Ageng of Tembayat that was strange. He and his ragged brown sarong were in need of a wash, and his waist-length hair was knotted. He carried a stick like a duster with which he languidly harassed the flies that came his way. There was nevertheless a queue of devotees wanting a blessing, a mantra or some advice. This process had to be interrupted at Romo's insistence. The king himself, he claimed, had required that the kiai give the small group his undivided attention.

Romo began the explanation of why they had come, with Sri

whispering a translation in Hodges' ear. He particularly wanted to know, he explained, whether truth was to be found in Islam or in the old beliefs of Java. This elicited some difficult words, but Sri could only understand them as meaning that they were the same, for truth was one.

Romo persisted in pointing out that the gates of the shrine at Bayat were the same as those at Brambanan, the gapura form like a cleft mountain. Did this mean that both were sacred in the same way? The response was again cryptic, and Sri had to intervene when Romo's language failed. Eventually she came back to Hodges in Portuguese.

'He insists we are too concerned with what is only the surface. The gate's form is unimportant. It shows the untutored that it is a passage from the world of outer form and suffering to inner meaning. The Sanskrit sages called it the way to the temple, *gapura*, but the Muslims see it as the place of forgiveness, *ghafura*, where sins are cast off. These outer signs may be in any language or form. What matters is the purity within.'

Romo persisted, asking whether it was necessary to pray five times a day, to be circumcised, and to avoid pork. He explained that he and Hodges followed the way of Jesus, with different names for god, different rules for prayer and for progress to holiness, different sacred places. Was it necessary to change these, or could they also reach the truth through these forms?

The question seemed clear enough, but the answer far from it. Again there was much discussion, of which Hodges could only catch the familiar debate between sang hyang and Allah. Sri appeared to be talking more than the kiai, trying to convince

Romo of something. Hodges grew impatient and insisted this exchange proceed in Portuguese so he could understand.

'I believe he is saying that no name in any language can express the ultimate truth. The Muslims have ninety-nine names for god, and the old believers have more. You may have yours. There are also numerous ways to progress on the path towards that truth. All are difficult, and require much concentration and stillness. If somebody says there is an easy way to do only this or only that, they must be mistaken. If somebody says only one word or entrance is the true one, they must be mistaken.'

'So is he saying the prince is wrong to require me to be circumcised, and to recite the Muslim creed?'

Sri did not translate this for the guru, but provided the answer she wanted.

'What the king requires is his business. This kiai cannot tell him what he should do to unite his kingdom or keep it in peace. He can only say these outer signs on the path are not the truth. You may use those that are helpful to you, but they are only the lower steps on the ladder to truth.'

Romo was not satisfied with this, and pushed the guru further.

'Are you a Muslim then? Does it matter whether you are a Muslim or not?'

The kiai seemed irritated by this directness. He resorted to muttering some formulas neither Romo nor Sri could understand. After Sri put the question more deferentially, some exchanges ensued that Romo struggled to follow. Eventually it was Sri again who believed she could explain it to the sceptical men.

'Everything is Islam, he is saying, and everything matters,

because everything is god, and god is everything. You must meditate on the ultimate oneness of truth, and the truth of oneness.'

Ki Ageng had had enough, and shuffled off. The other pilgrims looked as though they blamed the foreigners for his irritation. Sri said some words of gratitude or apology to them and led the two Englishmen out.

When they were back in the potter's house Sri needed a rest, and the two men reverted to plain English.

'I'm not sure if he is a mad saint or just a fraud, Romo. As far as I could tell, he did not answer any question. Only Sri made him appear half-sensible.'

'Whether he is saint or madman is not the point, Thomas. What we have to worry about is why Anggalaga and Kiai Wirajaya insisted we visit here and talk to him. It looks like they want to ask why we cannot accept the outer signs of Islam as merely steps on the ladder to truth, as Javanese followers of the old religions do.'

'So we should not get anxious about a superficial thing like losing a foreskin?'

'Exactly. If that is what the king requires of subjects, that is his right and a man of god should not trouble himself over it.'

Later Sri said much the same, and didn't see his problem. 'I like your little man fine as he is, Thomas, but what does it matter if the king wants to reshape him a little. Roast pork can be tasty, but you don't get much chance to eat it anyway. If you just give them the outer sign they want, you don't need to change what you believe deep down, and we will be able to live together in peace."

'Oh Sri, Sri, that is not so easy. My language has harsh words for those who betray their faith. I would not be able to return to my own kind.'

'Do you really want to, Thomas?' She placed his hand on her belly, so he could feel the little life within. 'I need you here, and he needs you here. Do you want to go back to your English wife, and your cold weather?'

Hodges had no answer, except to lose himself again in the wonder of her. She made the choice seem so simple and natural. Yet he despised the wretched Abdullah/Antonio who had betrayed himself, not just his faith. 'I need you too, Sri,' he muttered in English, 'so help me, god.'

# Fatherhood, 1611

The approach of a child drove Hodges and Sri apart as often
as together. They shared wonderful fantasies about the child,
usually as an extraordinary boy who could somehow be a hero
in both Java and England. Yet their dreams often diverged from
there, in ways they could not share. Though Hodges had thought
little about Margaret and Timothy since arriving in Mataram,
Sri's reactions to the presence in her womb brought Hodges
unexpectedly back to such moments in Margaret's pregnancy.
Could this boy end by taking Sri away from him, as Timothy had
Margaret?

The possibility of a girl entered Hodges mind only when they
discussed the question of names. The Javanese names Sri proposed
seemed prettier than the English ones in his mind. Not Margaret,
not Elizabeth, not Joan; no cold and awkward images he conjured
from his England would fit this child of Sri's. Of course Sri herself
was the image of every Putri, Dewi or Lakshmi he could imagine,
and he wanted nothing changed except her credulity.

Having brought to Bayat sobering news for Hodges, Buyung
had brought joy for Sri. Her mother, Raden Ayu, had heard
through her brother in Japara that Sri was with child. As quickly
as possible she had made the difficult journey from Banten
accompanied by one of her maids, an experienced midwife.
They were now in Mataram, impatient to be reunited. This news
transformed Sri. She insisted they return immediately. Hodges'

fears of a day of reckoning were swept aside. On the journey each of them turned inward. Sri thought only about her mother, who would be sure to take charge. All the physical and spiritual preparations for birth would be in order.

Hodges could think only of Anggalaga's demand. He reviewed time and again his schemes to dodge or postpone a decision, his hopes for some chance of escape with Sri and the baby. They had often discussed this issue in the past, with no plan proving practical. Sri had no patience to discuss it further as her time neared. Her reproach did not require words; her silence and her sad eyes were eloquent: 'Do you not want to stay with us?'

There were great rejoicings when they reached Mataram, though Raden Ayu scolded Hodges for dragging her daughter around the Java countryside. She had already calculated that the mitoni ceremony was overdue, and must be performed at once. This should have been done in the seventh month of pregnancy, but Sri was already into the eighth. The child at seven months was already thought to have a *semangat*, a spirit of its own, which must be attended to.

A meal was arranged with members of the adjacent houses whom Raden Ayu had already befriended, and the women carefully washed Sri with special water from seven wells. Hodges' only role as father appeared to be to cut open two coconuts, held to represent the same exemplary couple who had been worshipped at the shrine on the slopes of Merapi – Arjuna and Sumbadra. To avoid embarrassment at his clumsiness this was done for him, while his task was reduced to offering the juice from them for Sri to drink. It was claimed that somehow this would make the baby like Arjuna or Sumbadra. What rot! Hodges felt excluded and indignant as the superstitions multiplied and Sri slipped further into her Javanese world. He was grateful after all to be swept straight into his military tasks, drilling the Mataram artillerymen.

It was a boy. Nobody told Hodges about it until he returned late one night to find their hut still lit and full of women. Ayu announced the news with glistening eyes. Sri was safe, thank god.

'Hush, she and the baby are sleeping. Please go in quietly.'

He stood transfixed before the sleeping pair, and his heart turned. Whatever happened, he could not abandon them. The fine lines of Sri's face, the deep composure of her body, had become part of him. He needed this to be himself. And the boy was a darling: him and her, England and Java, robust but delicate. He lay down next to Sri and said nothing until morning. When she stirred, he held her very tight.

Though Anggalaga himself was again fighting in the east, Kiai Wirajaya and others in Mataram asked what he had learned in his pilgrimage and where he now stood on the vital question. He found himself borrowing the lines of Romo: Java had accommodated different religions so fluently, it must be able to make room also for Christianity. There seemed no conflict between the way of Jesus and the ways of the Javanese, and so forth. Pangeran Danupaja, the artillery commander, was firm: 'Good, you have learned. But we here acknowledge that Islam is the faith of the king, and so we accept it as a sign of our loyalty, whatever we believe in our hearts.'

Ever since his submission to his captors on the road from

Japara, Hodges had nursed a secret guilt. It was not hell he feared. That concept made even less sense since he had been with Sri. What he had betrayed was himself, whatever deep identity that gave him the courage to live and, if necessary, to die. He had tried to express this to Sri when those eyes seemed to ask: 'why would you not do this for me?' Whichever way he expressed it, she would pretend to bewilderment at the ways of men. 'You seem to need to create something to fight about. I don't know why.'

Talk of escape or finding a peaceful home somewhere safer was now out of bounds. They focussed on the immediate joys and demands of the baby. They had agreed to call him Andy in every language. For Hodges this was a baby form of Andrew; for Sri, Andi was a suitable title for a baby destined for greatness, but when she spoke Javanese to the women around her it sounded more like Adi, and sometimes the longer form, Adiwarna.

There were Javanese rituals to conduct after the birth, especially at the forty-day anniversary when the couple had to host a party for virtually all their friends. Romo and Buyung were the only non-Javanese, but both appeared more at ease with their sarong and headgear than did Hodges himself. When the offerings and hair-cutting were done, Romo quietly asked Hodges, 'May I give Andy a blessing?'

Hodges quickly warmed to this unexpected idea. 'Thank you, Romo. He needs a Christian blessing, and I suppose you need not bring the pope into it. Can you say it in English instead of Latin, just so there is no cheating?'

Romo smiled. 'To be honest I never have, though I keep changing the way I do it in Javanese. I have often thought about how I would have enjoyed blessing my nephews and nieces in English if I had had the opportunity. So it would be a pleasure, Thomas.'

Hodges was astonished at the wave of love he felt for this child as Romo placed his hand on Andy's head and quietly intoned, 'May the Lord bless you and keep you in his love. May you grow in his grace and wisdom. May his face shine upon you and give you peace.'

Sri was listening carefully, and when she joined him in an 'amen,' Hodges was in tears. He could not have explained why.

As he farewelled and thanked the guests, he took Romo aside. 'Thank you for that, Edward. I would like Andy to be a Christian, as well as a Javanese. Could you do a baptism for me?'

'It would be possible, Thomas, but it raises some bigger issues.'

'You mean will he be papist or reformed? Since these disputes no longer make much sense in Java, I hope he will make the right choices for himself when he grows up.'

'Very sensible. And fortunately a baptism is a baptism, whether performed by Catholic or reformer. No, this is about Sri. You need to sort out with her what your intentions are for Andy. I would rejoice in helping him to be both Christian and Javanese. Both Christian and Muslim is a tougher ask, that would require the mysticism of the strange kiai at Bayat. Let us talk about all that when you are ready.'

Talking to Sri sounded well and good, but what would he say? The easy part was to ask for equal time: *we have had the Javanese ritual, now let us have also an English ritual.* Sri wanted as much blessing as possible for the adorable boy. When she asked about the meaning behind the ritual of the water, he found himself as incoherent as she often was explaining the Javanese events. 'It's just what we do.'

It was Romo who insisted that Sri be aware of what was at stake, when he dropped by to discuss the issue the following week.

'I have great hope for your boy, Sri, being better able than any of us to bridge the misunderstandings between your culture and ours. I would dearly love to baptise him, but we have rules about these things – too many rules, too many words. I must explain that in this sacrament the parents and those present agree to nurture him in the Christian faith, and their agreement is part of the ceremony.'

'If that is what Thomas wishes, then I wish it too.'

'And if Thomas were to die?'

'Don't say that, Romo!' Sri recoiled. 'He cannot.'

'I am sorry, Sri, I should not have said that, though we live in difficult times.'

Romo realised he had gone too far, and quickly switched to the form of the baptism. He would be delighted to say some of the words in Portuguese as their common language, some in English for Thomas, and some in Javanese for Sri, her mother and friends. The boy would be christened as Andrew. St Andrew, he explained, was the first of the disciples to meet Jesus, an appropriate patron for this new beginning. Thomas wanted Buyung as a godfather, and Romo agreed to overlook his very flexible religious identity as long as he would agree to the words in the ceremony. Sri and Romo agreed that one of the ladies in his tiny flock could be godmother, having already befriended Sri.

Hodges was relieved, but clearly had more on his mind. Romo was not surprised that he appeared alone one evening at his house.

'You look troubled, Thomas. Has Sri had second thoughts?'

'No, Edward. For her this seems a simple matter. She thinks only men are bothered by the conflict between one thing and another, as if we like an excuse to fight. It's my problem. I am not married to Sri in the eyes of your church or mine, although we had a Javanese wedding. I should tell you, since you probably know it already, that I had a wife in England. Perhaps I still have, though if she lives she has probably found another man by now.'

'Do you have other children?'

'I had a boy, yes, but he died in infancy. After that my wife grew cold, and our marriage was like a prison.'

'I see. Well, I should say that my church holds that a baptism is effective no matter what the status of the parents. Since it is held to be essential to salvation, nobody should be denied it.'

'I am glad of that. But what about *my* salvation? I am a bigamist, and worse. I don't want Andy to be called a bastard, to be ashamed of his father, or to have to lie when he meets another Englishman.'

'Is it time for confession? What do you mean, "and worse", Thomas?'

Papist priest though he was, this man seemed to have worked out how to be a Christian in a strange pagan land. He at least understood what was at stake; what this English guilt could do to a man. Hodges had tried hard to forget the trauma on the road from Japara, but since the baby's birth it kept disturbing his sleep. He needed somebody's absolution, and this Jesuit would have to do.

'When they tortured me in my captivity, I denied my Lord, and agreed to become a Muslim. I wanted to live, for Sri, and for whatever purpose it was that had brought me to this cursed place.'

'Did you want to live for Sri, or to become a Muslim for Sri?'

'To live, to live. I had no desire to become a Muslim. What I did has haunted me ever since.'

'And what do you intend now, Thomas? Do you want to stay in Mataram with your lovely wife and child, or somehow try to return to your own kind?'

Hodges pondered how to put into words for the first time the frightening reality that had been gradually apparent to him since Andy's birth. 'I will stay in Java with Sri and Andy. I hope we can find a way to live in Japara or Banten, where we are further from the caprice of the rulers here. But I have accepted that I cannot return to England, and certainly not to my former wife.'

'Then things would be easier for you and safer for Sri if you do what Anggalaga wants, and accept Islam as the unifying faith of Java. After all, most of our countrymen accepted the church of Henry and Elizabeth in the same way, even though they might not have agreed with it.'

'No, Edward. *You* did not accept that church, and you have not accepted Mataram's kind of Islam. They may kill you, but you will respect yourself and trust in the god of your fathers. If I had died in that miserable prison I would have faced my maker with shame and guilt. Now I know that is not a path I can travel. If Anggalaga wants me, he must accept my difference. Java should be big enough for another religion alongside all the ones it has already. We have quarrelled in the past, but on that I have come to agree with you.'

'Bless you, Thomas. You have chosen a dangerous route – brave to the point of folly. That is what the church calls an act of contrition. Would you like me also to absolve your sin in the way the church has done for a thousand years?'

Hodges said nothing. He fell on his knees before Romo, who placed his hand on Hodges' head and recited the Latin formula. A wave of relief came over Hodges, not so much from the words as from the reassuring warmth of Romo's hand.

'... *ego te absolvo a peccatis tuis, in nomine Patris, et Filii, et Spiritus Sancti.*'

Romo dragged Hodges to his feet and embraced him. Hodges finally disengaged.

'Thank you, Father; I mean Edward, Romo, whoever you are. Thank you for that. Now can we talk about Andy's baptism. Will he be a bastard in the eyes of Christians and Englishmen?'

'If you intend to remain here that may not arise, Thomas. In the eyes of the Javanese here you are Sri's husband and Andy's father, and that is all there is to it.'

'Even if I cannot return to England, I hope Andy will do so one day. Somebody needs to tell people in Europe about the real Java, and I hope it may be him.'

'Amen to that. I had hoped to be that person, but I doubt I will ever be able to leave Java without losing everything I have tried to build here. But will it matter to Andy in twenty years' time, or to anyone in Europe, who his parents in faraway Java were?'

'I hope he can tell people in England that he is the son of Thomas Hodges, an honest seaman from Hampshire, and his lovely Javanese wife. Can you marry us, Romo?'

'I was afraid you might say that. Sit down, Thomas. This is a big question.

'As you know, the church feels obliged to take a harsh line in public against both bigamy and divorce. King Henry discovered that, but the line became even tougher at the Council of Trent. The Javanese find it hard to understand this. If one marriage has failed and the parties are far apart, as in your case, then they should be encouraged to remarry in a proper permanent way. The most important thing that should distinguish a marriage blessed by god from the many ways in which men and women engage with each other is the free and absolute commitment of love between two equal parties. I have found more equality and love in Javanese marriages than in most English or Italian ones, because it is easy for a woman to leave if she is mistreated. The hard line of the Council can make a woman like a chattel, the property of a man who doesn't love her.'

'What are you saying, Romo? Will you marry us or not?'

'Unfortunately I cannot marry you if you already have a wife, and I cannot establish whether she is alive, whether a divorce is possible, or whether the marriage was valid in the first place in the eyes of the church. As the Muslims say, "God alone knows the truth." What I have done in the past in Java is to bless the union in a form you may call a marriage. I and my church can call it a conditional marriage. If in god's eyes you are free to marry, then it is a marriage; if not, then it is a blessing. Will that do?'

'The argument sounds thoroughly Jesuitical, but I like the result. First a Christian marriage, conditional if you wish, and then a baptism. I think Sri will be very happy. To her a blessing is a blessing, wherever it comes from, and she cannot have too many.'

'Prince Anggalaga may not be so happy, if you stick to your decision not to accept a token Islam. You and I will both need all the blessings we can muster, as well as what you call Jesuitical guile, if we are to survive here.'

'And if I ever do make contact with the East India Company again, they will be less forgiving about my consorting with slippery Jesuits than you were about my giving in to Muslims.'

# Mixed Marriage

Sri was happy to have a less hurried ceremony than the one in Banten – a 'proper' wedding, even if a Christian one. Her mother, Raden Ayu, was quickly persuaded to the same opinion once Romo began consulting her about the right Javanese words and symbols for an effective marriage. He wanted the ceremony to be a showcase for his conviction that Christianity was no threat to Javaneseness.

Raden Ayu sent word through Buyung to her brother, Raden Kajuron in Japara, to make the journey, and a date was found to suit his plans. His presence made the event acceptable to other great men of the kingdom like Buyung's patron Pangeran Purbaya and Hodges' military commander Pangeran Danupaja. Once Kiai Wirajaya agreed to come, he became the target Romo wanted to impress. Hodges began to wonder what was left of Christian, let alone English, tradition in Romo's plans. There would be a passage of scripture in Romo's translation, but Romo insisted it be one that had the right effect on a Javanese audience. Romo proposed, to Sri's enthusiastic support, the passage in John's Gospel about the woman taken in adultery.

'That is the story my brother and his friends should hear,' she said. 'It is true that those who take his hard position on Muslim law will not come, but Javanese women will love Jesus for saying, "Let he who is without sin among you cast the first stone."'

Since nobody except the two Englishmen would understand

it, Hodges was allowed only one line in English. While presenting her a ring, Hodges would make his vow to honour and worship Sri in his own language, and she would respond in hers. Since that seemed to divide them, Sri was delighted with the compromise she had suggested, that they next recite words of mutual commitment together in the language they shared, Portuguese. The whole ceremony offered so many linguistic and cultural challenges that Romo, Sri and Raden Ayu could do little else for a couple of months than draft and redraft the Javanese words.

Hodges, on the other hand, was under increasing pressure. His commander warned against the course he was taking, even when accepting the invitation to the wedding-baptism event.

'Prince Anggalaga was not pleased when I told him about your ceremony,' warned Pangeran Danupaja. 'He asked why you chose this priest to conduct your wedding. When you debated in front of the king and prince, the king was pleased to see that you disagreed with Romo. You then supported the king's idea that he should decide which religion is right for his people. How else can there be harmony in the land? Now you ask this priest with his dangerous religion to conduct your wedding. You should invite a learned Muslim to bless your union with Sri. She is a Muslim, is she not?'

'She is, Pangeran, but I am not. We had our Javanese wedding already in Banten, but now I wish also to have a Christian wedding, so our union can be seen as blessed by me and my people as well as by her and hers.'

'The prince insists that those in his army should accept Islam. He has been gracious in giving you time to see that this is only a small step, which can do you no harm. He cannot force you while his father is king, who takes a different view. But as you know the king is sick. You have little time to show Anggalaga this small proof of your loyalty.'

Hodges made no headway with his argument that Java could accept many ways to god. He confided eventually to Romo his fear that the wedding would make his position worse in Mataram, even if it made his conscience easier.

'You may be right, Thomas. But at least we will have done our best to make the case that Christianity offers much good and no threat to Java. We may still fail, and Anggalaga may force Islam upon us, drive us out, or worse. But we will have done right, your wife and son can be proud of you, and my church of me. I have learned not to expect god to give me the satisfaction of small victories. We cannot know his purposes for Asia. It is enough to play our small part in our time.'

Hodges was not reassured. Although he had earlier resisted some of Romo's concessions to Javaneseness, he could now see the danger of appearing to resist Islam.

'Perhaps we should ask one of our Javanese friends who have accepted Islam also to make a prayer. That would be fair to Sri, as well as politic for me. How about Raden Kajuron, or my boss, Danupraja?'

'I see.' Romo pondered. 'The best would be Kiai Wirajaya himself. If he agrees to do it we will have the highest spiritual authority in Mataram, short of the king himself. If he blesses a Christian and a Muslim in their union, we can hope that means there is room for both in Java.'

It was Sri, her mother, and in the last days her uncle, Kajuron, who organised the ceremony with Romo. Hodges was increasingly absent, physically with his military demands, and mentally as the pressure on him mounted. Anggalaga insisted that Hodges lead an artillery unit against one of his half-brothers, whom he was convinced was manoeuvring for the succession. But first he must have an audience with both king and prince and make his allegiance clear. Only with difficulty had he twice delayed this moment of truth until after the wedding. For him, it now appeared, the wedding would be part of the test – was he Javanese enough to be loyal?

Raden Ayu was happier than she had been since losing her husband and daughter. She spent much time with her brother, Raden Kajuron, to ensure that he would find everything perfect about the wedding. She needed him to convince her son Khalid that Sri could remain Javanese and Muslim even though she had tied herself to this stranger. She spent time with the dalang selected to perform a wedding scene from the wayang kulit repertoire. The bride must be a beautiful princess, the groom a mysterious but powerful warrior, whom only love and marriage would tame to become a dutiful husband. The clowns could make fun of foreign ways, she allowed, but only to the point of underlining this happy conclusion. Romo tried to persuade the dalang to use a Javanese prayer he had written as part of the heavily philosophical part at the beginning of the puppet play, but was not sure he had succeeded. Sri herself was radiant, hardly seeming to notice the anxiety that was disturbing her husband.

The guests came in abundance, and were entertained in the

best Javanese manner by the music of the gamelan, the wayang performance and the food. Sri was breathtakingly beautiful, in gorgeous Indian cloths that Buyung had presented. She had reverted to the demure, innocent girl who had first entranced him, eyes downcast, but now with the mature love of a mother. Hodges boldly spoke the words of Cranmer's Book of Common Prayer, which Romo had granted could not be bettered: 'I, Thomas, take thee, Sri, to be my wedded wife, to have and to hold from this day forward, for better for worse, for richer for poorer, in sickness and in health, to love and to cherish, till death us do part, according to god's holy ordinance; and thereto I plight thee my troth.'

The gentle way in which Sri made the same vow in Javanese seemed from a different planet, with only their names recognisable. The contrast made Hodges feel he had stepped into the role the dalang had cast for him, a clumsy but powerful warrior tamed by love. They both faltered with emotion as they placed rings on each other's fingers and said the words in Portuguese – 'With my body I thee worship, and with all my worldly goods I thee endow.'

The rest of the ceremony was in Javanese, carefully chosen to appeal to the guests. Romo had used various words for god, as if to emphasise that Allah, Gusti, sang hyang, tuhan and deus were all reaching for the same absolute.

Raden Kajuron asked the blessings of Allah, the sang hyang, and the ancestors of both bride and groom on the proceedings. Raden Purbaya gave a traditional Javanese blessing, and Pangeran Danupaja one with more Arabic phrases. The blessing of Kiai Wirajaya caused Romo the greatest anxiety, not allayed when it began and ended with an Arabic invocation. Since this was unusual for him, Romo guessed that he had received instructions from the palace. In between he prayed for harmony in the bridal family, in the community and in the realm.

Afterwards, congratulating Hodges during the meal, Wirajaya made clear that Anggalaga's patience was at an end. 'It is a small thing; you must only accept Islam as the outer layer that binds us.'

To Romo he said, 'Thank you for this beautiful ceremony. You have understood us well, and made your way of Jesus comprehensible to us Javanese. You have only to show that the Christians and their faith are no threat to the kingdom. If Anggalaga is the arbiter of what that means, you may need to follow the example of the Javanese sages I love – worship how you wish but with enough Islamic coating to show your people and ours that you are part of *this* kingdom, and do not contest its fundamental choices.'

Both men were sombre when Romo shared this information with Hodges after most of the guests had gone. He had something else grave on his mind.

'Thomas, I will soon have to leave Mataram. Raden Kajuron brought me a letter that had been sitting in Japara for months without an address. I wish it had been lost on the way, but unfortunately it arrived safely, only a year late.'

'A ghost from your past?'

'My Jesuit superior in Goa has remembered me. I write to him myself every year – the last one I gave to Buyung. But I never know if these letters reach their destination. I believe I have been careful in reporting what I do in a positive and orthodox way. But some other news of me must have reached them from a critic.'

'There is no other Jesuit in Java, is there? How could they know what you are up to?'

'I would love to explain what I am doing to a brother Jesuit, believe me. No, I fear rumour has played its part, and probably started by someone like Antonio here. I try to talk to him, but I'm afraid he sees my very existence as a reproach to his embrace of Islam. He believes the worst of me and doesn't mind telling people.'

'He has a nasty tongue, I warrant. But we are so far from Goa. What can anyone there do to you?'

'My superior wants me to come to Goa as soon as possible to answer some questions. The language is formal. It must mean that the Inquisition is involved, and the Jesuits are not sure they can protect me.'

'That is ridiculous, Romo! You cannot let that evil institution destroy you. They know nothing of Java, nothing of science, nothing of free will and a man's conscience. You cannot accept that they have any right to burn you, or whatever they plan to do.'

'I don't think it will come to that, Thomas. I fear most for everything I have worked for here. I will try to make the case I have often rehearsed in my mind, how Christianity must complement and fulfil the beliefs of Asia, not destroy them. I will enjoy the argument, but I am not sure I will win it.'

'Of course you will not! Even in England your ideas would have you jailed or worse. They would burn you twice, as a papist Jesuit and a heretic.'

'Goa is not quite England. There are some Jesuits there whom I hope will understand me.'

'You must not go, Edward! Mataram needs you, and damn it, I need you. What purpose could possibly be served by your rotting in some dungeon in Goa?'

'I have taken a vow of obedience, Thomas. I am still a Jesuit, even if I hope to have become a Javanese one. I have to believe that the holy spirit is at work even in the church, with all its faults. Obedience has a purpose; I accept that.'

'Nonsense! That blind obedience gave you the Inquisition and popish tyranny. The letter has taken a year to get here. It would take you another year to reach Goa, and by then they will have forgotten all about it. Don't risk it all for those villains, Romo.'

Romo smiled and changed the subject.

'I do have a serious favour to ask. As you know, I have written some things, and at least to me they are important. Even if my mission fails here, my life will not have been in vain if they survive. My Javanese version of Mark's Gospel is complete, with thanks to Sri. That should remain here, until somebody devises a system to print Javanese characters. I have also some writings in Latin about Java and its religious system. I will take them to Goa to argue my case and to try to get them printed. But if I lose the argument they will be condemned and perhaps destroyed. That would break my heart. I have made a copy that I would like to leave with you here. It may be a long time before another European learns enough Javanese to understand this place and appreciate its civilisation. Europe needs to know this.'

'I would love to help, Romo, though my Latin is poor and my Javanese poorer. What's more, I am not sure my chances of survival are any better than yours.'

'Like me, Thomas, in your own way you have tried to understand Java, to build some kind of bridge between Europe and this island. We cannot know the future, but I would like to believe that what we have done will not die with us. You have a wife who has shared this adventure, and a son who is heir to both. Please try somehow to keep these things safe, until a happier future.'

Romo was shivering as they embraced. 'You are not well, Edward. Let me take you home.'

'No Thomas. It is nothing, a passing fever. You belong with Sri. Enjoy this day. I am sorry if I have dampened the joy. Our friend Kiai Wirajaya did not help either, did he?'

# Requiem

When Hodges and Sri visited Romo to say a sombre farewell and collect the manuscripts, it was clear that he had more than a passing fever. He was weak and sweating. He could swallow nothing but hot water and rice porridge, and had difficulty breathing. Sri suspected poison, often deployed in palace circles. This had come too swiftly, she said, for a normal fever. After more questions about the symptoms and what and where he had eaten, she went to the back of his house to consult with his old housekeeper about which remedies should be applied for his condition. She gave Lakshmi a few coins with instructions to get the crucial herbs in the market without delay.

Hodges tried again to talk Romo out of leaving. 'You cannot travel like this, Romo. Even for a fit young man it is a hard and dangerous journey. You will never make it.'

'Don't worry, Thomas. This will pass, and I will be off. I am all packed up and ready here.' He waved at some cloth bundles in one corner. 'I have left this house and the rest of its belongings to Lakshmi and my small flock of Christians here. Please try to see that no rascal from the court steals it from them.'

'Romo, just write to Goa and tell them that illness prevents you from coming. No, let me write. I can say what a wreck you are, too weak to write, let alone travel.'

'I have written to Goa and given the letter to Buyung. He should be able to ensure it gets there before I do. It explains that

I did my best to fulfil my vows.'

'How could you leave now, Romo?' Sri intervened. 'Our wedding was a wonderful triumph. Many people, important people, saw the beauty of your picture of Jesus and his teaching. Your work is just beginning. Mataram without you will not be the same.'

'Thank you, Sri. Believe me, I want nothing better than to stay. But if these good people liked my Javanese Christianity, and the church rejected it, where would that leave them? I hope they are strong enough to deal with persecution from the Javanese court, but to be persecuted by their own church would destroy them. No, I must go.'

Romo made sure they both understood the importance of the box of papers he was giving them.

'You are right that the way to Goa is dangerous. I do not fear for myself; my time to join my Lord is near anyway. I fear for my work. These writings are as precious to me as your Andi is to you. Even if condemned or ignored now, I believe they will one day be understood. I dreamed of printing the Javanese gospel here, as the Spanish are printing in Manila. Now God alone knows who will bring the first printer and cut the Javanese letters for it. If it is the Dutch, they will not want to print anything from a Jesuit hand. If I am condemned in Goa, no Catholic press will print it.'

'We will tell Andi who it was who married us, and brought peace to his father,' Sri whispered as she stroked his arm. 'Andi will know all the languages, and understand that there are many paths to god.'

'I pray for that, Sri. I have wrestled with the pride in me that hoped to see my name on a printed work, in Javanese or Latin. I have overcome that, it is not important. If it helps to get this work printed to put your name, somebody else's or no name on it, so be it. With your help, Sri, I have tried to write as truthfully as I can. If these words are worth anything, it is because they are true, not because I wrote them.'

Romo obviously thought he had not long to live. Hodges was too choked with emotion to speak. It was Sri who said what was needed.

'As long as we live, Romo, and Andi lives, you will be remembered and your writings will be treasured.'

Romo died two days later, without leaving his bed. His housekeeper sent word to Sri and her mother, who knew at once what to do. They began preparing rice and other dishes, leaving Hodges to his own desolate thoughts. Seeing his misery, Sri chased him out of the house, telling him to inform Buyung and their other friends, most importantly Kiai Wirajaya, the key to the palace. He found Buyung at home, and he readily agreed to spread the word among his aristocratic clients, including Wirajaya. He offered Hodges a smooth plank of wood.

'The Javanese men usually get busy digging a grave and carving a wooden grave marker, while the women prepare the food. You might want to add something English to the grave.'

Hodges was grateful for something to do. He was familiar enough with death – how many men had they piped overboard from the *Red Dragon*? But he was neither Javanese nor Catholic, and had little idea what was appropriate here. As he mulled over

Buyung's suggestion, he mustered some purposeful defiance. Romo was an Englishman, damn it, for all his popery and his Javaneseness. Hodges would dress as an Englishman, and write some words in plain English to remember him.

Sri protested when he started to put on his boots and jerkin, but withdrew when she saw his resolve. She even found him the black sash he wanted for his hat. At least he had a purpose now. The rest of the family dressed in appropriate coloured sarongs and carried the food to Romo's house. Hodges carried his wood and his English Bible. He was surprised to find at least fifty people gathered in and around the house, the women busily preparing food and the men talking quietly or watching those who were digging the grave.

'I didn't think Romo had so many converts in all of Java.'

'No, Thomas, all his neighbours must come, including the Muslims. The community must ensure his spirit is at rest and harmony restored.'

The body was laid out on a bamboo platform, and Lakshmi and two men were washing the naked body with damp cloths. They invited Hodges to join them, but he shrank back in horror. Eventually it was considered sufficient, and others joined them for the wrapping of the body in a white cloth. Lakshmi invited those present to walk past and make their last farewell. A file of people formed, as Lakshmi and the small group that must have been Romo's flock quietly chanted something in Javanese. He caught a word and guessed this was a Javanese *Ave Maria*. Another group chanted something Muslim, sprinkled with Arabic. Hodges busied himself finding some ink among Romo's things and writing his English words on the piece of wood. Only when Sri nudged him did he join the file and follow her example. Like her, he kissed Romo's cold forehead and muttered a 'thank you, Edward.' His awkwardness was forgotten in the grief for questions unasked and unanswered.

As the meal was nearly concluded, Kiai Wirajaya made an appearance. He greeted Hodges, Sri, and then Lakshmi who urged him to say some words. A respectful hush descended as he addressed the body confidently. Sri translated it quietly as: 'You came from afar, but learned to love the ways and the people of Java. We are grateful for what you brought us, new knowledge about the stars, about ourselves, and about your teacher Jesus. You have sacrificed much for us, but now you will enjoy your reward with Jesus. May Allah receive you.'

His words appeared to provoke Romo's ragtail Christian flock to feel they should also say something. They began nudging each other, but the older man they looked to shook his head and sat tight. Eventually a younger woman stood up, amidst clucks of disapproval from the elders. As Sri translated her words, she said: 'Romo, you taught us a way of humility, a way of service, and a way of love. You taught us how to pray. Please join Romo's prayer if you know it.'

She began, and gradually others joined until her voice was lost in the increasingly confident murmur. Sri could only catch the early words, but her translation was enough for Hodges to recognise the one prayer he knew. He murmured the ending in English: 'Lead us not into temptation, but deliver us from evil.' He caught up with the others for an 'amen,' the only word they shared.

Sri picked up an expectant look from the young woman who had led, and asked Hodges, 'Will you speak? I can translate something for you.'

Hodges shook his head in confusion. There was a well of emotion he wanted to release to the departed Romo, but he could hardly say it in any language, and certainly not to this confusing crowd of papists, Muslims, Buddhists and god knows what.

'Will there be a burial? I think I know how to bury an Englishman.'

'Yes, quite soon. The closest people, especially the male relatives, should carry him to the grave and say some prayers there to ensure his spirit passes safely. But we don't know how Christians do it, and he has no relatives.'

'Then I must go.'

While Sri conferred about this with the young woman and Lakshmi, Hodges busied himself with his board. By the time the eating was over and the procession ready to start, he had his inscription:

> Here lies 'Romo' Edward Trevithic, SJ
> born Cornwall 1548, died Mataram 1612
> He served God, loved Java, and sought truth
> RIP

There was more confusion as to who should carry the body on its bamboo platform, and who should accompany it to the grave. The head of the village thought he should be prominent. The young woman and Lakshmi appeared to have the clearest ideas, and allowed this only if Hodges joined him at the front of the bier. They found two men of Romo's flock to join in the carrying, but as others demurred the two women impatiently made up the six bearers themselves and set off. Seeing the boldness of the women, Sri and her mother joined the little group as they processed. Somebody had brought a gong and now banged it all the way to the newly dug grave at the back of the compound.

Hodges wanted to ask Sri what to do next, but she was out of reach. Fortunately Lakshmi and the younger woman appeared to know. They tumbled the body awkwardly into the grave, threw some earth on top, and invited others to add their earth. The village head proclaimed something that appeared more Arabic than Javanese. Hodges was trying to still his racing mind by rehearsing the English words he had heard every time a shipmate had been committed to the sea. He had only to replace 'water' with 'ground.' This was his moment, if he could get through it without breaking down:

'We have entrusted Romo Edward to God's mercy,
and we now commit his body to the ground;
earth to earth, ashes to ashes, dust to dust;
in certain hope of the resurrection to eternal life,
through our Lord Jesus Christ.'

He saw the Christian women kneeling and making the sign of the cross. Despite his firm intention to be upright and English, he joined them, and wept. Sri was beside him, sharing his tears, with a comforting arm.

# Decisions

'Tuan Hod. You are required immediately at the kraton. Come with me now.'

Danupaja had never before come to the house himself. This sounded like the moment Hodges had been dreading. Was he loyal or not; Javanese or English? He dressed quickly, embraced Sri and Andi in case he wasn't coming back, and followed Danupaja through the half-light.

'What is this about?' He could now manage simple conversations in Javanese.

'It is a new cannon, a present from the Dutch. The prince does not know what it can do.'

'Ah. That is interesting.' Hodges' relief was palpable. Kiai Wirajaya had reminded him at every opportunity, even at his brief appearance at Romo's funeral, that the palace needed a public demonstration of his loyalty. Evidently that moment had not yet come.

The gun proved to be a mortar, a squat little bronze tub that could launch a large shot in a high arc. This one was more elegant than the pair they had carried on the *Dragon*, with a separate explosive chamber. He barely had time to examine it before Anggalaga was barking his questions.

'What is it for?'

'It can shoot high, Majesty, over a wall or into a ship's rigging.'

'The Hollanders say they can use it to destroy any fortress.

They say they could capture Surabaya with such weapons. Is it true?'

'No, by itself it cannot do that. It could fire a large stone ball over the wall of the Surabaya fortress, but that would not do much harm. It is more difficult to aim than other cannons, so it would be very lucky to hit an important target within the city.'

'Is that true, Abdullah?'

Hodges had not noticed the Portuguese renegade in the shadows. It appeared that he was the bringer of the mortar. The Dutch had attempted a mission to Mataram to ask for control of all the trade of Java's ports, in return for military help for Mataram. Their envoys had been stopped at Pajang. Only Abdullah and a Javanese military escort had been allowed to talk to them and receive the gifts.

'The Dutch have many ships and many of these guns, Majesty. They have taken Portuguese forts in the Moluccas with such guns. They say this gun can fire not just stone balls, but bombs that blow up inside the fortress.'

'Is it true, Hod? I do not trust these Hollanders.'

'You should not. If they take your trade, and build forts in your ports to guard it, you will never be able to expel them. They could cut you off from the world outside.'

Hodges pointed to the mortar: 'Everybody would like to fire a bomb into a city with such a weapon, but it is extremely dangerous. More artillerymen have been killed by the bomb exploding inside the mortar than enemy soldiers brought down by it.'

'Our craftsmen are cleverer than theirs. We only need to get the powder right. We can make it work, and have no need of the Hollanders. Danupaja, take charge of this cannon and make more. Experiment with which size shoots higher and further.

'Hod, you will make a way to fire a bomb. We have different kinds of gunpowder. Work with these until you get it right. If we have a gun that will defeat Surabaya, we have no need of the Dutch.'

'You are wise, Majesty. You should learn from the Dutch, the English, the Portuguese, the Muslims; but not allow them to become strong here, as the Portuguese are in Malacca.' Hodges was relieved. Experimenting with the bomb-making would be risky, certainly, but this was the kind of risk he enjoyed. He might never succeed in firing an effective bomb, but he would certainly learn something useful in the process. And Anggalaga, unlike many princes, was smart enough to understand what was possible and what was not. Meanwhile, he would not be sent to the front and separated from his family.

'Another thing, Hod. If we reject the deal with the Hollanders, we will have more need of you to master these new weapons. You have had time to decide whether you wish to become Javanese and serve us loyally, including our way to god. You must decide now. If you wish to remain English and true to your English god, then you have no place here. You will be arrested and tortured a little to see if that changes your mind. We may keep you in prison for a year or two to see if the English will give a good price to have you back. You see I am a kind and patient prince. But ultimately, if the English do not want you, I will have you executed very publicly and cruelly as an example to other strangers.'

Hodges turned pale. 'But my wife, my son!'

'They are Javanese; they will remain your wife, your son, if you too become Javanese. If not, they belong to us.'

In despair, he could only play for a little more time. 'I am loyal to you, Majesty, as you know. But the matters of god are hard for me to express correctly in your language. May I bring my wife to help me to understand more clearly what you require, and to express my own thoughts?'

'One day only!' he barked. 'Come here tomorrow with your wife. She appears to have more sense in these matters than you do. Perhaps she will save you, Hod.'

Sri was waiting anxiously. She had not been certain he would return this time. The two soldiers who walked behind him and remained at the door spoke as eloquently as the dread in his face. She embraced him for a long time before speaking.

'Was it bad?'

'Yes. I must tomorrow agree to become a Muslim Javanese or face the consequences.'

She heard him out, but with growing impatience as he explained the choice the prince had set out.

'You stupid, stubborn man! Do you love your English wife more than me? Or your king?'

'No, no, no! I love you, love you more than life. You know that.'

'How can I believe that, if you will not do even this small thing for me? Would you die for nothing, would you leave me and Andi to become the playthings of Anggalaga? You must really hate us to want that!'

'No, no, Sri. I will not let that happen. But please help me to convince Anggalaga that what he is doing is unwise. He is an intelligent man, and should be able to see that Java will suffer if he forces all into one box.'

'Intelligent enough, indeed, to see that he cannot trust you if you keep hoping for that English ship; if you might flee to the feringgi rather than help the Javanese to fight them. If you love me, if you want to stay in Java, you have a simple choice. Just make it, you stupid man, before it is too late!'

Hodges knew he could not resist her tears, her anguish, the thought of self-inflicted separation. He would embrace the devil himself for her. He longed to hold her tight, but now she pushed him away as her body heaved in despair.

She no longer seemed to want to listen, but he pleaded with her softly. 'I promise, Sri, that by the end of the day tomorrow I will find a way to be with you forever – if need be as a Muslim, a Javanese, or whatever it takes. But I now see that Romo was right. Mataram needs to keep a door open to each religion, just as it did in the past, and value them all. If I become just another Abdullah I am useless to Mataram, for the Europeans will all despise me as a traitor and an infidel. Together you and I can be more than that. We can be what Romo tried hard to be, the bridge between Java and Europe. And Java can show the Christians and the Muslims that there is a better way to serve god than all their fighting. If everybody is forced to become a Muslim, it may unite Java but close it off to the new knowledge. Please help me to say this, for me and for Romo.'

The night was their longest, and bitterest. He did not know whether she was hearing him through her sobs, until she shrieked his words back at him. Each time he tried to embrace her she kicked and punched him, or curled into a tight ball in her misery. The urgency of his need for love on this of all nights only made her more wretched and resistant.

'You monster, you are trying to say farewell,

As the first cocks crowed, there was the truce of exhaustion and they slept briefly. Reluctantly she listened to him in the morning, and began to think how to translate his idea into something deferential that the prince might consider, without making him angrier.

Hodges had to report again to the armoury to begin work on the mortar-bomb. He left Sri wiping her tears to focus on Andi, and could only hope that in his absence she would be able to think the issue through. Without her he knew the case was hopeless, for he could not begin to understand Anggalaga's mind as she did, or convey a complex argument with the elaborate deference that the Javanese of the court demanded.

The two soldiers, who had scarcely let Hodges out of their sight all day, conducted the couple to the kraton as the heat of the day was passing. One of them told Sri to bring his basic belongings since he might not be returning to the house. This they ignored – Sri with more tears, Hodges with feigned bravado. He tried not to hug Andi with more than usual warmth, though the child began to whimper as though he knew something was wrong.

As they walked, he tried again to convince Sri that there should be another way. 'Tell him that Java needs the science of Europe.

For that he needs an intermediary like me who can talk to both Europeans and Javanese, import the books and instruments, teach the languages and techniques. We could be his representatives in Japara to meet each ship and select the new things Mataram needs.'

'You are dreaming again, Thomas. Anggalaga knows what he wants and doesn't seek advice from you. We will be lucky if he will listen at all. If he lets me, I will make the best argument I can for what you are trying to say, but he will only listen at all if he can see it as part of his own plan to become the great ruler of Java. Please just do as I say, and make sure you sound like a deferential servant. Start by bowing to the floor and saying these words.'

She repeated several times the words of homage, sounding ever more disagreeable to Hodges now that he half-understood the self-abasement they expressed. But of course she was right. The greatest danger was that the prince would get angry and shout some impulsive condemnation of Hodges that would seal his fate.

When finally admitted to an audience with the prince, Hodges did as he was told. He bowed as low as he could manage, slightly in front of Sri as she instructed, making it even harder for him to imitate her supple lowering of head and arms to the floor. Anggalaga roared something at them that sounded like a question that demanded the immediate answer yes. Sri poked him gently and he produced the practised Javanese words in a low voice. She immediately followed with her soothing words of apology. Hodges had trouble understanding it, but could see Anggalaga's demeanour softening as this lovely young woman sweetly flattered him. His interruptions became less frequent and less angry as she proceeded. Hodges too fell under the spell, forgetting his anxiety that her excessive slavishness might oblige him to protest. Despite the rage and tears of a sleepless night, she had somehow worked out how to reconcile Hodges' hopes with the prince's ambition.

As far as he could tell, it began with humble apologies for keeping the great prince waiting so long. England was so far away, its ways so different, that it took much time for Hodges to learn and understand the wisdom of Java. Thanks to the indulgence of the prince himself and his father the king, and the guidance of Kiai Wirajaya and others (even Romo got a mention), he now understood the superiority of Javanese ways, especially as improved by the wise prince himself. He had come as an envoy from England to Mataram, but now wished to serve only Mataram. Its wisdom should illuminate the whole world. Europe, which had fought too many wars about the way to god, was especially in need of Java's wisdom. He could now understand that because god was ultimately unknowable, men had worked out different paths to him in different parts of the world. Only in Java were people free to explore all these paths, making this the divinely chosen land.

Here Anggalaga interrupted with his commands, prompting Sri to murmur her assent: '*Inggih, Kanjeng*'. Twice she prodded Hodges to say the same. This was evidently the decisive moment of agreeing to become a Javanese and a Muslim. He felt mainly relief. If this was what Sri wanted, so be it.

But she was not done. She sweetly explained that yes, Hodges wanted to make the best contribution possible to Mataram's glory. He was clever with guns, and would do his best to improve those of Mataram. But one thing the feringgi were good at was making new guns and other machines that measured time and space. Mataram needed to give its great wisdom to the world, but also to learn these lesser skills that had some practical importance. He was an ambassador of England, but he hoped now to be an ambassador of Mataram, especially for ensuring all these new inventions come to Java. He humbly wished to serve His Majesty in the best way possible in helping Europe to understand Java's wisdom, and bringing in return the little tricks of the feringgi.

Something here made the prince laugh, and he supposed Sri had made a little wordplay at the expense of the Europeans. It was a good sign.

Sri went on to say that Hodges, like the late Romo, thought Mataram's glory could only be greater if the king had at his court Christians as well as Muslims and Buddhists. This would show the world more clearly the special wisdom of Java. But of course, she hastily added seeing Anggalaga's face darken, Your Majesty knows best, and we will obey.

They were dismissed after another stream of instructions from Anggalaga. It appeared that they were free to go home, with no sign of the guards. 'You were magnificent,' he murmured to Sri, hardly able to believe they were free.

'You may not think so when you understand what he wants. But what matters is that we are together.'

Anggalaga had in fact insisted, as Sri knew he would, that Hodges' public embrace of Islam and Javaneseness take place at the next royal senenan, only a week away. Thenceforth he would be considered a Mataram official and would dress like one. Sri's attempt to make a multi-religious court appear a strength for Mataram had not impressed Anggalaga. He appeared all too well aware of the quarrels of the Christians and the Muslims.

'What did he say about being a kind of ambassador for Mataram, to keep abreast of European inventions?'

'He dismissed it rather rudely. He said you had to earn that kind of trust at his side on the battlefield. Until then you would not be not allowed out of his control. Whenever you were out of Mataram, I would remain here as the guarantee that you would return. I'm sorry, my dear.' She stroked his arm. 'It was a nice dream.'

They hardly had time to return home and embrace Andi before Pangeran Sanjata made an appearance at their house. Hodges remained wary of his obvious fondness for Sri, but this time his message was for Hodges. As Sri organised the minimal hospitality in the back of the house, Sanjata asked him about the audience with Anggalaga. News of it had spread quickly around court circles.

'Are you content with the outcome, Tuan Hod?'

Hodges was immediately on his guard. Who had sent him and why? 'I am content to be a servant of Mataram, and to remain here with my family.'

Sri reappeared with a tray of betel and offered it to Sanjata as he was beginning to talk around the religious question with a subtlety that entirely escaped Hodges' grasp of Javanese. Seeing his mystified look, Sanjata directed a lengthy speech to Sri, which led to protests on her part, more polite indirectness on his. He understood only that this had something to do with Islam and the way of Jesus – *Nabi Isa*. Hodges insisted she explain.

'It is dangerous business. Be careful, Thomas.'

'What do you mean?'

'Pangeran Sanjata is saying that there is more than one idea in the court about how to handle Islam. He is now in the royal guard of the old king, Panembahan Krapyak, who has sometimes asked Sanjata about you. The king seems to think that his son is pushing too hard to make Islam the sole religion of the state. Anggalaga thinks he will always be strong enough to control the Muslims, but the king does not believe it. He fears that Islam will eventually bring division, and endanger the old ways and the monarchy itself.'

'What has this to do with me?'

Seeing that Sri was reluctant to answer his question in Portuguese, he asked it directly to Sanjata in his blunt Malay. The answer was again lengthy, indirect and Javanese, and left Hodges more bewildered than ever. Eventually it was Sri who took charge and ushered Sanjata out. He left a little reluctantly, not before saying in Malay as he took his leave from Hodges: 'Please think very carefully about it.'

'What was all that about?' asked Hodges when he was safely out of the way.

'The politics of the court are dangerous, Thomas, and you should not get involved.'

'So what did he want me to do?'

'He seems to know that you, like Romo, think that Mataram

should allow different faiths in the kingdom, including the Christians. He thinks that you do not really want to become a Muslim, and that you should not have to.'

'He thinks I could refuse Anggalaga? Who would protect me then?'

'Exactly. He seems to think that you would be better off shifting your allegiance to the king, who would not ask you to become a Muslim. He thinks, although without exactly saying so, that Anggalaga is gathering many enemies through his energetic policies, and that the king himself can better guarantee the survival of the kingdom.'

'Is he right?'

'Of course not, Thomas. You know better than I that Anggalaga controls most of the soldiers. Everybody knows that the old king is sick and erratic. He will die soon, if somebody doesn't poison him first. I told Sanjata he should not get you involved in these dangerous games. Even a slight hint of disloyalty to the prince would be enough to have you poisoned or mysteriously killed.'

'Would Sanjata be playing this game himself if it is so dangerous?'

'He knows how to be very careful. Anybody who survives for long in the kraton learns the art of speaking very indirectly and being deferential to all. He claimed he wanted to help you because you are more exposed as a foreigner. It is true that you are, but just because of that you should have nothing to do with this idea. He might be willing to see you take the risk that he would not take himself.'

'So you think I should go ahead and become a Muslim

publicly at the senenan?'

'Not only that. You should be even more careful now to show no sign of questioning this decision. That is done, and you will try to be a good Javanese – a strange Javanese admittedly, like Petruk, with a big nose and a beard.'

She pulled both to make him laugh and forget the idea. Was he tempted by this madness? She would be good to him tonight, to make sure he knew that he was home at last.

# Your Father, 1622

Adi was sulking again. He had been moody for months, ever since his stepfather had told him it was time to prepare for the *sunat* ceremony, his circumcision. But today Sri could do nothing with him. He spoke only to try to pick a fight with his inoffensive younger brother. She had had enough.

'Stop this Adi! If you don't tell me what is bothering you, it will churn around inside you until it rots your liver. Tell me at once or I will tell your father he must deal with you!'

Adi looked with alarm at where he thought his liver might be, then at his mother's unfamiliar fierceness.

'Why do the other boys hate me?'

'They don't hate you, Adi. Agus was just asking you to play tops and you chased him away.'

'You don't see it! They think I am ugly and weird. They make fun of my nose and these cursed freckles. When you talk Portuguese to me they say we are witches speaking devils' language.'

'Come here, you stupid boy. It is time we had a talk. You are not ugly; in fact you're a bit too handsome for your own good. The girls are talking about you too much for my liking.'

At last he accepted a hug from his mother.

'You know why you are better-looking than those boys, don't you? You are special because your father was Inggeris – "an Englishman" – and he wanted you to be one too.'

'I hate him. Why can't I be just normal like everyone else?'

'Nobody is "just normal", Adi. We are all different, each in our own way. We need sometimes to pretend to be all the same so we get along. But god made us all different for a reason, because we each have something special to give the world.'

'I don't want to be special, and I don't have anything anybody wants.'

'Yes you do, Adi. You have so much that is special that I can understand it hurts sometimes. Here, there are some things that will be yours, and it is time you saw them.'

She fetched a box that Adi knew was special to her, though he had never dared ask why. There were funny clothes in there, that looked far too hot.

'This is your father's doublet and hat, that he was proud to wear when he felt really "English". When you are ready to wear it you will be not Adi but Andy – he always called you that. When you are big your name will be bigger too. "Andrew. My name is Andrew Hodges, son of Thomas."'

She said the words carefully in English. She tried to get him to repeat it, but her tears were by now too obvious even for an angry boy to ignore.

'What's the matter, mummy?' He switched to Javanese as he always did when appealing to her softer side.

She stroked him as she struggled to compose herself. 'He was a fine man, Adi, and you must be proud of him. He is the reason you are very special.'

'Then why did he leave us, and leave me to be just a funny-looking kid?'

'He didn't leave us, Adi. Never think that. He gave up

everything for you and for me. He loved you so much. Look at this.'

She pulled the small English text of the gospels from the box. Opening the first page, she read to him carefully, struggling with the words. 'The book of the generation of Jesus Christ, the son of David, the son of Abraham.

'This is your father's precious book. The English call themselves "Christians". That means followers of "Jesus", our Isa, whose other name was "Christ". That funny language is "English". I cannot speak it well, but your father would love for you to learn it one day and read this book. He said it was important that holy books should be in the language everybody spoke and understood. He thought the Muslims were wrong, as Christians were in older times, to leave the holy book only in a foreign language.'

'Is it true? What do you think?'

'I thought it was lovely to hear the Christian holy book in my own Javanese language.'

'But you are a Muslim, aren't you? Aren't we all Muslims?'

'Yes we are. Even your English father became a Muslim, but he did that for me, and for you, because he could see no other way to stay with the people he loved. What he really thought was that everybody should be free to follow their own way, especially here in Java where we always had many faiths. His own way was the way of this English book.'

'So if I do not understand English, that cannot be my way.'

'Perhaps not. It is for you to decide. I think your father really hoped that you could learn English from him, as well as Javanese from me, and be the first to understand both peoples and explain them to each other. That is why you are so special.'

She reached again into the box to find a larger package carefully wrapped in cloth. As she unwrapped Romo's Javanese translation of Mark's Gospel, she explained.

'This is another reason you are very special. Your father and I had a lovely friend, the only other Englishman in Mataram. His English name was Edward Trevithic, but he tried very hard to be Javanese and liked to be called Romo. He believed very much that the Javanese needed to know this Jesus and the stories about him. He worked very hard to translate one of the books of Jesus stories into Javanese. I helped him too, and we finished this book just before he died. He hoped one day it would be printed, but now he is gone, your father is gone, and only you and I are left with this responsibility.'

'What does it mean – printed?'

Sri took the English gospels again and showed him how the letters were formed very uniformly, so that it was easy to read. 'The feringgi in Europe invented this way to make hundreds of books from one book, by cutting a model for each letter and using it again and again to print, like a seal, a chop, can be used many times.'

Adi looked again at the Javanese text, struggling to read the letters. 'There are hard words in here.'

Sri read the Javanese words as she followed with her finger. '"The beginning of the good news about Isa al-Masehi." Yes, there are many words we argued much about. It is hard to express big ideas about god in any language, and translating them into another language with different ways of understanding is even harder. Finally we made something beautiful, Adi, and it must not be lost. I hope you will treasure this when I am gone. One day you may meet feringgi who can fulfil Romo's wish and have it printed so all the Javanese can read it.'

'How could I do that? No feringgi come here except those horrible Hollanders our king wants to fight.'

'Yes, it seems this king will no longer allow feringgi like Romo to come here. We knew the king before he was king, when he was called Anggalaga. Then he was interested in everything and we could argue. When he became king he ruled that everybody should be Muslim, or at least pretend. Our friend Romo did not agree. He thought that Java could show the rest of the world how all the faiths could live together and learn from one another about god and creation. Perhaps he was a dreamer, but he had beautiful dreams. In the end your father died for that dream.'

'Really?' Adi was startled. His mother had never talked about her English husband like this. He could tell that her new husband, Adi's Javanese father Sanjata, did not like talking about this other father. He had learned not to ask. Now was his chance.

'Please tell me. How did my father die?'

'Thomas wanted to be an ambassador, to make peace between England and Mataram, between feringgi ideas and Javanese ones. He wanted to believe that the English were better than what he called the "fanatical Portuguese" or the "greedy Dutch", who just fought for what they wanted. He always maintained that the English only wanted to trade in peace and bring their clever inventions here to Java. Of course that didn't happen. He could only stay in Mataram with us if he agreed to be a soldier and a Muslim.'

'Was he a brave soldier?' Adi stood tall and menacing, like the soldier he played at being.

'Yes, Adi. Very brave, like you must be. He saved the king's life once, and tried to save my father.' The tears came again, and she hugged Adi closer before she could continue. 'But he was also very clever. He would say that fighting was one part bravery and three parts intelligence. The king we have now, I still call him Anggalaga, valued him very much because he was both brave and clever with guns. Anggalaga knew that he needed your father to fight against Surabaya, which he was always doing, or against the Hollanders when they became too greedy. He fought very well, and helped the king win lots of battles.'

'But how did he die?'

'I can only tell you what I know, Adi. Of course I was not there to see it. Your father was always sad when he had to go to war, especially after Romo died. I think he learned that fighting did not solve problems. It only made more. He especially hated it when the king forced the feringgi or Chinese he captured to become Muslims as a sign of loyalty. He said the god he knew was sad every time somebody said he believed what he didn't believe to escape death or torture. When I first knew him he got angry and confused about our Javanese ways, but once he learned how to be still and listen, he became wiser than any of us.'

'It doesn't seem wise to get himself killed. Why didn't he just stay with us if he was so wonderful?'

Now she was sobbing again, and the boy knew he had hurt her.

'Don't cry, mummy. I'm sorry. Just tell me how he died.'

She took a long time to be able to speak, and the answer came slowly.

'There was a fight against one of the king's brothers, who didn't agree with him. I suppose the king's army won that battle, but when they returned Thomas was not there. The king came himself to thank me for his bravery on the battlefield, and said he had been killed by the enemy. He tried to be nice, but in a horrible way. I knew there was something wrong with his story. I was angry and screamed at him. I never want to see him again.'

Now Adi's eyes were wide. 'Do you mean somebody else killed him? The king? Why?'

'It was your Javanese father, Sanjata, who told me the story. One day he may tell you too, though we both try to forget that awful day. He came to ask forgiveness, because he felt responsible. He was one of those who thought, like Thomas and Romo, that the different beliefs could live together peacefully. He had many soldier friends who thought the same, and some who were foolish enough to support the present king's father when he was alive, and then his rebellious brother. That was a stupid, dangerous idea. The brother was less friendly with the Muslims, but not half the man our king is. Your father was wise enough to keep his opinions to himself, and to just do what he had to do to keep the kingdom safe and stable. But he had some enemies.'

Sri was sobbing again, and the boy was now the one trying to comfort her.

'Yes, mummy. Please don't cry. Just finish the story.'

'Some of these enemies were horrible enough to poison the king's mind. It was already a bit poisoned because your father had spoken his mind before, and perhaps because of me. Anyway, the king must have allowed these enemies to do something to a cannon your father was firing, to make it blow up instead. That is what killed him. He was a very clever man and never made mistakes with the guns himself.'

'Who are these people? I will kill them when I am bigger.'

Adi struck a bold pose of the *penchak* martial art that he loved to practise.

'My brave boy. No, he would not want you to do that. What he would want you to do is to keep these precious writings here safe until you can make them known to the English scholars. For that, and for me, you must first stay alive. He would want you to learn English, as well as your beautiful Javanese, and to learn the way of Jesus as well as the way of Islam and the ways of Java.'

'How can I do that? Nobody speaks English here. Nobody even wants to speak Portuguese to me except you.'

'Not here, Adi. But in Banten there are English now, and sometimes they come to Japara. When you are ready, Uncle Buyung will take you to Japara and even to Banten to meet them. So we must keep speaking Portuguese, and we will learn together how to read your father's English bible. So you can say with pride, "I am Andrew Hodges, son of Thomas."'

# Historical note

As far as we know, neither Jesuits nor English East India Company servants found their way to Mataram in the early 1600s, though both came close and did visit other great Asian kingdoms.

Pangeran Anggalaga, the best-documented historical figure in our story, became Java's most successful king, known to history as Sultan Agung after he obtained the title of Sultan from Mecca in 1641. He ruled from 1613 until his death in 1645, bringing the whole Javanese-speaking area under his authority. His one great failure was the attempt in 1628-9 to conquer, with a vast besieging army, the stronghold the Dutch had established in 1619 at Jakarta, which they named Batavia. This defeat meant he could not extend his authority to Javanese-speaking Banten further west again, nor to the mountainous west of the island in general, where the inhabitants eventually became known as Sundanese.

He enforced his own brand of religious syncretism. All subjects were obliged to become formally Muslim, and Europeans and Chinese were free to operate in his domains only if they became Muslim as a demonstration of loyalty. Several Dutch and Portuguese who refused to do so were kept as prisoners for bargaining purposes, and sometimes executed. A Javanese translation of the gospels would have to wait another two centuries. On the other hand, the *wayang* repertoire of pre-Islamic deities remained extremely popular in court and countryside, and the king, rather than any learned Muslim ulama, was the sole legal and spiritual authority. A complex calendar, such as Romo might have helped devise, combined Javanese, Muslim lunar and Christian solar dating systems with the Javanese five-day week and Saka era.

The English East India Company had a difficult period following Keeling's profitable Third Voyage. The mighty *Trades Increase*, intended to overawe all opposition when launched in 1609 as the largest merchant ship of its day, had the opposite effect, arousing the hostility of both Muslim Mocha and the Portuguese. The damaged ship barely managed to reach Banten on 22 December 1612, but was finally abandoned and burned there in 1614 after its commander Henry Middleton and many of the crew had died of disease. The Company continued to send vessels to Banten, and occasionally to Japara (where they spasmodically maintained a presence in the period 1618-52) and the Spice Islands (Maluku). They had an office in Banten until expelled in 1683 by the Dutch conquest, which ended its role as a port open to all. In its desperation to stave off the Dutch threat, Banten sent two ambassadors to London in 1682 to meet King James II. But the English Company could not match Dutch naval strength in Southeast Asia. Its retreat was sealed in the Treaty of Breda (1667), whereby all English claims to bases in the nutmeg and clove producing Spice Islands were abandoned, while in exchange the Dutch abandoned their claims on New York and New England. English commercial interest shifted to India and the American colonies.

The Dutch and Portuguese proved the most plausible options as European allies for Sultan Agung. He preferred the Portuguese since the Dutch were the greater threat, but entertained envoys from both parties so long as they were prepared to provide rich presents as tokens of tribute to him. Only after Sultan Agung's death did his successor establish friendly relations with the Dutch, who were permitted to send annual missions interpreted as tribute by Mataram. Internal challenges to the authority of the ruler became endemic in the 1660s, however, and eventually made the Dutch Company the stronger half of the partnership.

*Red Dragon*